DRAGON'S CURSE

HEIR OF DRAGONS BOOK TWO

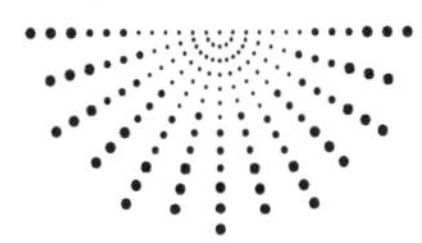

SEAN FLETCHER

To those with curses all their own

May you embrace them

May you break them

GET A FREE BOOK

To get a FREE novella and excerpts of my latest series with bonus content you won't get anywhere else, **Join My Newsletter**

You know you want to. We've got magic and stuff.

A RECORD OF LOST THINGS

There are many ways to kill a dragon.

Not that you'd need to, of course. Not that there are any dragons left that need killing. Not that there are any dragons left, period. Not anymore. Not really.

Right?

A blade could do the job. A well-forged length of steel or iron in the right spot is just as effective on a dragon as any human. Death is not particular about its manner of deliverance.

Magic will do it, too.

But not simple magic, that mundane spell casting and bumbling about of the arcane arts used nowadays.

No. What's needed is ancient magic. Deadly magic. Blood oaths. Summoning chants. Curses. Especially curses. Old, vicious things, full of spite and malice. Evil things. Always created with less-than-noble intentions, and yet always used with the belief that their intentions are, in fact, noble.

But none of that magic remains today, either. And that which does is safely lost or locked away, far out of reach of any man or beast wishing to use it for their selfish purposes.

Right?

CHAPTER ONE

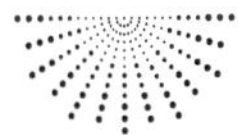

It was too cold for October, it was a school night, she had a geometry test tomorrow she still hadn't studied for, and yet Kaylee Richards crouched across the street from the apartment complex, waiting for the monster to emerge.

"You *sure* Damian gave us good info?" Kaylee whispered.

"Uh-huh."

"I know he runs the Slag Heap and has all this secret information, but he could be wrong. Heck, he could be lying."

"Uh-huh."

"Uh-huh? That's all you got? Are you even—what are you doing?"

Jade, Kaylee's best friend, sat beside her, back pressed against the tree. Her combat knife, a foot of glittering steel she normally had hidden up her sleeve, was clamped between her lips. She was scribbling furiously on a sheet of paper propped on her knee. Her fingers were stained with ink.

Kaylee leaned over. "Is that Mrs. Douglas' Chem assignment?"

"Maybe," Jade said. "What'd you get for number six? The stoichiometry problem? And can I borrow your lab later?"

"You're my dragon-kin Tamer. Aren't you supposed to be protecting *me* from evil stuff?"

Jade smirked. She scratched in another answer. "No one can protect us from the evils of Chemistry."

Kaylee checked that the parking lot of the apartment across the street was still vacant. It was. Just as it had been the last three hours. It didn't even look like *normal* people lived there, not to mention an unregistered magic user supposedly smuggling dangerous magical creatures.

She scooted closer to Jade and pointed to an answer at the bottom. "That one's wrong. I think."

Jade let out a frustrated groan and crossed it out.

"Why didn't you just do this earlier?" Kaylee said.

"No time. The Convocation wanted me to get more training hours in before I came on this mission."

"You already have plenty of hours. What do you need more for?"

"Don't know. Something to do with prepping for the Tamer test next year."

"Doesn't look like we'll be getting much practice tonight," Kaylee said. "I'm surprised the Convocation even let us come along."

"You mean let *you* come with *me*," Jade said. "Means they're finally letting you off their leash. Which I'm eternally grateful for. Waiting sucks, but you make it suck less."

Yes, Kaylee was surprised Alastair, the head of the Scarsdale Convocation, had allowed her to help a couple trained Protectors nab this rogue Merlin. Almost exactly a year ago, at the end of her first semester of freshman year of high school, Kaylee hadn't even been able to leave her hometown of Scarsdale for fear of getting attacked by Slayers.

But now the Slayers were reported to be far away, which meant Kaylee's training as a storm dragon-kin, a half dragon/half human with the ability to control storms, could resume.

And that meant nights camped out across from dingy apartment buildings in cities far away from home. How fun.

"Is that him..." Jade leaned forward. "Nah, never mind. I think it was just Edwin. Maddox needs to keep him hidden. He'll blow our cover."

"Maddox is Edwin's Protector, not his babysitter," Kaylee said. "Besides, Edwin can take care of himself."

"Uh-huh."

Jade settled back. She brushed her black hair from her face, her skin alabaster pale in the dark, her eyes, naturally narrowed, squinting to make out any movement in the low light.

Kaylee finished checking the positions of everybody else in the stakeout. She knew Josh, a wind dragon-kin from the Northern Scarsdale Convocation, and his dragon-kin Tamer, Tygus, were hiding to her right, cutting off any escape to the south. Which left only the rear of the apartment building, where two fully-trained Convocation Protectors were positioned. Not that Kaylee completely trusted their skills, fully-trained or not. It wasn't that the Convocation *couldn't* protect her. If it weren't for them, the Slayers and their overzealous (and misguided) hatred of all dragon-kin would have done her in a long time ago.

But the Convocation hadn't been there last year. They hadn't saved Kaylee and her friends from Lesuvius, leader of the Slayers, or his plan to use the Dragon Moon to steal all the dragon-kins' elemental magic. That had been Kaylee, barely controlling her storm powers, and Edwin, finally gaining enough confidence to cast spells, along with Jade and Maddox.

So yes, Kaylee was cautiously grateful Alastair had finally allowed them to go on a Convocation-sanctioned mission. She had to do something. She didn't think she would be able to sit around waiting to see what the Slayers and Lesuvius were planning next. And they *were* planning something. Edwin had told her they were, and if there was one thing that boy was better at than being socially awkward, it was knowing his stuff when it came to magic history and what the Slayers' next attempt to destroy them would be.

"They're moving," Jade said, nudging her head toward a pair of figures emerging from the darkened field at the rear of the building. "Bout time."

The two Protectors, dressed in black combat armor, casually made their way to the front door of the apartment in question. One knocked.

"Easy…" Kaylee said as Jade leaned forward.

"You should get ready, too," Jade said. "This creep isn't going to come quietly."

Kaylee breathed in, turning inward to the magic coursing just beneath the surface of her skin. This first level of magic was stable. Soothing, like a second layer of skin. Not like her other kind. The kind Kaylee hoped she wouldn't have to use tonight.

Kaylee coaxed the surface magic to her. The dragon within answered.

The skin on her forearms shifted to jet-black scales. Jagged claws replaced fingernails. Spits of ice-blue electricity arced between her palms, sending a comforting trill through her body.

The Protectors knocked again, harder this time.

"Can you hear anything?" Jade said. "Can you shift your ears yet?"

"Sometimes," Kaylee said. She kept her arms shifted and now directed her magic at her left ear. Not too long ago, changing more than one part of her body to dragon form at the same time would have been near impossible. It was still hard but, a second later, Kaylee's left ear swelled with sound as it changed.

"He's not here," she heard one of the Protectors mutter. "It's a bust. Let's call it in."

"One more," the other answered.

A final knock. A silence.

Then something else from within the apartment. Scuttling. A

hundred thousand tiny legs on hardwood and concrete. A growing hum of magic, building in power.

Kaylee knew that feeling. It was the same every time Edwin messed up a spell during their lessons. It was the same when she lost control of her storms. The sensation of tainted magic. Uncontrollable magic.

Without waiting, Kaylee sprinted straight toward the apartment.

"Run! It's about to—"

The Protectors swiveled on her, their faces shocked. They didn't see the outline of the door begin to glow behind them. They didn't hear the rumble.

An explosion rocked the earth as half the apartment exploded in white.

CHAPTER TWO

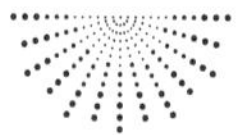

Kaylee was pretty sick of things blowing up on her.

In the past year she'd been assaulted, kidnapped, and stabbed; but more annoying than all those were the explosions. Sure, she'd technically been the cause of more than a few of them, but the novelty was already wearing off.

Such was her life.

A force like a punch collided with Kaylee's stomach, throwing her back. Her world whirled. The hard concrete came to greet her. Just before she hit, Jade dove, using her body to cushion Kaylee's landing.

Kaylee's ears rang. The world around her was nothing but a high whine, slowly descending into muddled, mushy voices.

"Maddox! Cover!" Jade barked.

"Already on it!"

The muscled frame of Maddox came into view. He wielded a spear, facing the billowing smoke pouring from the apartment. The Protectors lay in a heap nearby. Jade helped Kaylee up, but Kaylee couldn't take her eyes off them.

"Are they—?"

"They're okay," Edwin said. He had one hand held out in

front. Orange magic curled at the ends of his fingertips. In his other hand, he held a small leather notebook—his book of spells.

"Protection spell," Edwin said. "Their combat armor helped too."

As if to prove his point, the Protectors stirred. Dylan, military-buzz cut and pissed-off expression, wrenched himself to his feet. A faint magic sheen hung loosely around his frame. He helped up his partner, Beth. Edwin lowered his arm and the luster surrounding them vanished.

Dylan noticed them standing there.

"You were all supposed to stay in cover! You've exposed your positions!"

"Edwin just saved your life," Kaylee said. "You're welcome."

Dylan, still flushed in the face, began pointing back to the trees like he was directing traffic. "In position, before everything is compromised. We have to clean up this mess—"

"Not to break up your hissy fit," Josh said, appearing between Kaylee and the still-smoldering apartment. "Someone—or something—is still alive in there."

Edwin inched closer to Kaylee as they all faced where Josh pointed. There was movement within the rubble and hazy flames. The explosion had completely decimated half the complex. Kaylee dreaded to imagine the kind of person who would use such a volatile spell around an apartment building full of people.

Not that she was seeing any people.

"You hurt?" Edwin muttered.

"Never better. Thanks for the assist."

Edwin grinned, his cheeks blushing faintly. "If you stopped putting yourself in danger, I wouldn't have to do it."

"But what fun would that be?"

"More fun for me, that's for sure..."

"Are we really going to count how many times who saved whom?"

"Are we really going to do this now, you two?" Maddox said. He squinted into the flames. Something was moving closer, pushing its way through the rubble.

"This isn't right," Jade said.

"What gave it away, sweetheart?" Josh said. "Was it the apartment blowing up or that something's actually still alive afterward?"

Josh's dragon-kin Tamer, Tygus, all scrawny twelve-years-old of him, crouched more protectively in front of Josh. It was, Kaylee thought, the cutest, most futile thing she'd ever seen.

"I'm not seeing any civilians," Edwin said.

"That's the problem," Jade said. "Listen."

Kaylee did. Despite the explosion, there was no screaming. No sirens. No *people*. As if a muffling blanket had been tossed over the entire complex.

"Dampening spell," Dylan said. "Knew something was up. Nobody's probably been here for a while. He's turned the entire place into his personal lair."

An immense slab of concrete and splayed metal was hurled away from the nearest pile of rubble and landed with a crash twenty feet away.

Everyone took a step back.

"Now you all *really* need to get behind us," Beth said.

But it was too late.

A man, or what might have once been a man, hurled himself from the flames toward them, his arms flapping at his sides, his legs jutting out at impossible angles as he ran.

"Stop!" Dylan pulled his sword. The blade unfolded to a vicious point. "You're under arrest by order of the Scarsdale Convocation—"

The man swung. Kaylee had a moment to register that his arm was not an arm, that it was in pieces—fuzzy and disjointed, as if composed of a million dots—before it hit Dylan, the force of the blow sending him flying back. Kaylee blinked. Nobody short of a Merlin with an enhanced strength spell or a Slayer with a magically charged item could do that.

"Split!" Maddox yelled.

The group scattered. Kaylee, Edwin, and Josh stayed on the outside, conjuring magic to attack. Maddox and Jade, with no magic of their own, went with Beth straight for the man.

Jade swung her knife at the man's exposed mid-section. It was a good strike, impossible to miss at such close range. But at the last second the man's body split in two. Jade whiffed and stumbled past. A swarm of insects shot from the man's mouth and bashed her in the side. Maddox barely caught her as she tumbled.

"Scarabs! Don't let them reform!" Beth yelled, ducking beneath another attack.

The scarabs—hundreds of them, thousands of them—scuttled back into the man's form, pincers clicking, eyes glinting.

Kaylee pulled on her elemental magic and electricity answered. She'd been taking hand-to-hand combat lessons with Maddox and Jade for a while now, but this enemy would clearly require a little more force of the magical variety.

"Edwin, can you shield me?"

Edwin nodded and began chanting. The sweet tang of his magic covered Kaylee's tongue as his Shield spell fell on her. The effect would last only as long as Edwin could physically sustain it. And while he'd grown immensely better since the first time Kaylee had met him, she didn't want to put the extent of his magic to the test.

She rushed in, swiping with her clawed hands. A crackle of electricity sparked from the tips of her claws, skewering the mass of insects into two separate halves. This time they were slower to reform. The man's shapeless face turned on her. A gaping, writhing mouth lunged—just as a torrent of wind knocked it aside.

"You'll have to hit it harder than that, Kaylee!" Josh said.

"Give it some serious lightning," Edwin said. "That might be enough to disrupt it from reforming."

Josh summoned another burst of wind. "We'll give you an opening—no, Tygus!"

Josh's Tamer rushed forward as the man went for Josh. Josh knocked the strike aside and pulled the boy back by his collar. "You can protect me when we're not in danger! Go help Jade and Maddox. Now, Beth!"

Beth touched a carved talisman on her wrist. Kaylee recognized it as a magically charged charm the Convocation Merlins handed out to the magic-less Protectors. The charm glowed and Beth's sword ignited in flames. The scarab reared up, sending a wave of beetles her way. Beth's next strike broke through the mass and sent the group skittering back.

"Get ready, Kaylee!"

Kaylee called on her elemental magic again. The sensation was like trying to grasp a wriggling fish and use it as a weapon. She'd grown better the last few months, but Kaylee still felt she should have had more control by now.

The magic answered anyway.

Her electricity grew in power, balling in her hand. Her eyes picked out the electrical connections in the air around her; pathways of energy just waiting to conduct her power and enhance it.

"Now!" Beth yelled.

Josh summoned a final burst of wind. Beth swiped with her sword. The scarab screamed and fell back, exposing an opening. Kaylee charged. She raised her hand. The electricity sparked and snapped.

The scarab turned on her, hissing. Its eyes met her own.

But it wasn't the scarab anymore.

"Kaylee?" Brendan said.

Kaylee's throat seized. No. It wasn't possible. Brendan was—he was—

"Kaylee?" Brendan said again.

But he looked so real that she wanted to reach out and touch his intact face, so unlike the crushed, bleeding mess it had been when he'd died. When she'd—

"Kaylee!"

Jade's shriek jolted Kaylee back. There was no Brendan. There was only the scarab.

Its clawed hand slammed into her throat. Kaylee choked, seeing white spots. The scarab hissed, closing its grip. Tiny legs skittered up and down her skin. Pincers pierced at her flesh.

It's not him, Kaylee told herself. *He's dead.*

And why would that be?

Because I—

Kaylee thrust the ball of electricity into the scarab's face. The connections in the air ignited, coursing in an intricate pattern, feeding straight back into her attack, building in power.

The scarab's hand melted away. Its body puddled until there were only individual scarabs left twitching on the ground.

But still the magic grew around Kaylee. Her stomach clenched as she tried to wrestle it back. This was the feeling of overwhelm. The feeling of losing control, as she had with her storms. As she had when Brendan had forced the Slayers' dark magic into her. Too much. Too wild. Too uncontrollable.

Kaylee reined the magic back toward her. She drew it inside and held it there like a furious animal, the entire time her stomach tearing at itself. She clamped down harder, until the feeling fled and her magic receded back where it'd come from.

"Vas Ventir, Mar lo se!"

The beetles that had been scuttling in every direction were pulled back toward Edwin. Little by little, the black swarm vanished into the jar he held until there was nothing left and Edwin was able to cap it. He held it up.

"Thought we might need this," he said proudly.

In an instant, Jade was by Kaylee's side.

"What happened? You let that thing touch you!"

Kaylee moved her mouth, but the words wouldn't come.

"I thought you had your elemental magic under control," Josh said. Tygus was glaring at her from behind him, as if *she* was the threat.

"I did," Kaylee managed. "I mean, I do—"

"It didn't look that way to us," Beth said.

"She's trying," Jade snapped at them. "Believe it or not, it's a lot harder than it looks."

Beth snorted and sheathed her sword. She and Maddox helped a disoriented Dylan to his feet. "Let's scram, you guys. Now."

"What happened, Kaylee?" Jade asked in a smaller voice.

"Nothing happened. I screwed up. Sorry." Kaylee stood. Jade searched her face. She could read her better than anyone, but Kaylee made sure her expression was blank. She couldn't tell Jade she'd seen Brendan's face again. Jade thought she was over that. Kaylee thought she was too. The guy was a psychopath. Sadistic.

Dead.

You didn't mean to do it, Jade had said.

But did that make it any better? She had barely held onto her powers that night with the Slayers and it had almost cost her friends their lives.

Now she was losing control again.

"I said move out," Beth repeated. "We got what we came here for."

She, Maddox, and Dylan hurried off toward the van, parked out of sight across the street. Josh didn't move.

"If there's a problem, we need to know about it," he demanded, eyes narrowing. "I know our elemental powers are a little finicky—"

"You don't know anything," Kaylee snapped. "Stay out of this."

Tygus' glower deepened. Josh snorted.

"Sure, whatever you say. But I hope you figure out whatever it is before you *really* hurt someone."

"Too late for that," Kaylee whispered as he and Tygus walked off.

Jade put a reassuring hand on her shoulder. "We can talk more later. If you want."

"Thanks."

Jade nodded and followed the others.

When Kaylee looked up, Edwin was staring at her, his head half-cocked, his eyes deep and unreadable. He didn't say anything. He didn't ask if she was okay or what her problem was. He just stayed with her. And for that, Kaylee was immensely grateful.

"Come on," Kaylee said, leading the way back across the vacant parking lot. "Let's go home."

CHAPTER THREE

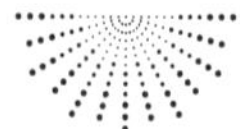

Edwin's family's mansion sat on a hill overlooking Scarsdale, in probably the nicest neighborhood in the city. The gates were wrought iron. Marble statues were more common in front yards than discarded children's toys, and there was a distinct difference in the air Kaylee could only describe as 'wealth.' Either that or badly burned pizza.

It had been two days since the scarab attack. By now, Kaylee had almost forgotten the nightmares she'd had since that night; frightening visions of teeth and claws, dark magic and a dead boy's face that wouldn't leave her alone.

Once school was out, she and Jade booked it to Edwin's house and up the long, winding path to the front door. Tibbs, Edwin's morose butler/housekeeper, let them in and led them to a room in the back of the house that Kaylee had never been to. It was a library, with floor to ceiling bookshelves, full of neatly arranged titles ranging from cracking, ancient spines to the latest thriller release.

"Misses Richards and Azuma to see you, Master Edwin," Tibbs droned when he let them in.

Edwin, curled in the nearest leather armchair with his face stuck in a book, grunted.

"Translation," Maddox said in the chair across from him, "thank you."

Tibbs inclined his head and backed out of the room, closing the door behind him.

"You think this is the best place to do that?" Jade asked Maddox as he used his lacrosse stick to toss a ball back and forth to himself. Maddox grinned, flipped the ball again, and caught it, his stick barely missing a pricey-looking globe on the nearby table.

Kaylee trailed her hand across the spines of the books. "All these are Alastair's?"

Edwin grunted. Kaylee cocked an eyebrow. She noticed the neatly arranged wooden desk near the window, every item on top of it meticulously arranged. "I should have guessed. Based on the state of Edwin's room, there's no way his library would be this neat."

Edwin snorted.

"Translation: very funny," Maddox said.

"I'd like to hear Edwin say it," Kaylee said.

"Edwin will be with you momentarily," Edwin said, burying his face deeper into the book. Maddox laughed.

They were quite the pair, Merlin and his Protector, Kaylee thought. While Maddox's bulky body and wide shoulders were splayed across most of his chair, Edwin's lanky, slender frame molded to his spot like water. His hair was curly brown to Maddox's straight black. And, if you got close enough to Edwin—which Kaylee had a couple times—there was the faintest splatter of freckles on the bridge of his nose beneath the bridge of his glasses.

Edwin shut the book with a snap and Kaylee jumped, realizing she'd been staring. Maddox fumbled with his lacrosse ball and narrowly missed skewering a nearby oil painting.

Edwin's eyes settled on Kaylee, drinking her in. "How are you feeling?"

"Why wouldn't I be feeling great?"

"I don't know. Why wouldn't you be?"

Kaylee glowered at him. He stared right back.

"I'm fine," Kaylee said.

"And I bet even if you weren't you probably wouldn't tell us, would you?"

"Annnnyway," Jade said as Kaylee made for a sharp retort. "Edwin, what have you found?"

Edwin finally pulled his eyes from Kaylee. "What makes you think I found anything?"

Jade nodded to the book in his hand. "You were reading. In Alastair's library. Which means you were probably looking for something related to the Slayers and Lesuvius."

"Am I that easy to see through?"

"Clear as glass," Maddox said brightly.

Edwin ran his fingers down the ridges of the book. "I haven't come up with anything yet. At first I thought this guy with the scarabs might have been involved with the Slayers somehow. Maybe they've been trafficking dangerous creatures similar to what they were doing with the illegal spell components last year. But the Convocation, at least here, hasn't actually been attacked by any magical beasts."

"Except for the sphinx in Mantinoba," Maddox said.

"Or the grindylow outbreak in Florida," Jade said.

"But both times, like with the scarabs, the creatures only attacked when we went after them," Edwin said. "And the Slayers weren't behind them."

"Plus, you told me most Slayer activity has moved west," Kaylee said.

"For now. It's only a matter of time before they swing our way again."

"So they're not using creatures, then," Jade said. "Then what's it going to be this time?"

Edwin cracked the book, but he was clearly not reading anything. "Not sure yet. I have a feeling it's going to be magic-based again."

"We stopped their last spell," Kaylee said. "We'll stop this one."

"That's why they won't do another spell," Edwin said. "At least not the same exact type. Too unstable. Not a high enough guarantee of success. I'm thinking they'll use an item to concentrate their power. Something powerful. Something the original Slayers tried to use back when they were still part of the order of St. George."

"The Convocation would have hidden or destroyed anything that powerful a long time ago," Maddox said. "We're safe then."

"But if they *were* to find something," Jade said, "you think it could be..." She extended a hand toward Edwin. "...what?"

Edwin uncurled from the chair and carefully replaced the book on the shelf. "No clue. As great as the texts are in here, nothing's...taboo enough to give me any ideas. Either about a possible item they could use or Lesuvius. For that info we'd need to go...somewhere else."

He glanced at Kaylee. She knew exactly what he was thinking. Baba Menorah, their magic instructor and immensely powerful Merlin, had a secret, spell-guarded room they'd snuck into once. It hadn't gone well. They'd managed to make it past the sentient rug guarding the place and even find the counterspell Edwin had used to defeat the Slayers last November. But when Baba had caught them she'd made it clear the next time they entered the room without permission would be their last.

Kaylee believed her.

"That option's out," Edwin said, mirroring her thoughts. "Until I can get access to similar texts there isn't much more I can learn about that, or Lesuvius."

"I thought I made it explicitly clear you were not to investigate anything relating to him," Alastair said, stepping into the room.

Maddox scrambled to sitting. Jade stood. Even Kaylee found herself straightening.

Alastair Dumas, Edwin's father, had the kind of presence that commanded attention. And for good reason. He was head of the Scarsdale Convocation. He also dressed the part, always wearing a charcoal-colored, three-piece Italian suit that only magnified his authority. It was either that or the dragon-kin in him. Though Kaylee knew he was a powerful forest dragon-kin, she wasn't quite sure what his powers could do. Much like the true strength of Baba's magic, she wasn't sure she wanted to find out.

"Well?" Alastair said, looking at Edwin. "What did I say?"

Edwin faced his father, shoulders squared. The two held their positions for a couple seconds before Edwin casually gestured to the book he'd just replaced.

"We weren't looking into him, but if we're talking about the Slayers his name *is* going to come up."

Alastair gruffly nodded. "He's heading the Slayers for now. That's all you need to know. Miss Azuma, Mr. Rudd, your instructor decided to have lessons out by the pond today. Please go join him."

Jade and Maddox nodded.

"Oh, and Dylan and Beth gave me their report from the other night. They said you both handled yourselves well under pressure and adapted to the situation. Jade, this speaks highly going into your Tamer test next year. Maddox, I may have to recommend your test be moved up, too."

"Thank you, sir," Maddox said, inclining his head.

"Yeah, thanks," Jade parroted. When she inclined her head, Kaylee caught her brief dark look.

"Edwin, you too, please," Alastair said once Jade and Maddox had left. "Tibbs would like some help cleaning the second dining room. This would be a good chance to practice inanimate animation magic on some of the mops."

"Sure," Edwin said. He paused beside Kaylee. Up close, she could make out each line of concern etched into his face.

"You sure there's nothing you want to tell me?" he said in a low voice. "I'm not buying that 'I'm okay' act for a second."

"Edwin—"

"I looked into cases like what happened to you, where someone's forced to take on more magic than they can handle. Granted, the cases were for Merlins, but the application's the same. They said the victims experienced hallucinations, lost control of their powers—"

"Edwin, please—"

Edwin leaned in. "Saw things that weren't there. *People* that weren't there. Sound familiar?"

Kaylee's breath caught. He knew. Of course he knew. After training so much together, he knew her almost as well as Jade, and now he'd figured it out. It was a horrifying relief. And yet… not. Because her guilt…that was still hers and hers alone.

"You can always talk to me, you know that," Edwin said. "When you're ready."

"I know that," Kaylee said. "And…I just…I will. Later. After I figure this out."

Alastair cleared his throat. "Tibbs is waiting, Edwin. You can see Kaylee after."

Edwin squeezed her hand, sending a rush of warmth shooting up her arm. "Just don't wait too long. See you soon."

Alastair's gaze lingered on the doors after shutting it behind Edwin.

"Am I in trouble or something?" Kaylee said.

Alastair laid his suit jacket across the back of his chair and settled on a corner of the desk. "No, not precisely. In that same report, Dylan and Beth also described your little…episode."

Kaylee stiffened. Episode? Way to make her sound like a

psych patient. Was that what her dragon-kin powers had been reduced to? Moments of total control interspersed with spastic outbreaks?

"It was the first time that's happened, Alastair," Kaylee said. That she'd told them about, anyway.

Alastair held up a placating hand. "They didn't condemn you for what happened. In fact, they praised your ability to control the magic when it got loose."

"But there's still a problem," Kaylee guessed.

"Yes." Alastair sighed. "Losing control isn't the problem. It's just a symptom of an underlying issue. You've done immensely well training with Baba—"

As if on cue, the study doors burst open and Baba Menorah strode in. Kaylee couldn't have been more shocked than if she'd fallen through the ceiling. It was one thing to see the portly, stringy-haired old grouch actually out in public; it was quite another to see her wearing something other than her normal, ratty bathrobe. In this case, canvas jeans and a corduroy shirt, with boots two-sizes too big, their tongues flapping with every step.

Baba made herself at home in one of the leather chairs. She propped her boots up on the center table and pulled out a flask.

"Baba..." Alastair said with a strained grin. "Glad you could make it."

"Not happy to." She took a swig.

"I'll have to ask you to refrain from drinking in my study. We have another room for that across the house."

"By all means, ask away," Baba said, taking another sip. "You tell her yet?"

"Tell me what?" Kaylee said.

"I was getting to that," Alastair said. "Kaylee, you've done well controlling your powers under Baba's tutelage—"

"I'd call it passable," Baba said. "But acceptable."

"—but the truth of the matter is that we believe you've reached the limit of what Baba can teach you."

"The...limit."

"Your dragon-kin elemental magic is strong, girl. Very strong," Baba said. "Like 'Stair said, you've kept it pretty much under wraps, save for a stray lightning bolt here and there. But that's not enough. You need another trainer. Another dragon-kin. Preferably one with similar elemental magic to yours."

Kaylee looked between each of them. "You mean I won't be taking lessons with Edwin?"

Baba snorted into her flask. "Told you she wouldn't take it well."

Kaylee clamped down her fingers, which had begun to grow warm with sparks. "I'm in control, if that's what you mean. But..."

This wasn't supposed to happen. Sure, not too long ago just the thought of training with Edwin had infuriated her, but they'd been through a lot since then. She'd helped him become a better Merlin, and he'd helped her when the struggles of being a dragon-kin and Slayer's target were too much. They'd fought together, nearly died together. It was the kind of mutual experience that tended to bring people closer.

Kaylee touched the small wooden charm around her neck. Edwin had made it for her to help her calm down when their training had grown overwhelming. The magic in the charm had long since worn off, and though Edwin would usually only recharge it before a big test, she wore it all the time anyway.

"Have you told Edwin?" Kaylee said.

"No," Alastair said.

"It ain't like you'll never see the boy again," Baba said. "Don't be so dramatic."

Breathe, Kaylee told herself. *Murdering Baba wouldn't help anything.* "I'm not being dramatic."

Baba stomped her feet down and see-sawed to standing. She

placed her hands on Kaylee's shoulders. Her breath reeked of scotch. "Listen close, girl, 'cause I ain't gonna say it again: you did good with me. Not great. Nothing to write home about. Your shifting still needs work and your elemental magic needs tempering, but considering how terrible you were when you arrived, you suck less than you did then."

"Thanks, Baba," Kaylee said, knowing that was as close to a compliment as she was ever going to get from the old woman. But she cared, Kaylee knew that. Baba hadn't confessed to it, but she'd been the one to pull Kaylee from the wreckage of the barn before it collapsed on her. Not letting her die had to count as some kind of affection.

Baba pounded Kaylee's shoulders once more. "I said my piece. Don't get used to it."

"Who?" Kaylee said, not sure if she wanted to ask, "Who's going to train me now?"

"We're not sure yet," Alastair said. "I'm the only fully-trained Convocation dragon-kin in the Scarsdale area and, unfortunately, I don't have the time. I also don't think I would be much help. You don't just need a trained dragon-kin, you need one with at least some similar elemental magic to yours."

"But how many other storm dragon-kin are there?" Kaylee said. "Unless you're talking about—"

She clamped her mouth shut before the rest of her thought could flutter free. Baba didn't appear to notice Kaylee had been about to mention the only other storm dragon-kin they both knew: Baba's former best friend, who had holed herself up alone somewhere after accidentally killing innocent bystanders with her uncontrolled elemental magic. If the subject of breaking into Baba's secret room was touchy, the isolation of her best friend was even worse.

"We've put out a call for candidates, so don't get your knickers in a bunch, Alastair," Baba said. "The elemental magic component won't be that big a deal either. She's a storm dragon-kin. Who wouldn't want the chance to train her? Maybe we're looking at a light elemental dragon-kin, maybe that dark dragon-kin I've heard about in Manhattan."

"Absolutely not him—"

"Heck, even a wind dragon-kin would do. Best would probably be electric, but there aren't many of those in the Convocation, are there?"

"No."

"Hmm..." Baba's mouth squeezed to a thin line. "You don't know of a single one?"

"Not in the Convocation, so no," Alastair said sharply.

Baba's lips stayed thin. "Very well. Though you should know it's her skin you're putting on the line by leaving her untrained, not your own. Kaylee," Baba waved a hand, "scram. 'Stair and I have business to discuss."

"And Kaylee," Alastair said when she reached the door. "We're sorry. Truly."

Kaylee nodded, not because she agreed, but because they couldn't be as sorry as she was.

CHAPTER FOUR

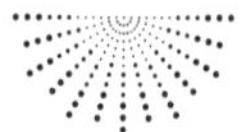

"You told Edwin already?" Jade said. "How'd he take it?"

Kaylee stuffed whatever she didn't need for her first classes into her locker. The movement was haphazard. Jerky. Her head wasn't in it, not after talking with Edwin for almost two hours yesterday and seeing the hurt look on his face when she'd told him they wouldn't be training together anymore.

"He...didn't take it well," Kaylee admitted.

That was an understatement. He'd been furious. But not at her.

"I know you're a dragon-kin, and yeah, you've had some problems," Edwin had admitted. "But this won't help. We can figure it out together. We're partners, yeah?"

Kaylee tried to forget how her stomach had fluttered when he'd said that.

"He's talking to Alastair about it," Kaylee said. "I told him not to. Not that I don't appreciate it, but it's not going to help anything."

Jade closed her own locker and leaned against it, observing the mixed mass of students as they streamed by toward their first classes.

"Honestly, and I know you're going hate me for saying this, but I agree with Alastair."

"That I shouldn't train with Edwin?" Kaylee said hotly. Jade shook her head.

"That you need a better teacher." She smirked. "I wouldn't *dream* of taking you away from Edwin."

Kaylee's face flamed. "What does that—?"

"Kaylee, I don't think you realize how strange your situation is. Not only did you discover your dragon-kin powers way later than usual, but you've never even had a properly trained dragon-kin teach you. You know how uncommon that is? In a normal Convocation there're at least two or three older dragon-kin who help teach the young ones."

"I have—had—Baba."

"Which was great, for a time. Now she's not."

The bell for their first class rang. Jade pushed off her locker and the two of them headed for Government.

"Besides, I thought you and Baba didn't get along all that well," Jade said.

"We don't. I mean we do. It's a mutual-dislike-but-grudging-tolerance sort of thing."

"Ah," Jade said, nodding sagely. "The most stable of all relationships."

Most of the other students had filtered away to class, save for the lingering few who darted in and out of the attendance office. All the major hallways in school led to a large four-way intersection. The attendance office was on the right, band hall to the left, straight ahead were the gyms, and at the other end, the outer quad, bisecting the school into two separate halves.

Dani stood in front of one of the bulletin boards in the center of the crossroads. She brushed her hands to straighten her jeans and sweater. They were both slightly stained at the fringes, as if she'd splattered mud on them running here.

"Dani!" Jade said.

The other girl turned, and Kaylee was briefly taken aback.

Dani was by far one of the nicest people Kaylee knew, and one of the prettiest. She had golden hair that shimmered almost as brightly as her attitude, and was involved in more clubs than Kaylee had friends. She was the kind of person who was so cheery it almost bordered on disgusting, but thankfully never quite reached that point.

But now…when she smiled at them, it didn't quite reach her eyes. There were strained lines on the edges of her cheeks. Her cheeks were a bit sunken, as if she hadn't eaten well in a little while.

"Hey, guys! Running a little late, too?"

"Voluntarily," Jade said. "Mr. Tuttle won't dock us if we're a minute late."

"Hit some trouble?" Kaylee said, nodding at the mud on her sweater.

"Did I—oh." Dani fingered the splattered hem. "No, I—just a little misstep in the parking lot. No biggie!" She laughed, this one sounding unusually hollow. "Anyway, I heard what happened, Kaylee," Dani added seriously. "The training, I mean."

"You heard too?" Kaylee groaned inwardly. Did *everyone* know what was going on with her life?

"Maddox told me," Dani said in an apologetic tone. "I know you'll find a great teacher. And that doesn't mean you can't still hang out with Edwin. Maybe outside of training."

Dani gave her a wink, but the move seemed like a great effort, like she hadn't done it in quite a while.

"I'll see you guys around," she said. Then she disappeared down the hall, leaving Kaylee with unanswered questions cartwheeling in her head.

~

KAYLEE MANAGED to survive the first half of the day with

minimal suffering. It was so close to Thanksgiving break now that most teachers (with the exception of Chemistry, of course) had pretty much given up trying to teach anything, but instead handed out busy work. Kaylee was totally fine with that. Having the horror of busy work was nothing compared to what she'd been dealing with last year at this time: the rise of the Dragon Moon and what the Slayers had been trying to do with it; mainly, steal all the dragon-kin's elemental magic. Permanently.

Yeah, she'd take the busy work.

They met up with Maddox at lunch. They were able to get a few seats down from Maddox's lunch buddies from the lacrosse team, but not right with them, which Kaylee was silently grateful for. The lunch room was an almost unbearable din of noise, and at least half of it seemed to stem from that part of the table.

"Word to the wise, if you can avoid taking AP Calculus, do it," Maddox said, putting his tray down next to them harder than necessary. Flecks of mashed potato spewed onto Jade's sandwich. "Seriously, I think my brain is officially mush."

"You're in AP Calc?" Kaylee said.

Maddox gave her a shining grin. "Not just a pretty face, huh?"

Jade finished brushing off the rest of Maddox's collateral damage. "Just because he's *in* AP Calc doesn't mean he's passing it."

"Which is why we're studying again Sunday night, right?" Maddox said. "I've got another test right after break I want to get a jump on—"

"Kaylee, you want to join?" Jade interrupted.

"What?"

"For studying Sunday. Don't you have Speech to work on or something?"

The way Jade asked made Kaylee feel like this was about more than studying. It was a question to ease the guilt of Jade and Maddox spending time together without Kaylee. That wasn't anything new. The two had been training together in the Convocation for years.

But this wasn't training. This was them, together, in a non-Convocation setting. Apparently they'd been doing it for a little while, too. The somewhat-secrecy combined with the setting somehow made it all the more personal, and the way Jade's eyes kept flickering guiltily to her sandwich told Kaylee she felt bad Kaylee had even found out about it.

"Thanks, but you guys go ahead," Kaylee said. "Maybe I'll catch up on…maybe I'll…Edwin and I can do something."

Jade's eyes lit up. "That's a great idea! There's that new horror movie at the theatre you said you wanted to see. Maybe you two could go."

"Jade…"

"Maybe he'd even ask you—"

"Jade. Not helping."

Maddox looked between them both, his expression that of bewildered confusion.

"You guys just slipped into a different language there for a sec."

"Maddox," a guy from down the table yelled. "You gonna join us or what?"

Maddox waved him off with a grin. "That reminds me, practice is going longer today 'cause of how close the season's getting. I'll have to meet you guys at Baba's later than normal."

"Not me," Kaylee said quietly.

Maddox paused with a large scoop of peas halfway to his mouth. "Ah. Right. Crap. Sorry."

"Way to go," Jade said, in a slightly chastising voice.

"You have any idea who'll be taking over for the Baba?" Maddox asked, trying to salvage the conversation. "I'm sure you're not sorry to see the lessons with her end, am I right?"

"Kind of," Kaylee said. "And I have no idea who it'll be. According to Alastair, training me would be a 'great honor,' so I might get every glory-seeking whack job dragon-kin for five-hundred miles."

"Maybe you'll get that guy from the Saginaw Convocation Edwin was telling us about, Jade," Maddox said, elbowing her. "Remember?"

"The earth dragon-kin they named the Trainee Torturer?" Jade said.

"Let's...talk about something else," Kaylee said. Her stomach was starting to hurt just thinking about it.

"Sorry," Maddox said. He stood with his tray. "Just joking around. I'm sure whoever you get will be awesome."

He nodded at them and joined the guys down the table. Kaylee ignored a wink from the nearest one (Bleached hair? Seriously?) and searched for something else to distract herself from the thought of not going to training today.

Dani was two tables away with her usual group of friends from the girls' soccer team. She laughed loudly at a joke one of them had just cracked. *This* Dani seemed fine. Worlds apart from the one they'd met earlier.

"Did Dani seem off to you this morning?" Kaylee said.

Jade swiveled to where Kaylee was looking. "Off how?"

"Just not herself."

"Probably had a bad morning. Even bottomless rays of sunshine have cloudy days."

They did, Kaylee agreed. But this had seemed more than that to her. But maybe she was reading too much into it. As if she didn't have enough problems of her own, she now had to try to find them in other people.

"She's been hanging around the Convocation more often, which is good," Jade said. "My instructor thinks she might have a future working behind the scenes for them."

"Huh..." Kaylee said.

"Hey, don't worry about your new instructor," Jade said,

misinterpreting Kaylee's silence. "I'm sure you won't get the Trainee Torturer."

"And if I do?"

Jade flashed her a playful grin. "Then it was nice knowing you."

By the time the final bell rang, Kaylee was almost glad she didn't have lessons with Baba to go to. Her mind was a thousand different places except for school, and the last thing she wanted to do was try to rein them all in by *focusing*.

Kaylee said goodbye to Jade at her locker before her friend left for her own training. There was a painful pull in her chest as she watched her walk down the hall. She and Jade had never not walked home together, even when they'd had a big argument. Now, Jade didn't even have to be around her all the time. The Scarsdale charms and Convocation reports would be enough to keep Kaylee safe until the Slayers showed up again. And now... Kaylee didn't have a reason to go to Baba's anymore. Sure, she *could* go, but Baba had made it clear she was done training her. And standing around there would be awkward. She could go to see Edwin, but...

Kaylee slammed her locker shut. She had lingered after the last bell and most of the other students had dispersed outside to freeze for their respective sports or trickled to band or after-school clubs. Kaylee briefly wondered which one Dani was going to, if at all.

Does she seem...off?

Kaylee was so lost in thought, she didn't notice the brief shadow falling over her, or react in time when a shoulder clipped hers. Her backpack hit the ground, the contents spilling like a broken bubble gum machine.

"Ouch! Sorry."

She stooped to pick up her stuff. She noticed the boots—ragged, chipped, with pieces of leather treatment peeling off them—stayed in place.

"Thanks for the help," Kaylee muttered.

She scooped up the last of her things and stood.

A girl stared back, not even pretending to act concerned. At first, Kaylee thought a female version of Damian from the Slag Heap had transferred to their school. The girl wore rumpled jeans and a frayed jacket with the sleeves cut off, matching the fingerless gloves on her hands. Half her head was shaved, the other long and brushed back over her shoulder. The girl smirked and crossed her arms, revealing tiny tattoos of symbols Kaylee couldn't read on the knuckle of each finger. Piercings dotted her eyebrows, lips, and nose.

"Thanks for apologizing," Kaylee said. "The death metal band doesn't play until four."

The girl smirked wider. "So you're it, huh? Got some spine in you. I like that."

An uncomfortable drop settled in Kaylee's stomach. "I'm it? What does that mean?"

The girl brushed past her. "Later."

"Hold on!" Kaylee scrambled to zip up her backpack before chasing after the girl around the corner.

The hallway was empty.

Kaylee blinked. She must have taken a wrong turn. Maybe she'd gone right instead of left. Maybe she was hiding.

Kaylee opened the nearest door. A storage closet. Empty. Beside it was a classroom. Also empty.

"Excuse me?" A girl poked her head out of a nearby room. "Can you stop slamming doors, please?"

"Sorry—did you? Was there another girl passing by here just now?"

The girl shook her head. "We would have heard her if she was as loud as you."

Touché, Kaylee thought.

Then she saw the fox. The door to the outside quad running between the two halves of the school was propped open, letting in waves of chilly air. The fox sat in the doorway, staring at her.

It was made entirely of electricity; that much Kaylee could tell. Its body roiled with a continuous current, from the tops of its ears to the tips of its nine tails.

For some reason, this stuck out to Kaylee most. Maybe it was because, now that she was part of a world where people could cast spells and she could summon thunderstorms, that the idea of a fox made of electricity wasn't so surprising as much as what *kind* of fox it was.

If it was possible for a bundle of electricity, the fox regarded her with a mix of curiosity and boredom, before turning and zipping away outside. Kaylee wasted no time in following it, out through the quad, around the rear of the school between the science wing and the athletic field, and over toward the woods on the western edge of the school where fewer people were.

It dawned on her that this was *exactly* what someone trying to hurt her would do, but already she was slowing. The fox had reached the very edge of the student parking lot, mostly separate and exclusive from the rest. This part was where the seniors paid a hundred bucks to paint their own personalized spaces. A few cars still remained. And a man.

Kaylee ground to a halt, her body tilted halfway toward the man in case he...did something. She wasn't sure what.

From the hundred yards or so between them, Kaylee could tell he was big. He was draped in a thick leather jacket and jeans, and a helmet and sunglasses obscured most of his face. He was casually leaning on an idling motorcycle.

The fox scurried up to him. The man flicked his hand and the fox dissipated, the electricity flowing up his arm and away.

The two of them stared at one another for a full minute.

Despite the sunglasses and distance, Kaylee knew—*knew*—the guy was smirking at her.

"What do you want?" Kaylee said loudly. She immediately felt stupid. Maybe he was a parent picking up a kid. On a motorcycle. Dressed like a gang member. Far away from the pick-up zone. With a magic nine-tailed fox avatar.

Kaylee took a step toward him. As she did, the man kicked his motorcycle into gear. He gave a last nod to Kaylee then rumbled out of sight.

Only then did Kaylee realize she'd shifted her hands to claws.

THANKSGIVING PASSED without anyone dying or the Slayers trying to kill her. Not surprisingly, it made the holiday that much more enjoyable.

The next week was a battle for Kaylee to stay focused. Finals were squashed between their upcoming Christmas break and, on top of that, she and Jade had been kept busy with their respective training; Kaylee trained by herself, trying to mimic the intensity of the lessons she'd had with Baba, and utterly failing. Jade continued practicing for her test to become an official Tamer, which would take place the following year.

Kaylee's parents had been a little more concerned lately too, and it showed with their increased questioning about finding her a new trainer. They hadn't been the most involved in Convocation business, but now that Kaylee had stopped the training that would supposedly help her actually survive until at least college, they'd visited Alastair a couple times to figure out what was going on.

"You're in trouble..." her little brother Jeremy had said one night when their parents had gotten home from their latest meeting.

"Shove it, squirt," Kaylee said, pushing his head down. The

move wasn't as effective as it used to be. Jeremy had shot up over the last summer. Now he was one of the tallest seventh graders in his middle school, a fact he continually reminded her of.

Kaylee had asked her parents if Alastair had found someone yet.

"No one suitable," her mother had answered.

"They will," her father had said cheerily. "Think of it like training for the Olympics. You have to find the perfect trainer to make it to the gold!"

"That's...not a great analogy, Tim," her mother said.

"Unless the gold is not dying," Kaylee said.

KAYLEE KNEW something was wrong the moment she stepped out of her last class. Instead of being packed and ready to go to her after school training, Jade was waiting in the hallway for her, a serious look on her face.

"Problem?" Kaylee said.

"We're not sure yet," Jade said. "Get your stuff. Quick."

Jade stayed uncomfortably close to her as the pair of them threaded through other students to their lockers. As Kaylee pulled the books she needed, Jade kept a keen eye turned toward the outside doors.

"You're kind of scaring me," Kaylee said, laughing weakly to try to lighten the mood. She lowered her voice, but it was impossible for anyone to hear them over the relieved end-of-school chatter. "Should I be prepared to...you know? Shift?"

Jade's eyes briefly widened. "No! I mean, hopefully not. You should never do that in front of normal people. Unless, you know, you're in mortal peril."

Kaylee closed her locker and they crossed to the doors leading to the quad. "And *will* I be in mortal peril?"

Jade didn't answer. She double-checked the coast was clear, then pushed the door open.

Maddox screeched to a halt in front of them. Jade went for the knife in her sleeve, stopping a second short as Maddox threw up his hands.

"Friendly! Friendly!"

"Idiot!" Jade hissed. "Maybe try jumping out of the bushes next time! Where is he?"

"Gone," Maddox said. "Pulled out of the parking lot a few minutes ago. A Protector swung by to tell me they're trying to track him."

"Let's get her home."

But as they talked, an uncomfortable feeling had started in Kaylee's gut. "This...person, this guy...Was he wearing a leather jacket? Riding a motorcycle?"

Jade and Maddox stared at her.

"*Please* tell me you didn't talk to him," Jade said.

"No! Of course not!" Kaylee didn't mention she *nearly* had. She already felt like enough of an idiot, waltzing into danger like that. "I saw him once, about a week ago."

"Great. Who knows how long he's been here," Maddox said.

"Who is he?"

Jade pulled her arm and they started across the parking lot. For once, Kaylee wished she had a vehicle to go with her shiny new driver's license. It would have been so easy to simply throw their things in and drive off to safety.

"We don't know who he is, only that he's been around the Convocation safe houses and places of operation. He also seems to know a lot about how the Convocation operates."

"And about you," Maddox said.

"Thanks, Maddox. Like we needed to worry her any more."

But as the two of them flanked either side of Kaylee and hurried her down the street, Kaylee wondered if there was a very good reason to be worried.

"GET INSIDE," Jade said when they reached Kaylee's house. "I'll stay out front for a bit. A Protector should check in soon."

"I'll go update Alastair," Maddox said. He jogged off in the direction of Edwin's house, pulling out his cell phone as he went.

"You should come inside with me," Kaylee said.

"Na-ah. Someone's got to stand guard."

"Jade, I'm a little better at protecting myself than I used to be. And you won't do much good protecting me if you're out here."

Jade pointed to herself. "Tamer." She pointed to Kaylee. "Dragon-kin. Now get inside."

Kaylee sighed. They'd had this debate before and there was no arguing with her. Jade swore she wasn't Kaylee's dragon-kin Tamer out of obligation, but as her best friend. Still, no matter how many times she said it, Kaylee would never feel good about her best friend being in harm's way for her sake.

Kaylee went around the side gate, toward the back door. She paused as she passed the garage.

Odd. Her mom's car was home. And her dad's? They weren't supposed to get off work for hours.

Nervousness prickled the back of Kaylee's neck. There was probably a good reason for them being home early. Maybe Jeremy had gotten in trouble at school again. That had to be it. Nothing sinister or unusual about that. All the craziness of the last hour had sent her internal alarm bells into overdrive.

But as she put the key in the back door and cracked it open, she turned, sensing something out of place. It was a hiccup in the normal uniformity of their backyard—a disparagement in the usual outline.

Kaylee held in a gasp.

There, leaning against the shed, partially obscured beneath a ratty tarp, was a motorcycle. And not just any motorcycle: the one she'd seen the man riding the other week.

Something shocked her leg.

Kaylee let out a startled yelp of alarm and stumbled inside as an electric fox slipped past her.

"Kaylee?" a gruff voice said. Kaylee froze. She should run. She could make it back to Jade before the creep could grab her.

"Kaylee?" her mom said.

Oh no. Her parents. Maybe even her little brother. She couldn't leave them here. She'd never be able to live with herself if they got hurt.

Kaylee forced her nerves to settle and stepped the rest of the way inside and into the kitchen.

Her parents stood, arms crossed, near the refrigerator. The motorcycle man leaned on the bar, eyeing her with interest.

"There's my favorite niece," he said in a voice low and grating. "Technically, my only one, but who's counting? 'Bout time we saw each other again."

"Who are you?" Kaylee demanded.

The man chuckled. "Oh, you know me, girl, though you were just a spit when I saw you last." He raised one hand and electricity crackled between his fingers. "I'm your Uncle Randy."

CHAPTER FIVE

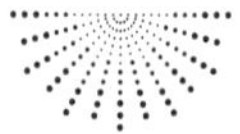

Kaylee's arms shifted before she realized she'd done it. Goosebumps prickled the skin on the back of her neck as the temperature dropped. The windows fogged, then frosted.

Uncle Randy cracked an eyebrow. "Well, I wasn't entirely sure if I believed what they'd said about you. Glad to see I'm not completely wasting my time."

"Kaylee, what have I told you about magic in the house?" her mom barked. "Away, now, young lady!"

"He was at my school. A week ago," Kaylee said, not moving. "He's been following me."

"Not *following*," Uncle Randy said. "Scouting."

"You went to her *school*, Randall?" Kaylee's mom said. "Do you have any idea how creepy that is?"

"In retrospect, not my finest idea. I wanted to see her before ol' Alastair got a whiff I was here. Wasn't sure if he would actually let me meet her."

"Gee, I wonder why that would be," her dad said. "Maybe because you're dangerous?" He pointed to the door. "You need to leave, right now."

"Calm down, *Tim*," Randy said. "I'll leave when I've said my piece. And why don't we stop this idiocy?"

He brought up one muscular arm and waved his hand in a swirling motion. The electricity rotating around Kaylee's hands was pulled into the center of his palm. Randy closed his fist and the electricity vanished.

"There. Glad to see they didn't completely skimp on your training, though when I heard they had Baba Menorah teaching you..." Randy shuddered. "Glad you're still alive, kid."

"How did you do that?" Kaylee said, her curiosity temporarily outweighing the immediate threat.

Randy winked. "Pretty cool, right? You can learn, if you want."

"What are you doing here, Randy?" her mom said. She snapped her fingers. "Kaylee. Dragon scales away. I won't ask again."

Kaylee reluctantly shifted her arms back. Randy held up a hand.

"I'll explain everything in just a sec. Let's let the rest of the party arrive—ah, here they are."

Kaylee hadn't heard Alastair or the others come in. In an instant, a Protector blocked each door to the kitchen. Alastair himself stood in front of them, his sleeves rolled back, his hands clawed. It was an intimidating display of force. Randy looked unimpressed.

"Oh look, the rest of the party."

"Back up, Kaylee," Jade whispered behind her. "Let them handle this."

Kaylee stayed in place. After the initial shock at seeing her uncle again had worn off, her common sense took over. This was Uncle Randy, not Lesuvius or some rogue Slayer. The guy had visited once when she was a kid and hadn't hurt her then. He also could have attacked her at school but hadn't. If he'd wanted her dead, she would be by now.

"Alastair." Randy nodded. "I see the Scarsdale Convocation is still as alive and kicking as ever. Though your outer perimeter security is a bit lacking. It took your guys almost a week to figure out I was hanging out at all your Convocation hotspots."

"What are you doing here, Randall?" Alastair demanded.

"Just heeding the call, like a few other trained dragon-kin."

"Heeding—" Understanding dawned on Alastair's face. "Absolutely not. That position and any position like it was closed to you a long time ago."

Randy settled his weight on the kitchen bar. For such a big man, the movement was almost delicate. "Circumstances have changed, my man. Clearly, if you're having to—" He paused. He motioned to the Protectors still hovering around the edge of the kitchen. "Can these guys leave? We're trying to have a decent conversation."

"They're here to escort you out."

"If you're worried I'll hurt Kaylee or anyone else, don't be." Randy sucked in a deep breath. A prickle shot up Kaylee's spine. The overhead lights blazed twice as bright, forcing everyone to cover their eyes. When Kaylee put her hand down, she could see a cage of electricity surrounding Randy like a coil of snakes. An occasional bolt lashed out toward Alastair. The Protectors surrounding him took a step back.

"If I wanted to hurt them, I would have," Randy said simply.

"No magic in the *house*!" Kaylee's mom yelled. "Enough, Randall!"

Randy let out another long breath, his eyes never leaving Alastair. The electricity vanished. "Whatever you may have heard about me, I would never hurt my family. I'm not a monster, Alastair."

"I never said you were. I also never said you were someone to trust."

"Why don't you try giving me the chance to earn it?"

The two held their gazes a second longer, then Alastair reluctantly waved a hand to the Protectors. "Outside, but stay alert. That means you, Jade."

"But—"

"Now, Jade. Thank you for bringing Kaylee home."

Jade eventually nodded then joined the other Protectors as they left. Kaylee stepped closer to her parents. Alastair and Randy continued to face off.

"I still won't allow it," Alastair said.

"You *did* send out a call, didn't you?"

"For any teacher other than you."

"I'm sorry, are my qualifications lacking?"

"Your methods are not how we handle things in the Convocation—"

"Has anyone died?"

"That's not—"

"But no one's died."

"...No."

"And the people I've stopped deserved it."

"It's not about deserving it—"

"And I'm an electric dragon-kin, which is probably the closest elemental magic you'll find to hers, unless you have another storm dragon hiding beneath that ridiculous suit. Plus, I'm family."

Randy stepped closer to Alastair. "So what you're really saying is you don't want me training her because I didn't pledge allegiance to your little club."

"*Did* you come here to train me?" Kaylee said. "You're applying to be my new teacher?"

"Yes. And as far as training..." Randy eyed her. "You've got spark, I'll give you that. I've heard of Scarsdale's storm dragon-kin darling. We'll have to see if there's any truth to the stories."

Kaylee's dad stiffened. "If you think for a moment I'm going to let my daughter train with you—"

"Tim," Kaylee's mother said in a warning tone, but her dad cut her off with a slice of his hand.

"No, Brianna! This guy vanishes for years, then just shows up and expects to be let back into our lives?" He pointed a threatening finger at Randy, and for the first time during the entire conversation, Kaylee felt a ripple of unease. She had never seen her dad lose his temper like this. "She's not going to train with you."

"That's not your decision, *Tim*," Randy said. "Do you want what's best for Kaylee?"

Her dad's face grew so purple Kaylee was afraid it would explode. "How dare—"

"If you want what's best for her then she needs the proper training. And that's with me." He turned to Alastair. "And I think you know it."

Alastair glared at him a moment longer.

"Um...don't I get a say in this?" Kaylee said. "He's going to be *my* teacher, after all."

"Kaylee, we've got plenty of other teachers who I'm sure would be more than happy to take you as their student," Alastair said.

"You mean like the Trainee Torturer?"

Alastair grimaced. "Viktor's methods are a little...uncouth, I'll admit. But he gets results."

Randy let out a rumbling laugh that reminded Kaylee of a car with a dead battery trying to turn over. "Viktor and the other two idiots I know applied couldn't teach a baby how to cry. You really think an earth or sky dragon-kin know the first thing about her kind of magic?"

"About as much as you."

"I want Randy," Kaylee said.

The room hushed. Her dad's mouth hung slack.

"Kaylee..." her mother said.

Randy beamed at Kaylee. "Good choice, kid. We can start with the basics and move to—"

"*Wait.*" Kaylee's mom didn't speak forcefully, but again the conversation came to a grinding halt. Kaylee had heard her mother use that tone only a few times before, and none of them had ended well for the person her fury was directed at. It was almost as if she'd gone beyond simple anger and entered a whole new level of reprimanding.

"Randall, you come motoring into town after years traveling God-knows-where, never having written, called, spoken to us *once*—"

"I came by when Jeremy was born!" Randy protested.

"And nearly caused an electrical fire and burned our house to the ground!"

Randy shrank back as Kaylee's mom advanced, finger raised. The way he stared at it made it seem as if she wielded a sword aimed straight at his heart.

"As if that wasn't enough, you tried to traumatize Kaylee—"

"I was seeing if she had any latent dragon-kin abilities."

"She was three, Randall!"

"Turns out I was right, though, wasn't I—?"

"And after that, you zoom off into the night and we don't hear from you until now. Please explain to me how any of that sounds like the kind of responsible adult who should be teaching my child."

The room held its breath when Kaylee's mom finished. Her dad gently patted her hand. All eyes were on Randy.

He looked between each of them, a half-cocked grin on his face, eyes beseeching for some leverage. Some way out. When he didn't find it, his expression sobered.

"Okay, okay, okay. No, I haven't been here, or stayed in touch, or any of that. But you, of all people, should know that's not how I roll, Brianna."

"That's a pathetic excuse," Kaylee's mom said. "And I wouldn't know 'how you roll.' You never let me find out. Not when you spirited off every chance you got. Not when you left me and our parents without a word and just—"

"Enough!" Randy roared. The lights flickered again. One

shorted, raining sparks down on Randy who brushed them away as casually as a dusting of ash. He took a deep breath and the lights settled. A Protector rushed in, but Alastair waved him down, still expectantly facing Randy. "I'm the best not because I stay in one place or I'm the best role model to your precious princess," Randy said. "There's a reason I travel around. Settling ain't my style. But you know what I am the best at?" He pointed out the now-darkened kitchen window. "Knowing what she's going to face when she finally leaves this crummy city, and how to deal with it."

"Mom," Kaylee said. "He's right."

"How do you know that, Kaylee?" her dad said. "Surely there's someone more qualified. More stable. More…sane."

But Alastair was reluctantly shaking his head. "I hate to say it, but if half of what I've heard Randall has done is true then he is equipped for the danger Kaylee may face. And his elemental magic is close to hers.

"A dragon-kin should have a say in who they have as their mentor, and Kaylee has picked Randall," Alastair continued. "We'll see if it turns out to be the right choice."

"Yeah, we'll see," Kaylee said, giving Randy a hard look. He smirked.

"Randall and I are going to have a very long chat tonight before Kaylee begins lessons," Kaylee's mom said quietly. "We have a few things to iron out."

Randy's smile dropped. "I look forward to it, sis."

"And while you are training Kaylee or residing in Scarsdale, you are hereby under Scarsdale Convocation rules and order," Alastair said. "You follow our laws, you confer with us before you do anything, or there *will* be consequences."

"Sure. Whatever. Maybe with me here you'll actually get your little rogue dragon-kin issue packed away."

"How do you know about that?" Alastair said sharply.

Randy grinned, tapping the side of his head. "Oh, I'm half as good as they say, Alastair. There's a lot I know that I'd just *love* to share with you. I'm sure you wouldn't mind the extra helping hand of a fully trained dragon-kin every now and then, would you?"

The temptation was evident on Alastair's face, but he managed to stamp it down. "It…wouldn't hurt."

There came a cry of alarm from the hallway a second before Jeremy stumbled in. He froze when everyone stared at him.

"Hi…" He gave a sheepish grin. "I, uh, found your dog-thing, Uncle Randy."

The electric fox sauntered in behind him, looking rather pleased with itself.

"Completely forgot about that," Randy said. He waved his hand and vanished the fox before rustling Jeremy's hair. "You've gotten big!"

"Were you eavesdropping again, squirt?" Kaylee said.

Jeremy made a face at her. "It's not eavesdropping if you can hear everything from the stairs."

"That's enough for tonight," Kaylee's dad said. "Jeremy, set the table. Kaylee, homework."

"Randall," Kaylee's mom swept her arm toward her office. "Let's talk."

"Right." Randy straightened his rumpled jacket. "Interrogation time." He ruffled Jeremy's hair again and walked past Kaylee.

"Training starts tomorrow, Kaylee," he called back. "Hope you're ready."

The office door slammed shut.

"He's *so* cool," Jeremy said. "Think he'll let me drive his motorcycle?"

"I hope you made the right choice, Kaylee," Alastair said, staring at the office door.

"I hope I did too," Kaylee said.

CHAPTER SIX

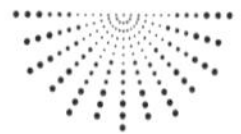

Kaylee hadn't thought she'd regret choosing Randy so soon. Definitely not the second she walked out of school and saw him casually kick standing his motorcycle in the parking lot's pickup circle.

"Subtle he is not," Jade muttered beside her.

Another van honked at Randy and he lazily raised one gloved hand and waved them around. Another honk, and the hand began dropping fingers down to one.

"Randy!" Kaylee hissed.

"Hey! Princess!" Randy called. He patted the seat behind him. "Daylight's burning!"

"You *did* pick him," Jade said, almost regretfully.

Randy raised his hand to shout again and Kaylee nearly zapped him right there, witnesses or not.

"I'm coming!" she shout-whispered. "Just give me one second!"

Randy smirked and put his hand down. He winked at a mom in a minivan behind him.

"Just take a deep breath and try not to kill him," Jade said. "We can hang out tonight, when we're both done."

"I'll need to."

"Just think about Friday."

"What's on Friday?"

Jade patted her arm gently. "You really are out of it. Maddox's first lacrosse game? We were talking about it at lunch."

"Oh, right." In all honesty, Kaylee had completely forgotten; though, lately, Jade never failed to be on top of anything Maddox was doing.

Randy yelled again. Kaylee ground her teeth, pulling her backpack straps so tight they hurt. "See you tonight."

She ignored the small group of students gathering around the pick-up lot. Kaylee spotted Dani, her jaw slack.

"*You know him?*" she mouthed in disbelief.

"*I'll explain later,*" Kaylee mouthed back.

"You sure took your sweet time," Randy said when Kaylee reached him.

"I'm perfectly capable of walking to wherever it is we're going."

"I haven't even shown you where it is yet."

"Doesn't matter. I'll walk across the country as long as you don't come here again."

Randy snickered and shoved a helmet into her hands. "Strap that on and hold tight. I'm not having any niece of mine splatter her brains out on my watch. That's to do on your own time."

Kaylee settled herself on the back and reluctantly wrapped her arms around Randy's midsection. A buzzing current of electricity traveled up the length of her arms, as if just beneath his skin was a live-wire waiting to break free.

Randy revved the engine louder than necessary, then peeled out into the flow of traffic, cutting off another mini-van and eliciting a chorus of angry honks in his wake.

"I think I'm gonna like it here!" Randy yelled back to her.

~

Kaylee recognized where they were the second Randy turned from the commercial district of Scarsdale and onto a more rural country road. Though Kaylee had only ever taken the foot path out to this place, the checkerboard fields of tan, dead plant stalks and groves of intermittent splotches of trees were familiar.

"I have some questions for the hag," Randy said. "Want to see what she has and hasn't covered."

The motorcycle skidded on gravel as Randy took a sharp turn down a long drive leading to Baba's house. Even though she wasn't taking lessons from her anymore, Kaylee's stomach clenched with nervousness as Randy parked and shut off the engine.

From the state of her house, it would appear Baba had taken special care to make it look as uninviting as possible. There were more rotting side boards than Kaylee remembered from just a week ago. The columns supporting the roof of the back porch were bent, some splintered like a man with his teeth punched in. The windows were all stained yellow and more than one (though Kaylee was to blame for this) were cracked.

Baba was standing on the back porch before Randy had even dismounted.

"Stay here," he said. "This'll only take a sec."

"Kaylee!" Edwin appeared behind Baba, and despite it having only been a couple days since she'd seen him last, Kaylee was beyond relieved. At least here was one friendly face she could count on.

"I didn't say you could stop training," Baba griped.

"I'm taking my break now," Edwin said, then gingerly slipped past Randy on the stairs. Randy rolled his eyes and stopped in front of Baba.

"Randall," Baba said.

"Baba," Randy said.

"Never thought I'd see you crawl out of whatever hole you'd buried yourself in."

Randy spread his arms. "Behold, I have risen again. We need to talk. I have a few questions about the girl."

Baba nodded over her shoulder. "Inside. You like scotch?" she asked as they both vanished. Edwin whistled.

"Ookay…my dad told me, but I didn't believe it. Is that guy for real?"

"Seems like it," Kaylee said glumly.

"He's really your uncle?"

"Unfortunately."

"And *you* actually picked *him*?"

"I didn't have another choice, Edwin. I need to keep training and he's an electric dragon-kin. And my uncle. Family has to count for something, right?"

Edwin nodded slowly, rubbing his chin. Kaylee noticed a thin dusting of stubble had grown there and, for a brief moment, she imagined reaching out and running her fingers along it. Much like him defying Baba to come speak with her, it was something she never would have imagined doing a year ago.

"He teach you anything yet?" Edwin said, and it took Kaylee a moment to bring her thoughts back to their conversation.

"Just how to ruin what little reputation I had in school."

Edwin grinned, and the small movement lit up his whole face. "Important life skills. I like it. Baba's been keeping me on the same track as before. Maybe ramping up the offensive magic, though she's as pissed as ever about my progress. Needs to get more creative with the threats."

"I miss training with you—with her—us together," Kaylee blurted out before she realized she'd voiced what she'd been thinking.

Edwin looked at her. A pink tinge was on his cheeks, though Kaylee told herself that was from the cold. "Yeah, I missed you too. I mean the lessons with you. Both?"

"Which is stupid because we literally just saw each other a

couple days ago and we're seeing each other Friday night," Kaylee said. She laughed, but it sounded awkward to her ears.

"Friday night?" Edwin said. "Are we going to something Friday toge—?"

"Maddox's lacrosse game?" Kaylee said quickly, for some reason scared of what he was going to finish that sentence with, but not sure if she was happily scared or terrified about it.

"Right. Of course. Of course I'm going. I've never missed any of his opening games since he started."

"Great!" Kaylee said.

"Great," Edwin echoed. He cleared his throat. Kaylee kicked the ground.

"So...find anything more on what the Slayers are up to?" Kaylee could have kicked herself. That was what she almost *always* asked him. And now she was just being a chicken because there was maybe something else Edwin wanted to talk about, and it definitely did *not* involve the people who wanted her dead.

But Edwin looked excited as he said, "Nothing new yet, but I did find some more interesting reading in my dad's office. And I'm thinking of asking Baba for permission to enter the secret room." He chuckled at Kaylee's horrified expression. "I know, it sounds insane."

"Why the heck would you want to do that? She almost killed us last time, Edwin!"

Edwin lowered his voice. "It's the only place I can think that might have more info on Lesuvius. Plus, we found out what the Slayers were doing last time in there, didn't we?"

"I guess..."

"Besides, there's been nothing much going on other than your uncle showing up, and the rogue dragon-kins appearing again."

"Randy mentioned them last night. I didn't know they'd come back around here." Kaylee peered up at the house, but Baba and Randy were still nowhere to be seen. "You don't think he's part of..."

"I don't," Edwin said. "From what my dad's said about Randy, even a gang of rogues is too much order for him. But it's a little weird they came in at the same time. Anyway..." Edwin scratched his stubble again. "If I don't find anything else about the Slayers soon then I plan to go talk to Damian."

Kaylee gave him a sharp look. "I'm not sure he'll want to talk to us. Not after last time."

Edwin chuckled weakly. "I'm sure he's forgiven us. We didn't destroy *that* much of the Slag Heap."

"You think he knows something?"

"Not sure yet. But if anyone will, it'll be him. I have to ask."

"*We* have to ask."

"We? Just you and me?"

"Jade and Maddox too. All of us."

"Of course." Edwin rubbed the back of his neck. "Of course. Yeah. L-listen, Kaylee. I've been meaning to ask—"

"Load 'em up, kid!" Randy bellowed, tromping down the steps. He nodded at Edwin. "Alastair's kid. Glad to see you don't look like as much of a prick as he is."

"Glad to see you're not as ugly as he told me you were," Edwin shot back.

Randy laughed, then slapped Edwin on the back so hard he stumbled. "Keep training with that she-beast and in ten years you might learn to make a good comeback."

Kaylee barely had time to grab hold of Randy again before he started up the motorcycle and tore out of the drive, spewing dirt and rocks behind him.

"Do you have to be such a jerk?" she yelled.

Randy just smiled.

~

KAYLEE HAD BEEN RIGHT: she could have walked to where Randy

was staying. But then, she supposed, Randy wouldn't have had his fun completely embarrassing her.

They left Baba's house, entered city limits and the condensed snarl of suburbs, passed Kaylee's house, and only a minute later had hit rural farmland again. There was only one other house along the narrow gravel road that wound to the edge of a private drive.

"You have got to be joking," Kaylee said when Randy parked at an unmarked mailbox and stepped off.

Randy pulled off his dust covered goggles. "Does this look like the face of a man who jokes?"

No. No it didn't. But it did look like the face of a man who ate car exhaust on a daily basis and had never heard of the concept of moisturizer. But Kaylee knew Randy was just trying to goad her for his own amusement. That was his game, and she wouldn't let him win.

Randy stepped into the ditch behind the mailbox and kicked a For Sale sign farther down into the drainage pipe. Behind him, Kaylee noticed movement between some of the trees surrounding the property. Men in black clothes and sunglasses.

"Are those—?"

"Alastair's pet Protectors, yeah," Randy said. There was a note of grudging tolerance in his voice. "He insisted. As did your parents. For now, at least, they don't trust me."

"I don't blame them. I don't trust you."

Randy got back on the bike. He kicked harder than normal to start it. "Home sweet home!"

'Home' had never been sadder.

It looked as if someone had attempted to start a hobby farm, then promptly gave up halfway through. A half-finished chicken coop with loose boards stacked beside it sat next to a lazily roped off snaggle of dirt that might have been a garden. Kaylee couldn't tell. The 'dirt' was more rock than soil. To the left was a somewhat respectable shed, but the house itself wasn't much better than Baba's. And that was no small feat. Two stories of white trim with a sharply slanted roof and a gloomy, vomit-colored paint job.

"This place is a dump," Kaylee said, gingerly stepping off the bike.

"Then I guess it's a good thing you're here to clean it," Randy said.

Kaylee snorted. Randy didn't.

"You're serious?" Kaylee said.

"Just call me Mr. Miyagi. And I'd start with those rocks in the garden. They look heaviest and we don't want you getting tired before we start the real work."

Then, whistling, he wheeled the motorcycle away.

KAYLEE COULDN'T BELIEVE what a waste of time this was. After Randy had stored the bike in the shed (he'd made extra sure she wasn't able to peek inside) he'd gotten Kaylee clearing the rocks from the back. The loose boards were next, making a stack of them on the side of the house. Then it was raking the gravel path, trimming the tree blocking the view from the kitchen window, and helping Randy load the rest of his stuff onto the porch, but not the house. He didn't let her go in there, either.

Throughout all this, the only training Kaylee felt she received was strengthening her patience in not summoning a storm and zapping the place to charred embers. The only attention Randy paid to her was when she tried to get into the shed.

"What's in there?" Kaylee asked.

"Nothing for you, that's what," Randy said.

He pulled her over to a large dirt patch Kaylee had cleared of rocks and raked into a fine, smooth patch. They stood spaced apart, facing each other. Kaylee tried to ignore the meandering Protectors as they patrolled in a wide pattern around them.

"Baba gave me the lowdown on what she'd already worked on with you," Randy said. "I wasn't impressed. You can shift your arms and ears—"

"And feet," Kaylee added.

"Sometimes, according to her. But not wings, a tail, or midsection armor yet." Randy rapped his stomach with his knuckles. It sounded like hitting iron. "Midsection counts as one of the two things a dragon-kin can shift safely, but it's invaluable in a fight. We'll need to work on that. Then there's the progress on your elemental magic. You can barely control a storm and are only using a fraction of your secondary elemental powers: ice, electricity, temperature manipulation, I'm thinking even some mastery over wind. All in all, not a gold star report."

"I've done okay!" Kaylee protested. "I just started a year ago. *And* I beat those Slayers last November."

"Beat, huh?" Randy shook his head. "That's not how I heard it. More like 'scraped by.' No, it's not enough. Especially the older you get."'

Kaylee crossed her arms. "Yeah?"

"Yeah."

"So if my teaching was so bad, who taught you?"

"I didn't have an instructor. I learned on my own."

Kaylee's mouth dropped open. "And you're teaching *me*?"

"Welcome to 'check your teacher's credentials 101.' I mastered my powers because I learned something a Merlin could never teach you."

He walked over and poked her in the forehead. "A Merlin uses books and charms to cast spells. They think. Movements and drills and dusty old words, that's their world. You and me..."

Randy pointed to his heart. "We aren't like them. Magic is loaned to a Merlin to be used one second and lost the next. For a dragon-kin, our magic is within us. Our gift is our curse. We are always two different halves trying to be whole, but from that weakness we draw strength."

"My friend Maddox said something like that to me," Kaylee said. "He said I have to embrace what I am to truly let it be a part of me."

"True enough," Randy said. "You've been thinking for too long. It's time to start feeling."

Kaylee looked him up and down. "The six-foot-three tattoo-covered biker dude is going to train me to embrace my feelings?"

"Hey, I'm a sensitive guy. Which is why…" Randy took three loping steps back and spread his arms wide. "I want you to hit me. Ice, electricity, heck, even a storm. Bring it on."

Kaylee hesitated for only a moment. She'd seen enough outlandish teaching techniques from Baba to know when to just roll with it.

She shifted her arms and drew a ball of lightning in her hand. She'd been working to summon it as a continuous power around her, much like what Randy had done, able to lash out at her command. So far…the ball was all she could manage.

"That's it?" Randy said.

Kaylee hurled it at him. Randy brushed it aside like swatting a fly. The ball fizzled out behind him like a defective firework.

"I like how you attacked an electric dragon-kin with electricity. That's critical thinking right there."

Ice came next. Sheets of it. At least, that's what Kaylee tried to do.

Instead, small stinging flakes erupted from the center of her palm and rocketed toward Randy in a powerful stream. He sidestepped it. He scuffed the ground with the toe of his boot and a jolt of electricity zapped up Kaylee's legs, making her yell in surprise.

"Move your feet," Randy ordered. "This isn't target practice. This is you versus them, and the more you stay stationary the easier it'll be for them to hit you."

Kaylee circled him, still trying to keep up her assault all while avoiding the occasional ground attack. It wasn't working. Every time she tried to focus on her hands, her feet would stop and Randy would shock her. But when she moved, she couldn't use any magic.

"This isn't training!" Kaylee said when another painful jolt caused her left foot to temporarily go numb. "You're not teaching me how to fight, just how to take hits! If I wanted abuse I would have stayed with Baba!"

"I am the crucible through which you will be forged," Randy intoned. He held both his hands up and slowly brought them together like he was piecing together two halves of a coconut.

"You have two parts right now, and neither one knows what to do. That's why you can't get a hit on me. You're thinking too much and trying too hard. I bet you'd have no trouble with moving and using magic in a real fight, when all your sense is gone and you're left with nothing but instinct. Come back to that. Use it. Bring your two sides together as one."

"I don't even know what that means!"

Randy leapt toward her. Kaylee found herself forced back as Randy swiped and kicked at her, exchanging physical blows for bursts of magic seamlessly. Dust swirled around them. The air sparked as Kaylee pulled on every fighting technique she knew to stay one step ahead of him.

If Kaylee had any doubts that Randy was as strong as he claimed, it vanished in that instant. It vanished again every second he shifted to counter her attacks. Every time he easily dodged. Every time her fist met his stomach and merely clanged against hard scales. Kaylee was forced to duck as a tail whipped out from behind him, nearly taking her off her feet.

"Hit me!" Randy yelled. "Stop holding back! Hit me with what I know you can do!"

Pressure built behind Kaylee's eyes. The smell of thick ozone clogged her nose. But she forced it back. If she lost control here—

"Why are you stopping?" Randy bellowed. Kaylee tried to duck again but she was too slow this time. Strong claws gripped her forearms, trapping her in place. The magic inside her yearned to unleash but, almost as quickly, images flashed through her mind:

The barn up in flames, skeleton timbers collapsing.

No.

A spell glowing a hellish blood red, men chanting, the wrongness of the magic the Slayers forced through her.

No.

Brendan's final expression before death. His eyes resigned and tired and regretful in his last moments.

NO.

"Kaylee!"

Kaylee jolted back to herself as Randy shook her again. His dragon-slitted eyes changed back to normal. She was lying flat on her back, staring at a clear gray sky tinged with the final remnants of a sudden storm.

Had she done that? No, she would have realized it. Wouldn't she?

"Apparently Alastair didn't tell me everything," Randy growled. "Up you go." She took his offered hand and pulled herself up to sitting. "Hands on your head. Breathe slowly."

"Did I—?"

"Lose control? Yes." Randy sighed. "Alastair failed to mention it, but Baba told me this would be your greatest struggle. You've never been able to control your strongest elemental magic."

"I've been *trying*. It's not like any of you have to control a freaking storm!"

"It's not the storm I'm worried about." Randy's face was tilted to the sky. "You handled that well enough. Kept it together and dispersed it when it grew too big. A storm—a dragon-kin's main elemental magic, really—draws on the user's physical energy and reserves of magic greater than that of any other type they use. If you had lost control of that, it would have continued to pull from you until you were empty. Or dead."

Kaylee shuddered. "Then why didn't that happen? What *did* happen?"

"Hold still."

Randy placed his hands on her back. A numbing pulse of energy—strange, but not unpleasant—rippled through her. He frowned.

"Physically, there's nothing wrong. I can't use healing magic like Merlins, but my electrical impulses can sense irregularities in magic and physical structures within someone. There's nothing out of place inside you."

Kaylee pushed off the ground. She dusted her hands on her pants, ignoring the alarmingly large, Kaylee-shaped dent in the ground. "I know that."

"Of course you do. Which means the reason you're losing control now is your body is using its magic to attack something your mind sees as a threat. My question is," Randy said, staring hard at her, "since I know quite a lot about traumatic experiences, why don't you tell me what really happened that night with the Slayers?"

"Alastair already—"

"Told me what he knew, and his report of those events came from you. But I'm not buying it."

"You think you know—"

"I know I know, Kaylee. But I can't help you get better, control your magic, even accept your magic, until I know what I'm dealing with. I'm not asking as your mentor, I'm asking as a concerned uncle."

Kaylee looked up at him. His arms were draped at his sides, his face a mask of concern. This wasn't the uncle she'd seen so far. This wasn't even the uncle her parents had told warning stories about for the last year.

"What did you and my mom talk about last night?" Kaylee said.

"Mostly about none of your business. And don't try to change the subject. I know about dark magic, Kaylee. I know that whatever those Slayers did couldn't have been easy to handle. I also know you can tell me about it."

It was that last way he said it, so raw and honest, that made Kaylee relent. Once she started talking, it was as if the words were a faucet she'd broken the handle to. She told him about how she'd discovered her powers, about how Brendan had attacked her, and what the Slayers had done since then. About that night when she'd brought the barn down.

Randy didn't interrupt once. By the time Kaylee finished, they had migrated away from the dirt patch to the front porch of the house. There were no chairs so Randy leaned on the half-rotted bannister while Kaylee sat on the steps.

"You've got a pretty great group of friends there," Randy said after she'd finished. "That Edwin kid seems pretty sharp, too, to figure out their plan like that."

"Yeah. He's great."

Randy fell silent again, and Kaylee looked up to find him staring off into the distance.

"We get to choose a lot of things in life. Being a dragon-kin isn't one of them. I don't know much about this Brendan kid, but it sounds like he made his choice and you made yours. I'm not saying he deserved what he got, but what they did to you—what he's still doing to you—that's not your fault."

"I don't think it's my fault."

"Don't insult my intelligence, kid. Your magic just went haywire trying to attack what I'm guessing is his ghost or something."

"How did you know that?" Kaylee snapped.

Randy chuckled. "Because you just confirmed it for me. Am I right?"

Kaylee wrapped her arms around her knees. "Yes—not just now, but yes. I've seen him a couple times. I don't even know why it bothers me, after what he—they—tried to do."

"It bothers you because you're a human with feelings and not a monster. I told you to embrace your dragon side. To truly accept it. But there is such a thing as too much of either. It's about balance. And as for Brendan..." Randy sighed. "I've made some mistakes like that, too. Mistakes that cost people everything. Some who deserved it. Some who didn't."

"But I thought you told Alastair you'd never—"

"I lied."

"Oh." Kaylee let this revelation process. Randy had killed people. Maybe not intentionally, but he had.

But when she opened her eyes, Randy was the same as he'd been before he'd told her. "How'd you deal with it?"

"Day by day," Randy said. "Just like I dealt with accepting I was a dragon-kin. I did it, and you will too. But, Kaylee?"

His sorrow-filled tone made her meet his eyes. "As a dragon-kin, I can promise you that by the end of your life—whenever that is—you'll see more people get hurt."

CHAPTER SEVEN

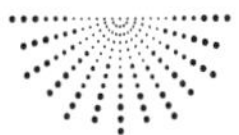

Kaylee was being followed. She was sure of it.

Although it was nearly impossible to pick out any one person in the massive crowd that had assembled for the lacrosse team's first game, a couple times she'd felt a tingle in the back of her neck; a prickle of unease. And it wasn't just from all the times Randy had shocked her during their training that week.

"Kaylee?" Jade had already bought their tickets and stood waiting for her on the other side of the gate. Kaylee scanned the parking lot one more time. Parents, couples, (lots of couples, most of them hanging off each other like their skin had fused together), and kids. Nobody suspicious.

Except…there. The brief flash of a figure slipping between the cars. The furtive movement of someone trying to see without being seen. Kaylee glimpsed them for only a moment, but she was sure they'd been looking right at her.

"Trouble?"

Jade had joined her side. One hand clutched their tickets, the other had disappeared up the sleeve of her Scarsdale Lacrosse Team hoodie. Maddox had practically forced each of them to buy one as part of his team's fundraiser. Kaylee was sure Jade had already sewed her concealed knife sleeve into the inside of it.

"It's nothing," Kaylee said. "I thought I saw something."

"Hey, kids, move it through the gate. You're holding up the line," the attendant grouched.

"You can't ever assume it's nothing," Jade said. "Not when you're dealing with Slayers."

"They're still out west," Kaylee said.

Jade didn't say anything.

"Jade? They *are* still out west? Plus, they wouldn't attack us with all these people around."

"They're out west for now. And remember the djinn giant at the mall? I wouldn't put it past them to unleash something else nasty just to draw us out."

"Hey!" the attendant snapped. "I said scooch!"

Kaylee gave a sheepish wave to the growing line of annoyed ticket holders and together she and Jade hurried through the concrete tunnel to the stadium's inner ring. Ahead was the playing field, and to the right and left concrete columns and overhead strip bulbs led the way to more upstairs stadium seating. Lines of patrons shivered their way to buy hot chocolate and cider, their breath fogging the corridor. Outside on the field, an announcer had begun booming an advertisement about *Dave's Lumber.*

"The Slayers don't want me anymore," Kaylee said, following Jade up a flight of stairs to the spot where Edwin had texted them he'd be sitting. "My magic can't help them power that spell again."

"Doesn't mean they don't want you dead," Jade said. "The Slayers will do anything to target dragon-kin, and Alastair doesn't let on how much you could be used by them. Remember what Edwin told us about your magic?"

"Er...vaguely. To be honest, when he gets into research mode he doesn't make sense half the time."

Jade laughed. "I know what you mean. Maddox doesn't get

into research mode at all and he still doesn't make sense half the time. Edwin said your magic was both destructive and constructive. You can store it to be used for anything they want. That means you could be a high priority target. And *that* means if you think you see someone suspicious, you tell me."

They reached the second floor. Kaylee was surprised to see Josh in a group of guys huddled outside one of the gates. Tygus wasn't with him, though Kaylee supposed—Tamer or not—having a twelve-year-old hanging around would have cramped his style.

Josh saw her. He gave a subtle nod. Kaylee hadn't seen him since the night of the scarab mission. Alastair oversaw both Convocations in Scarsdale, including the Northern one Josh was part of, but the relationship had been strained since last year when she and Edwin had broken into the other high school to protect a magical object from the Slayers. They'd gotten it anyway, and the Northern Scarsdale Convocation had gotten pissed.

"I think the game's about to start," Jade said. The noise growing from the field seemed to agree with her. The two of them weaved through the crowd to their seating section. Kaylee spotted familiar curly brown hair and glasses and filed in beside Edwin.

"'Bout time!" He yelled over the roar of the crowd. Below, small black and white figures carrying sticks were taking the field. "You can help me interpret."

"Interpret what?" Kaylee said.

Edwin held up a small booklet: *Rules of Lacrosse*. "Read it twice. Still can't make sense of it."

"Our team puts tiny ball in opponent's goal," Jade said.

The crowd cheered louder. A sea of Scarsdale's black and red flowed over their side of their stadium. The other side looked lonely and bare in comparison. Kaylee wasn't entirely sure who the team they were playing was, but Maddox had told her they were from somewhere out of their district.

A whistle blew and the game began. At first, Kaylee tried to keep up, but between others yelling conversations around her, and Edwin trying in vain to shout the rules to her, it wasn't long before she was lost. The marching band played through a slew of songs. The cheerleaders on the track chanted and flipped, and Jade scoffed as the nearest one did a front handspring.

"That is so easy. *And* she's not even holding a knife."

"How forgetful of her," Kaylee said.

"Just saying, it'd make things more interesting." Jade suddenly waved over Kaylee's shoulder. "Dani! Hey, Dani!"

Dani broke away from the group of friends she was with and clambered over to hug them.

"I think we're winning!" she said cheerily.

"I'll take your word for it," Jade said. Edwin frantically flipped through the rule book.

"I think that's a foul—no, that means a penalty, which is the same thing as a foul, isn't it? Or is that a goal?"

"To me, they're still boys running around with sticks," Kaylee said. Dani grinned, and Kaylee was glad to see that most of her usual cheeriness was back, though there was still a dullness behind her eyes; a porcelain doll with cracks showing through.

"Who cares what the rules are?" Jade said. "We're here, that's all that matters."

"Just supporting Maddox, huh?" Dani said, and Kaylee could tell she'd noticed the rest of Jade's outfit, as Kaylee had earlier.

Jade had told Kaylee all the merchandise was helping Maddox's fundraiser, but Kaylee was pretty sure buying a lacrosse sweatshirt, keychain, wristband, button, and commemorative season schedule was a little excessive.

An hour passed in no time. Despite having no clue what was happening below, Kaylee was having a blast. She and Edwin shared the rule book between them, him pointing out players and movements, and Kaylee content with listening and pretending—if only for a moment—that this was just like how their lessons used to be. An easy camaraderie and banter between them. A sudden swell of loss welled from inside, but she squashed it. There was no point in moping about the past.

"Is it halftime?" Jade yelled as the marching band picked up with their school's fight song and moved onto the field.

Kaylee blew into her hands. "Not sure, but I'm going to get some hot chocolate. You guys want some?"

"Totally," Jade said.

Edwin grunted, absorbed in reading, which Kaylee took as a yes.

"Dani, how about—you okay?"

Dani had been furiously scratching at her left arm, wincing.

"Dani?"

Dani jumped. "What? Sorry, didn't hear you."

Kaylee nodded to her arm. "Chapped skin?"

"Cha—yeah." She nudged her head back up the stands. "I'm going to get back to my seat. See you guys later!"

She clambered back over the bleachers. Kaylee watched her go for a moment, then took the stairs to the concession stand.

Apparently, everyone wanted hot chocolate. The line near their entrance was ridiculously long, so Kaylee followed the signs to one of the more secluded concession stands on the ground floor. She took a spot in line just as two more people slipped in behind her.

At first, Kaylee didn't think anything of them. Her mind was on Dani, and Jade, and Edwin, and how he seemed to be having as much fun as she was tonight, and how she wished she could do this more often, and the strange, almost scared look Dani had given her, and the way Jade had been almost flustered when Kaylee had brought up all the stuff she'd bought from Maddox and—

"Next!"

She ordered and took the drinks. The game must have started again, because when she turned around the ground floor had cleared out. She was alone.

Except for the two people still behind her.

There was blurry movement. The two people each grabbed an arm and pulled her down a narrow passage behind the bathrooms, rushing her out of sight before anyone could see. It took Kaylee's mind half a second to catch up to what was happening. Another half for her training to kick in and assess the situation as Jade had taught her.

She was being kidnapped. By Slayers.

Finally.

Once Kaylee controlled her initial terror, she felt only relief. Here she'd been waiting, wondering, watching for them, always unsure of what they'd be up to next, and here they were, dragging her away beneath the stands, while the muffled cheers of the crowd thundered overhead.

Kaylee slowed her breathing and let herself be taken. Her heart thudded but her muscles tensed. She wasn't the same clueless girl she'd been the last time they'd attacked. She'd wait until there were no witnesses.

Then she'd make them pay.

The tugging hands paused when they entered an open concrete space far below the bleachers.

"Hey, Z, we got—"

Kaylee threw her hot chocolate. Most had spilled during her abduction, but the rest of the burning liquid coated the nearest Slayer. He let out a cry of pain. Kaylee could almost hear the satisfying sizzle.

The Slayer's partner tried to re-double his grip on her, but Kaylee spun away and delivered a punch to his gut, her scale-hardened fist meeting with soft flesh. The man stumbled back with a squeak of pain. Kaylee went to finish him.

But they weren't alone.

Kaylee wanted to smack herself. Of *course* they weren't bringing her down here by themselves. Two Slayers would never be enough to take down a dragon-kin.

They'd brought her to their friends.

Slayers materialized from the edges of the darkness, becoming illuminated in the pus-colored maintenance lighting. Kaylee was on the nearest one before they could come any closer. The first she downed with a swift front kick, the next a punch to the face. Her elemental magic strained to be free, but she couldn't risk it. Not yet. Not with so many innocents nearby.

But it didn't seem like she'd need it. These Slayers sucked.

Kaylee beat back two more. There were shouts of alarm. Chaotic voices. Frantic cowering.

Yeah, these Slayers definitely sucked.

Then a fist launched from her left. Kaylee failed to move in time. The blow glanced off her ribs, but she managed to grab it and pull her assailant close, raising her claws for a counter-attack.

A boy's terrified face stared back.

Kaylee's arm hovered mid-strike. "Who're y—"

Another blow landed on her shoulder blades. Kaylee threw the boy away and spun on her new attacker, not holding back this time—

Claaaang.

It was like hitting a street pole. The shock reverberated back on her, sending shock waves of pain up Kaylee's spine.

"We meet again."

Kaylee stared. It was the girl she'd run into at school. The one with the crazy hair and infuriating smirk.

"Not as much of a weakling as I thought. Good. I was worried," the girl said. She shoved against Kaylee, forcing her to dig her heels in to avoid getting thrown back.

"I didn't think Slayers left their dirty work to children," Kaylee spat.

A flash of movement as the girl brought her other hand up. Scaled claws shone in the light, gun-metal gray.

Kaylee blocked in time, but the attack knocked her back into the center of her assailants. The circle closed in around her.

"Enough!" the girl yelled as a few of the older kids lunged for Kaylee again. "No reason to have her kick your sorry butts again, idiots."

"But Z—"

"I said enough."

The circle reluctantly widened. Now that the frenzy of battle was gone, Kaylee could see these weren't Slayers at all. A girl just a bit younger than her wiped a trickle of blood from the corner of her mouth. A couple kids—no older than her little brother—were clutching their stomachs.

"They'll be fine," the girl said. "And the lesson will be good for them. Morons. Told 'em about a million times to never underestimate an opponent."

"And you are?" Kaylee said. She took a moment to get a good look at who she was dealing with. Only this girl was older than her; the rest of the kids ranged anywhere from ten to fifteen-years-old, dressed in a variety of clothes. Some wore rags, while others had outfits that could have been pulled from a department store mannequin. Some kids carried magic in their palms, while others still had dragon scales. "*What* are you?"

"Pip. Gunner." The girl waved a hand. "Go keep watch. Holler if somebody's coming."

That broke the stalemate. The two hurried off while the other kids took more relaxed positions around them.

The girl's hand shifted back to normal and she stuck it out. "Zaria."

When Kaylee didn't take it, Zaria rolled her eyes. "You don't like getting attacked? Violence is our standard greeting. Get used to it."

Kaylee gripped her hand then, pushing a small jolt of electricity through her arm. It stopped when it hit Zaria's arm, as if hitting an impenetrable block.

"You're a metal dragon-kin," Kaylee said.

"What gave it away? Was it the metal claws?" Zaria released her hand. "And you're Kaylee Richards, the often-blabbed about storm dragon-kin."

"Blabbed about?"

"Underground won't shut up about you. Not that they want to *do* anything to you. That's the Slayers' shtick. Most are just curious."

Kaylee swore the tips of her ears were burning. Just how many people knew about her? And how had she not known?

A sudden realization hit her. "You're the rogue dragon-kins."

"And the lightbulb appears," Zaria said, giving a mocking bow. "Technically dragon-kin and Merlins, if you care to know. Dragon-kin recruitment numbers are a little thin lately, so we had to bolster our numbers."

"Gee, I wonder why. Maybe because their leader orders all her 'guests' to be kidnapped."

"Hey! Show Zaria some respect!" one of the older boys yelled, the one Kaylee had splashed hot chocolate on. Kaylee shifted her hand to claws and held it up to him. The boy backed off.

Zaria chuckled and lounged on a steel bracing. "I don't blame you for what you think of us. I'd hate us too if I believed all the lies the Convocation spread to keep other young dragon-kins from joining."

"They say you're dangerous and don't follow Convocation rules set out to protect our kind. So far I'm not seeing anything disputing that."

"We're dragon-kin, not beasts to be ruled by laws or others of our kind. Tell me, when Randall Conners arrived in town—"

"How did you—?"

"What was Alastair's condition for him if he wanted to stay?"

"He...had to follow Convocation rules."

The others let out a hiss.

Zaria leaned forward. "And do you know why they wanted that? Fear. They're scared of what he can do. Just like they're scared of any one magic user having too much freedom."

"That's so nobody gets hurt. What would happen if dragon-kin were allowed to use their powers whenever they wanted?"

"Freedom."

"Chaos."

Zaria waved her hands. "Sometimes those things are closer than you think. What is freedom, if not the chaos to do as you please?"

"Zaria," one of the younger girls said meekly. "You're...talking all confusing again."

"I hope you aren't here to debate me on philosophy," Kaylee said. "Seems you already do what you want anyway."

"Darn right we do. We do what we want, free from the Convocation that abandoned us."

That caught Kaylee's attention. "What does that mean?"

Anger flashed in Zaria's eyes. "This may come as a shock, Kaylee Richards, storm dragon-kin of the Scarsdale Convocation, but most dragon-kin aren't as important as you are. Like I said, I'm a metal dragon-kin. Impressive, but nothing exceptional."

She pointed to one of the younger boys who was wiping his nose with sleeves far too long for him. "Another wind dragon-kin. I think you already have one here. Only difference between these two is the Convocation where he was left to die when he was captured by Slayers." A girl came next. "Merlins, too. Slayers want dragon-kin dead, but they'll happily kill all who oppose them. Marica was left homeless after Slayers killed her family. And guess who never bothered to help? Guess who saw the risks as too great for the life of one, weak, puny girl?"

Zaria pushed off her spot and stalked closer. Kaylee backed up, one hand at her side prepared to shift, but holding back.

"And me," Zaria said softly. "A dragon-kin *just* important enough to warrant the Slayers taking...special interest in me. But still not enough for the Convocation to consider stepping in when I was taken."

She whipped up her arm. Kaylee flinched, but Zaria merely pulled down one sleeve to reveal a line of quarter-sized pock marks in her flesh, roughly shaped like dragon scales. "Did you know metal dragon-kin scales are fun to study? So many *fascinating* properties and uses. The applications were truly endless. Until the person they're taking them from has enough and decides that help isn't coming, that they didn't care enough to save her, and the only person you can really rely on is yourself and those who have been through exactly what you have."

Without meaning to, Kaylee found herself rubbing the spot on her arm where Brendan had taken a scale of her own for the Slayers' spell last year. Losing one had been painful enough.

"I'm not going to say sorry," Kaylee said after a pause. "You don't want my pity."

Zaria grinned, then patted Kaylee on the shoulder roughly. "You're right, I don't. Pity died along with our childish ways. I have a new family now. One I love and who loves me."

"Then what do you want with me?"

"You," Zaria said. "We want you."

Kaylee tried not to show her surprise. "Why?"

"Like I said, you're tougher than I thought. I'm looking for a little extra help for something. There's a spot that needs filling in our ranks and I thought you'd fit nicely."

"That didn't answer my question."

"I don't have an answer to your question. Not here."

"Then where?"

But at that moment there was a disturbance in the hallway. Feet shuffled. Voices rose.

"Hey! This part's closed! You can't—"

"Hey!"

"Back up! I'm warning you—"

"Aserath Vevan caji!"

There was a bright flash of light and the snarl of offensive magic. The two people Zaria had sent to keep watch were blown into the room, stunned. The smell of singed clothing filled the air.

Edwin rushed in, an expansive orange screen of light held in front of him. Kaylee had never seen him conjure anything quite so solid before. His eyes found her and he visibly relaxed. Then tensed again when he saw Zaria.

"Kaylee's coming with me."

Zaria gave Kaylee an amused look. "Overprotective boyfriend much?"

"Everybody just stop," Kaylee said as those around her began to close in on Edwin. "Put the magic away, Edwin. They just want to talk."

Edwin didn't move, but Zaria casually waved a hand. A couple of the older kids helped the stunned ones up. The group began trickling into the hall.

"We're done talking for now," Zaria said. "If you want to know more about my offer then we need a little more privacy. Find me when you're ready."

"How?" Kaylee said.

"You'll figure out a way if you want to badly enough. Or maybe ask that uncle of yours." Zaria smirked. "I'm sure he's hiding all sorts of things the Convocation doesn't know. Until then." She gave a small salute and joined the rest of her group, the younger ones warily sidestepping Edwin who kept his shield up.

The second he was sure all of them were gone, Edwin dissipated his shield with a relieved sigh. It was then Kaylee was able to see how much the effort had drained him.

"Are you okay?" he said.

"I'm fine, Edwin." Why was everyone always asking her that?

Like she was a house of cards, brittle and ready to collapse at any moment. "Why are you here?"

Edwin looked slightly hurt. "You were gone a long time. I wanted to make sure nothing was wrong."

"Well nothing was."

Edwin jabbed a finger toward where Zaria had just stood. "Clearly that's not true. Were—"

"Edwin." Kaylee rubbed her temples as sudden pain hit her head. The events of the last few minutes were catching up to her. She didn't know why, but something about his concern was annoying her right now.

"Did they say anything? Anything about the Slayers?"

"No. Well, maybe. I'm not sure yet. They wanted me to visit them and talk more."

"Which of course you won't do because it's clearly a trap of some kind."

Kaylee glanced at him. His hands were stuffed into his pockets, his pose reserved, yet confident. Reliable. Even now, when they didn't train together anymore, when their lives had begun to drift different directions, he was still the rope tying them together.

"But…" he added. "You're you, so you'll probably go anyway."

"Probably."

"Which means I'm coming too."

"I know."

"Whenever you jump into the fray, I'll be by your side."

And it was that, Kaylee suddenly realized, that scared her the most.

CHAPTER EIGHT

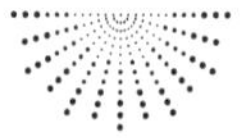

Christmas swooped in like a hawk on a baby rabbit, full of sound and fury, a blur of talons and training and merciless exams.

December storms had snarled full force the last week leading up to the school break, bringing in cold weather and wind stronger than anything Kaylee could have ever managed to conjure with her magic, shoveling in a whopping three inches of snow over the last couple of days. The pure, glistening white made Kaylee's relatively short walk from school to Randy's farm peaceful, as it dampened all noise save for her crunching boots and her soft sighs at the quiet landscape around her.

It also told her Randy wasn't home.

The front porch creaked as she stepped up to it. Already, Kaylee noticed the usual absence of sound. Usually she could hear Randy banging around inside, or tinkering in the shed, the door locked tight.

"Randy?"

Kaylee stood and tried to peer in one of the windows. Whether he'd meant to or not, Randy had mimicked Baba in that he'd never let Kaylee inside his house without permission, usually meeting her on the porch before leading her to wherever they were training that day.

Nothing moved inside.

Then again, he hadn't mentioned them having practice today, and she'd gotten out of school half a day early for winter break. That had to be why he wasn't here. It made more sense than him cancelling lessons because he'd found out about her meeting with the rogue dragon-kins. All week during training, Kaylee had watched for any sign that Randy knew what had happened to her. Any sign, really, that he knew more about them than he was letting on. Zaria's words had echoed in her ears long after the game: *I'm sure he's hiding all sorts of things the Convocation doesn't know.* But what those things might be, Randy gave no clue. He'd just been his usual gruff, annoying self.

Kaylee turned from the window and peered around the farm. The wood was already stacked in place, the drive clear. The shed doors were open.

For a moment, she just stared, her mind playing over the consequences of snooping around. The house was empty. Randy probably wouldn't be back for a while. And although she'd trained with him for over two weeks, she still barely knew anything about the guy save that he loved Chinese food, and loved making her suffer during training.

Basically, she knew squat.

She took a deep breath when she reached the shed, steeling herself for what she'd find inside.

It was empty.

Kaylee walked in and spun in a circle. She hadn't known quite what to expect, but not this. Not *nothing.*

She groaned in frustration and kicked the center beam. The rope and worn tack on the wall chattered in response.

There was a spot worn down for Randy's motorcycle, and racks on the walls that might have held tools, but that was it. Kaylee checked the loft, the back, even stomped for a trap door beneath the dirt and long-sour hay. Nothing. It was as if the man had picked everything up and vanished.

That still left the house.

Kaylee made it to the front door before something stopped her. It wasn't magic, but rather a feeling she didn't think she'd ever have when it came to Randy. Guilt. The guy clearly wanted privacy, and here she was, trying to break into his place.

Do it, a small voice said. *It's for your own good. You need to know who he really is.*

Some people keep secrets for a reason, another voice answered.

You deserve to know.

Do you?

Kaylee glanced at the vacant road. Randy could be back any minute. Who knew when it'd be before she'd get another chance to look, if ever.

Kaylee shouldered her way through the front door, the long-rusted lock Randy had failed to replace giving way in her hands.

The house was bigger inside than Kaylee had thought, but in a state of complete disrepair. Her feet scuffed the floorboards as she moved down the hall between the stairs and dining room. A gust of wind caused the shutters to knock against the siding. The entire house felt like the thin shell of a long-dead beast rather than a place of comfort.

Except the kitchen was bare and homey; the sink and refrigerator clean. The den too, was meticulously absent of any stuff thrown around. Kaylee took a walk around, looking for anything out of place. She had to admit, this part of the house looked nice. At least, as nice as it could. She never would have pegged Randy as a neat freak.

The rest of the bottom floor was just as empty. That left upstairs, but something was out of place. It wasn't until her foot hit the landing of the second floor that she knew what it was: there were no personal touches, no pictures or plants or anything else that truly made this place home. Kaylee hadn't expected

Randy to spruce the house up, but she'd expected *something*. This...this was how he had lived his life? In nothing but husks of houses and cold drafts wending their way through silent, bare halls?

Kaylee shivered.

The door at the end of the hall was slightly ajar. Kaylee had a brief flashback of sneaking into Baba's secret room, and listened extra intently outside. With Randy's motorcycle, she figured she'd get a thirty second head-start to get out before he came barging in.

She pushed the door open.

It was a study, just as bare and unassuming as the rest of the house, save for a single wooden desk in the corner.

"Bingo."

A neat stack of papers sat in one corner. The rest of desk looked as if it might usually have held other things, but had been scooped away with Randy wherever he'd gone.

Kaylee, still pushing her snooping guilt aside, wasted no time in peeling aside each page.

Times. Dates. Meeting places. Road maps. Nothing dark or secret or—

A picture fell out.

Kaylee placed the papers down and picked it up. Of course Uncle Randy would have printed off pictures, even in the age of cell phones and computers.

Kaylee's breath caught when she turned it over. It was her. A school photo she'd had taken last year. It had been right before freshman year had officially started. Before Brendan. Before the Convocation. She was dressed in a new shirt Jade had helped her pick out and had done her hair in a braid she normally never would have bothered with under normal circumstances.

Kaylee had trouble looking into her eyes. Did *this* Kaylee know what was about to happen to her? Was *this* Kaylee ready for how her life was about to change?

The Kaylee in the picture continued smiling, as if to say, *Look! Look at all you'll never have again! Look at the life that's gone away, drifted off out of reach—*

Kaylee flipped it over. On the back, Randy had scratched, *Looks just like Brianna.*

She did? Kaylee had never thought she looked anything like her mother.

There was another picture stuck to the bottom of the papers. It was a Thanksgiving photo her family had taken just after the Slayers' attack. Looking at it, Kaylee was shocked by how much had changed. Yes, she hadn't been fully recovered yet. Yes, she'd been in a lot of pain, but the girl who stared back in this picture was—in a word—haunted. Her mouth smiling, but her eyes hollow.

Kaylee certainly hoped she wasn't that. She had her problems. Brendan still lingered. But this...she wasn't...she couldn't.

Randy had written something on the back of this too.

She's ready. She can help.

Help what? And how long had Randy been planning to come out here? He'd made it seem as if he'd simply answered the call for her training on a whim, but clearly he'd had it in mind for some time.

Kaylee was all at once aware of how long she'd stood there. The wind outside had settled, as if the house had sucked in a giant breath, pre-shout, to alert the world where she was. She quickly replaced the pictures, but as she did, another one tucked between the pages nicked her hand. Kaylee pulled it out.

A girl. Her age, maybe a bit older. Blond hair instead of Kaylee's brown, but her face was so similar there was no doubt they were related in some way. Could she be Randy's—?

Kaylee almost screamed as something slammed downstairs. She shoved the picture back and slipped down the stairs to the front door and outside, expecting Randy to be furiously waiting for her there.

The shutters slammed again. Kaylee saw them, but she didn't relax, her heart still thudding in her ears. She was tempted to go back in but now that she was outside—now that she had seen those—it seemed like more of a violation than it had before. Randy was hiding something, and exactly what, Kaylee didn't know. She wasn't even sure she wanted to.

~

"HAVE you guys tried the pie yet?" Maddox asked, shoveling another spoonful of it into his mouth.

Jade, a slightly grossed-out expression on her face, shoved him slightly. "How are we supposed to when you keep eating it all?"

Maddox steadied his plate. He pushed himself against the wall as Mr. and Mrs. Azuma slid past them, each carrying glasses of wine.

"Don't spill anything, you three," Mr. Azuma said, then vanished into the family room.

Kaylee's house was organized chaos. Whereas on Christmas Eve the years before their family had often celebrated by inviting Jade's family over, this year they'd had Maddox and his parents stop by, with the promise of Edwin's family later on. Food and people shuttled back and forth from the kitchen. The lively hum of conversation filled every room.

Kaylee, Jade, and Maddox shuffled into a small lounge at the back of the house. Snow fell thickly outside, white splotches against a darkened sky. The adults were gathered in the family room, so for a little while the three of them had been able to dodge more prying questions about school or training. Meanwhile, Jeremy had been allowed to invite a couple of his friends over, and they were currently busy terrorizing the upstairs. Kaylee had made it painfully clear that if any of them entered her room it would be grounds for instant electrocution. Only Jeremy knew how serious her threat was.

"Your mom sure goes all out with the decorations, doesn't she, Kaylee?" Maddox said. He brushed his hand over one of the cut-out snowflakes decoratively placed on every windowsill and shelf. This was matched by mistletoe her mom had hung in every doorway (Kaylee nearly died from embarrassment when she'd done this. Maddox had already jokingly made a couple moves on Jade and she'd threatened to punch him in the jugular). Even the stockings her family had had since they were little hung below the holly-draped mantle of the family room fireplace. Kaylee imagined her dad in there right now, regaling the other adults with embarrassing Christmas baby stories.

"Maddox, I already had some!" Jade said, shoving Maddox's hand away as he offered her pie. "Seriously, aren't you supposed to be on a lacrosse season diet?"

Maddox patted his stomach. "We've won all our games so far. And *I'm* not the one prepping for the big Tamer test—"

He cut off, realizing what he'd said. Jade glared at him. Maddox looked to Kaylee to back him up, but she merely shrugged.

"You dug that hole."

"Sorry, Jade," Maddox said.

"Forget it," Jade said. "It's Christmas, let's talk about something else."

It had been a while, Kaylee realized, since she'd had a normal conversation with her friends, one that didn't involve magic, or dragon-kins, or Slayers. As they talked, she was relieved to hear she hadn't missed much of what was happening in each of their lives. The way the last few weeks had gone Kaylee had felt almost isolated from them all, and it was good to be brought back to where they all were with everything.

Even so, a couple times the conversation paused, and despite the unspoken decision *not* to talk about anything relating to the Convocation, Kaylee felt the urge to tell them about what she had found at Randy's. The problem was, she had no idea *what* she'd found at Randy's, and Randy hadn't been back the rest of the week so she couldn't even confront him about it. Not that she would have. When it came right down to it, she didn't think she could face him yet.

And the weirdest thing about his absence? Kaylee was...actually worried about him.

Randy hadn't been around for most of her life. She shouldn't have cared if he took off on another one of his vanishing acts. But for the first time since becoming a dragon-kin, she had known someone who had not only been able to train her, but had understood what she was going through. Had empathized with her. Had been in the exact place she was now and gotten through it, though he gave her little to no details on that part of his life, and Kaylee wasn't sure she wanted to know.

That was why, the couple times she'd gone over to Randy's to see if he'd returned yet, she hadn't snuck back into his house to try unearthing more secrets. It didn't seem right anymore. She had to content herself with hoping that, as her uncle, he'd tell her anything important.

Wouldn't he?

"Ambush!"

Jeremy and his friends whipped around the corner, firing nerf guns at them. Barely moving, Jade and Maddox caught three of the darts mid-air and dropped them to the floor. The boys gaped at them. Kaylee suppressed a smile.

"Gonna have to try harder than that," Jade said, casually taking a sip of her cider.

"Scram, brats," Kaylee said.

Whispering fiercely to themselves, Jeremy's friends headed back upstairs. Jeremy threw an annoyed look Kaylee's way.

"You're no fun anymore."

Kaylee summoned a small ball of electricity to the tip of her finger and waggled it at him. "Beat it."

"Did you see their faces?" Maddox chuckled. "Classic."

"Yes, because that's why I joined the Convocation," Jade said. "To shock the bejeezus out of punk middle schoolers with access to foam weaponry."

"It's why I joined," Maddox said with mock seriousness.

The doorbell rang. When Kaylee answered, she found Alastair and his wife, Amelia, standing in front of a shivering Edwin. He shot her a grin as Alastair said, "Merry Christmas, Kaylee! We bring good tidings and cheer!"

"And alcohol," Edwin said.

"But none for you," Alastair said.

"Alastair!" Kaylee's dad called from the hallway as they bundled in. "Glad you could stop by. And is that Mortlach Single Malt?"

"Good man," Alastair said, raising the bottle to the light. "You have fine taste."

Edwin rolled his eyes toward Kaylee. "I have *no* idea how he decides what sort of gift to bring your dad."

"It must have been an agonizing choice," Kaylee answered, feeling a smile creep up her face. Their eyes caught each other's for a moment. Edwin opened his mouth—

"Kaylee, please take their coats," her mom said, leading Amelia into the family room while Alastair went to the closet.

"Jade and Maddox are in the back," Kaylee told Edwin. He nodded and went to join them.

"Thank you, Kaylee," Alastair said, taking the rest of the coats from her and putting them on hangers. "I'm happy to say we were able to get away from Convocation business for a couple days. Things have slowed down on all channels. I suspect even Slayers celebrate Christmas."

"You haven't heard..." Kaylee bit her lip. "There hasn't been anything from..."

"I'm afraid not," Alastair said. "Randy hasn't been in contact with anyone from the Convocation for the last few days."

"But I thought he was running errands for them. Wouldn't any mission he does here be under their orders?"

Alastair readjusted the sleeves on his suit jacket. "I can't say whether what he's doing is or is not Convocation business."

"Oh, come on, Alastair—"

"But," Alastair said over her, "he should have checked in. It is a bit unusual that he hasn't." He noticed Kaylee's glum expression. His voice softened. "Don't worry about him, Kaylee. I may have just started trusting him to train you, but if there's one thing about Randall I will always trust, it's his ability to take care of himself."

"And you know that because of all those rumors you heard about him?"

"Maybe."

"Are they real?"

"That's for him to tell you, if he wants. Not me."

He put a gentle hand on Kaylee's shoulder. "I'm glad to see you're worried about him—"

"He's just screwing up my training, that's all."

There was a twinkle in Alastair's eye. "Of course. But I promise if we don't hear anything within a couple more days, I'll send out a team to find some answers."

"Thanks. I appreciate it," Kaylee managed.

"Now go have some fun, and *don't worry*. We'll be doing plenty of that per usual once Christmas has passed."

Maddox was in the middle of telling Jade and Edwin a joke involving the use of one of the cut-out snowflakes and a slice of ham from his plate when Kaylee returned.

"Hey," Edwin said, scooting over on the couch to make room for her.

"Hey yourself. I thought you'd be throwing a sick party at your house with the rest of the Convocation."

Edwin grimaced. "We tried that a couple years ago. Let's just say that too much spiked eggnog can make even trained Merlins a little crazy."

"Was that the time you told me Dylan got on the roof and—"

"Yes," Edwin said. "And I *highly* recommend you don't mention that to him. It's still a sore spot. Oh, I just remembered..." He dug into his pocket and pulled out a small wrapped gift. "I—uh—made this. For you. I mean...I made this for you."

Kaylee unwrapped it. Out tumbled a small carving, woven into an intricate pattern, lacquered and polished so that it shone lustrously under the light. Kaylee held it up. It was a bolt of lightning, circled by a dragon eating its tail.

"Edwin, this..."

"I thought your other charm might be a little worn and I saw this symbol and I'd gotten a lot better at carving so I thought you'd like it, so yeah," Edwin said in one breath.

Kaylee's fingers brushed the original charm Edwin had given her soon after they'd met. Despite the magic being gone when not charged, she still rubbed it whenever she felt nervous so that now the wood was worn and smooth in the shape of her fingerprints.

"If you don't like it, I can make another."

"No! No, this is great, Edwin."

Kaylee unclasped the old one and stuffed it into her pocket. She held her hair back while Edwin fastened the new one. Instantly, a sense of calm befell her, though Kaylee wasn't sure if that was the new magic he'd infused it with, or the fact that something Edwin had given her was once again so close to her.

"You have gotten better at carving," Kaylee noted, turning the new design over in her hand. "Where'd you see this?"

"It's a design from ancient times," Edwin said. "It means 'wisdom is power.' I modified it a bit with the lightning bolt. Thought it'd match more."

"That's cool the dragon circles like that. It's like the infinity symbol. I never thought—"

There was a small noise from the couch across from them. Kaylee was suddenly aware that she and Edwin had receded into a bubble of conversation all their own. Jade was giving her an amused smirk. Maddox had perched his chin atop his folded hands. He fluttered his eyelashes at Edwin. "And what did you get me, big boy?"

Kaylee was glad the doorbell rang just then. She was pretty sure if Edwin didn't die of embarrassment, she would.

"I'll get it!" Kaylee's mom called.

"I—uh—thought Kaylee would appreciate a gift like this more than you two," Edwin sputtered. "And, Jade, the last time I carved something you said it looked like a drunk woodpecker had gotten hold of a band saw."

"Yeah, that was pretty clever, wasn't it?" Jade said proudly.

Kaylee's mom gasped. In an instant, they were all up, funneling into the foyer just as Alastair and the others swooped out of the family room.

"Brianna?" Kaylee's dad said. "What—?"

Randy stood on the front porch, the snow swirling around him. For a moment, nobody moved. Randy rocked slightly back and forth on his heels, looking more uneasy than Kaylee had ever seen him. Despite the number of people there, his eyes never left Kaylee's mom, searching for something.

"Randall," Kaylee's mom said.

Randy held up a plastic bag. Inside were two boxes of donuts, giant red SALE stickers pasted on them. The kind the store probably gave away before they went stale.

"I brought dessert."

Still nobody moved.

"Brianna?" Kaylee's dad said.

Kaylee's mom stepped aside. "Hurry up, Randall. You're letting all the heat out."

A smile. A true, full-blown, unhindered smile broke out on Randy's face as he stepped inside and dusted the snow off his arms. "Thought you were gonna leave me to freeze, sis."

"Don't tempt me."

It wasn't until she had a proper look at him in the light that Kaylee could see Randy wasn't quite all right. One hand was slightly blackened. A fresh, angry bruise splotched just between his left eye and earlobe. He winced, just barely, as he shrugged off his jacket.

If anyone else noticed, they didn't mention it.

"I'm starving. Hope you have leftovers," Randy said.

"Randy?" Kaylee said. "Where have you—?"

"Good to see you too, kid." He ruffled her hair as he stepped past her, leaving everyone in stunned silence in his wake.

"NO OFFENSE, KAYLEE," Edwin said an hour later, "but your uncle's kind of awesome."

"He sure makes it seem that way, doesn't he?" Kaylee said. They both glanced at Randy sitting at the kitchen counter. He was digging into his fourth nearly-stale donut. Kaylee briefly wondered why she'd worried about him at all. The man looked a little beat up, but he'd promptly made the rounds with the family after he'd stuffed his face. Alastair had even given him a grudging handshake. "Good to see you're all right, Randall."

"Never better," Randy had said, slapping him on the shoulder so hard Alastair's knees had buckled.

No less than three times since he'd arrived had Kaylee tried to ask where he'd been, but each time Randy neatly evaded her with a strategic retreat into another room or, incredibly, offering gifts to distract them.

"Is this real?" Jeremy turned over the pocket knife Randy had given him, his eyes lit with mischievous wonder. "I can keep it?"

"Only if you promise not to tell your parents," Randy said with a wink. "Picked it up on my way back. Handle is made from Samarian shadow dancer bone. Promise me you'll only ever use it to smite evil-doers?"

Jeremy flipped out the blade. His grinned widened. "Dude, I swear. This thing's legit."

"Hope you brought me some answers for Christmas," Kaylee said when Randy had turned to her.

"Even better," Randy said. He reached into his pocket, then pulled out his hand and patted her on the back. ""For you, a hearty congratulations. Here's to surviving a week without me."

Kaylee's glare of disgust could have melted steel, but it merely glanced off Randy as he moved onto someone else.

"I mean, he's a little eccentric," Edwin admitted as they now both sat together on the couch. Jade and Maddox had already headed home, as had Alastair and his wife. Randy was picking up his fifth donut now, and Kaylee and Jade's parents were still in the family room, their voices at the more-than-two-glasses-of-wine-hush-level.

"He's infuriating," Kaylee said.

"Is he teaching you how to control your elemental magic?"

"I mean, yeah, I guess."

Kaylee thought back to their last lesson. Her powers had gone haywire again, but Randy had managed to calm her down. She wasn't sure if that counted as learning how to control her magic. However, she did seem to be getting better. Slowly. *Very* slowly.

"Every time I'm close to having a breakthrough, he leaves without a word. I don't even think Alastair completely trusts him yet. Then there's the—"

Edwin glanced at her when she stopped. "The what?"

"Nothing." She had almost blurted out about the pictures she'd found at Randy's house. That seemed a little too personal, even to share with Edwin. At least before she got the truth directly from Randy.

Edwin was eyeing Randy, tapping his fingers on one of his crossed legs. "Think I should ask him what the Slayers are up to next? I've hit a dead end."

"Why would he know?"

"If he's out on Convocation business that could involve Slayers. My dad and the sub-elders would be idiots not to use him while he's here. I mean, the stories I've heard..."

"Like what?" Kaylee asked, narrowing her eyes. She'd heard a lot of these supposed 'stories' mentioned and the more she heard, the less she believed they were true.

"Well, believe it or not, he actually *was* a rogue dragon-kin for a little while," Edwin said. He scooted so their legs were nearly touching and lowered his voice. "Then they say he may have even been a bounty hunter that took out high-ranking Slayers single-handedly."

Randy stuffed an entire donut into his mouth, downed it with a full glass of milk, then let out a satisfied belch.

"You're positive about that?" Kaylee said doubtfully.

Edwin shrugged. "What I heard. You'll have to ask him."

The clock above the fireplace chimed. Edwin stood and stretched. "I'd better head home."

"I'll walk you out."

Kaylee followed him until they entered the hallway. Here, Edwin stopped so abruptly Kaylee nearly ran into him. Kaylee nudged his back.

"You okay?"

Edwin stood frozen in place, barely breathing. Kaylee was about to touch him again when he spun to face her.

"I...had a lot of fun tonight."

"Oh. Yeah, me too. And thanks for the..." She pulled the charm up from around her neck. "You know."

Edwin brushed his fingers over it. His eyes flickered upward. Kaylee suddenly noticed the mistletoe hanging innocently above their heads. A knot of nervousness coiled in her stomach.

And then Edwin was leaning toward her and a trill of energy stronger than any magic she'd ever conjured shot from her toes to her head. She wasn't ready for this.

She was *so* ready for this.

What if she—?

He was close now, the space between them almost gone.

"This is so cliché," Edwin muttered.

But he didn't stop, and Kaylee's heart threatened to beat out of her chest.

The doorbell rang.

The sound was like ice cracking on a frozen lake they both stood upon. Kaylee's eyes flickered open. Edwin stood upright so fast he nearly smacked into the doorframe behind him.

"I got it!" Randy said. He gave them both a questioning look, then opened the front door. His body went rigid.

"Who is it?" Edwin said.

Randy continued standing there, and Kaylee peered around him to see—

"Reese!"

Her older brother stood grinning on the front porch, his face chapped red with cold. "Merry Christmas, Katy-did."

Kaylee tackled him and Reese laughed, nearly tripping off the porch into the snow.

"You didn't tell me you were coming home!"

"I thought I'd make it a surprise. Clearly it worked."

But as the rest of the family came to see who the visitor was, Kaylee couldn't help but notice the deadly expression that flickered across Randy's face, before he stormed back inside.

CHAPTER NINE

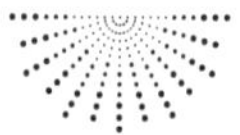

Kaylee ducked and rolled, barely avoiding the bolt of electricity that snapped at her heels. She whirled, drawing her magic to herself in the smooth motion Randy had helped her perfect. Randy's bolt of electricity reared, then struck, but Kaylee thrust her hand forward and pushed her own magic to intercept it. Her lightning split the attack in two, dissipating it to either side of her. But no sooner had she done that then Randy was there, one quivering claw hovering inches from her face.

"You lose."

"I didn't know *you* were going to fight me."

Randy dropped his claw. The gentle hum of power filling the forest around them ceased. "I was attacking you with magic. What part of that meant I *wasn't* going to fight you?"

"I mean, not you physically..."

"You were being lazy. Lazier than normal."

Kaylee bit her tongue as Randy picked up a towel hanging from a snow-covered branch and wiped his face. There was no point arguing with him. He'd been in a bad mood for the last week and a half. Ever since Reese had come home.

"I tried," Kaylee said. "At least I did better than last time."

"I don't want excuses."

"School's started again, and I was up late talking to Reese—"

Randy threw her a water bottle. It came so hard Kaylee barely caught it before it nailed her in the gut.

"When's he leaving?" Randy said.

"Not until fall."

Randy nearly choked as he sipped his own water.

"That long?" he demanded. "What happened to college? I thought he was getting a degree!"

Kaylee shrugged. "He's taking a semester off. Wanted time to figure things out."

"Stupid millennials," Randy muttered. "They just need to pick a direction and charge blindly ahead without thinking about it. Worked for me."

Kaylee's parents hadn't been too happy either when Reese had told them his plans for a break. She could still hear their voices carrying up to her from downstairs; confused, upset, but tinged with a hint of curiosity, as Reese explained he needed some time to think about what to do next.

"He's amazing," Kaylee said as Randy took up his position again. "You should talk to him. I think he'd be really interested to hear about the Convocation—"

"Don't."

Kaylee blinked and suddenly Randy was in front of her, a wavering finger nearly touching her nose.

"Do *not* tell him about the Convocation. Or that you're a dragon-kin. Don't tell him about any of it."

Kaylee shoved Randy's hand out of her face. "Why not? He's my family."

"Kaylee, he cannot know about the Convocation. It's bad enough you told Jeremy."

"Jeremy would have found out eventually. We live in the same house. He's not that oblivious. And Alastair said having our family in on it will help normalize our lives."

"Alastair is wrong. The more of your family who knows, the more danger they're all in."

You're just a puppet to the Convocation. Doing whatever they say.

"Look," Randy said in a gentler tone. "I know you're excited he's back, but...just wait a bit before you tell him. Can you promise me that?"

Kaylee had never seen Randy so serious about anything before. It scared her a little.

"Yeah...Yeah, I can wait. If it's that important."

"It is, and thank you."

"But he'll find out eventually, even if I don't tell him."

"Just as long as it's not yet."

Randy pointed behind her. Through the dips and low-hanging branches of the tangle of trees was another clearing.

"Your Convocation insertion team has been compromised. The Slayers are on your tail and ahead is a safe zone magically cordoned off by Merlins. You have to reach it before they get you."

The wind was already stirring as Kaylee drew it to her. Electricity crackled around Randy's feet. He raised a claw.

"Go."

It was by far the hardest lesson Kaylee had experienced with Randy. If Baba had been verbally abusive, then Randy was every bit as bad when it came to pushing her to her physical limits.

Just when she felt her reserves were drained, he would force her to do another drill. His power seemed bottomless and he controlled even the strongest of attacks with casual ease that simultaneously made Kaylee respectful and envious. Well, if he could do it, then she would learn too. She could still remember his face the night he'd come to announce he was training her: he didn't think she could handle what he threw at her. That she couldn't take his intensity.

She'd show him. Eventually.

Everything hurt as the two of them crossed the snow-covered field back to Randy's house. Kaylee winced every other step, her feet seizing from how many times Randy had shocked them when she'd stayed in one spot too long. Randy caught her arm as she stumbled. He dipped his chin.

"You'll have to learn how to shift those soon. Most dragon-kin's talons are resistant to magic."

"Then why aren't you teaching me to do that?" It was true Kaylee had gotten a lot better at controlling her magic. Not quite up to totally-controlling-a-storm levels, but her shifting had improved and her control over secondary elements like ice and wind was better than it'd ever been. But Randy always stopped at that. For all his intensity, it seemed there were in fact lines he wouldn't cross yet.

Randy threw their training gear on the outside of the shed. "We'll move on when you're ready."

Kaylee threw up her hands. "*Why* would I not be ready?"

"You're ready when you stop seeing that boy you killed."

So he'd noticed. Of course he had. Every time Kaylee assumed he was blind and oblivious Randy proved her otherwise. The visions hadn't been bad today. Certainly no worse than the last two weeks, but still enough to catch Randy's eye, it seemed. He must have noticed the second's hesitation in her counterattacks; the brief pause just before she first drew on her magic.

"You will kill others," Randy said. "Not because you want to, but because you have to, in order to protect those close to you. Isn't that more important?"

"Don't you dare try to justify it!" Kaylee snarled. "How do you know what's important? What others mean to you? You, who runs off for years and who's probably never—"

"Don't," Randy said in a dangerously low voice. "Don't say things you don't know about me."

Kaylee almost blurted that she knew about the girl. Only fifty yards away in his house was his big, bad secret, and she knew.

But it wasn't right. Not now. She wanted to ask when she wasn't so angry, and she actually had a chance of him answering instead of closing off like he always did when she tried to learn anything about his past. For now, she'd deal with the fact that he was just another mentor who didn't think she could handle her own power, or the truth. But she was ready. She'd struggled, and would keep struggling, with her magic, but she was ready. The visions were hers and she'd own that. She could handle seeing—

"Kaylee?"

Brendan.

She turned and there he stood in front of her; his face, scared and flecked with blood; his eyes, pleading and shocked as they had been seconds before death.

Kaylee's rational mind screamed that it wasn't possible. This was too real. She must have been tired and now—

Kaylee closed off her magic before it could rush to her aid. She blinked furiously and Brendan turned into Reese, concern written on his face.

"Katy-bear?"

"Reese!" Of course it was Reese. His short blond hair looked nothing like Brendan's long brown. His face was more angular too, his eyes kind. "What are you—how'd you know I was out here?"

Reese took a good look around. "Mom mentioned you usually came here after school." His eyes narrowed on the house with distaste. "No offense, but what are you doing—?"

"She's helping me."

Reese tensed. Randy put one massive hand on Kaylee's shoulder. "I pay her to do odd jobs around the place. Isn't as easy when you get to be my age."

"Uh-huh," Reese said.

"We're done for today. Go get your things, Kaylee."

"Okay…sure."

Kaylee snagged her backpack from the front porch. Reese and Randy hadn't moved from their spots. Reese was glaring holes at him. Randy was picking at his teeth.

"I guess it's good to see you again, Uncle Randy," Reese said. "It's only been, oh, what? Thirteen years?"

"Around that long, I guess. Can't remember, exactly. Was that back when you hid in your room and refused to see me?"

"A relative who was basically homeless, traveling around doing questionable things, yeah. Wonder why I thought you were someone to avoid."

Randy chuckled. He turned and started walking back to the shed, waving over his shoulder. "I'll see you next time, Kaylee."

Reese caught Kaylee's arm as she tried to walk to his car. His grip was like iron. "If he's hurting you, or doing anything—"

Kaylee almost laughed, until she realized he was being serious. "No! No, he's not, Reese. Seriously, he's been nothing but nice since he got here."

Not *exactly* true, but Randy needed all the praise he could get. And if it got Reese to pull his glare away from Randy's back then she'd heap it on him.

Reese eventually let her arm go. When he looked at her, he relaxed, a bright smile lighting up his face again.

"Say, rumor has it my little sis has her license." He tossed her the keys. "Why don't you show me how much you've learned?"

THEY FELL BACK into easy conversation on the short ride home. Kaylee filled Reese in on the non-Convocation parts of her life and he told her a little about his first year and a half at college. By the time they'd pulled into the driveway, however, Reese had lapsed into thoughtful silence, picking at a circle of beads on his wrist. He went to help with dinner while Kaylee headed to her room to start homework. Her phone buzzed on her way up. It was Edwin, asking if she had free time to talk about something. Kaylee answered yes, butterflies taking flight in her stomach.

They had seen each other a few times since the Christmas party, but Edwin had acted about the same, which both annoyed and relieved her. Maybe she had imagined the whole thing that had almost happened in the hallway. Maybe she was reading too much into how close he sat to her on the couch, how he gently touched her arm when he cracked a joke. Maybe she—

Kaylee nearly dropped her backpack when she opened her room and saw Edwin waving at her from outside her window.

"*What* are you doing?" she hissed as she threw it open.

Edwin looked bewildered. He made a short gesture, and the wooden plank he was levitating up to her window rose a little higher. "Uh, you said you could talk?"

"I didn't mean right this second! And stop doing that before Reese sees you!"

"Your brother? You haven't told hi—?"

But Kaylee yanked him inside so fast Edwin's shins barked on the windowsill and he collapsed with a pained groan on the other side of her bed.

"Oh, stop whining before my parents hear you," Kaylee said.

"But it hurts…"

Kaylee quickly closed her door. When she turned, Edwin had pulled himself up onto her bed. She nearly choked, suddenly realizing what she'd done. Edwin was in her room—*on her bed.*

Kaylee forced herself calm, hoping she wasn't blushing. She was making a big deal about nothing, and they had to stay quiet. If her parents came in now…no, she wouldn't think about that.

She took a seat in the chair at her desk, facing Edwin. "What…did you want to talk to me about?"

Edwin held her gaze for a moment, as if he knew everything

that had just gone through her head, then pulled out a leather-bound book from beneath his jacket. "This."

"That?"

"Yeah, this."

"Nothing else? Nothing else *at all*?"

"Uh, no. Why?"

Kaylee sighed, waving a hand for him to go on. To be honest, she was relieved. Between Reese's return, Randy acting weird and...*whatever* was going on between her and Edwin, the last thing she needed was another confusing boy in her life.

"I think I found something that might point us to the Slayers' next move," Edwin said. "Here, take a look."

He made a space for her on the bed. Kaylee sat next to him and scooted closer as he flipped through the pages.

"It looks like a log book," Kaylee said.

"That's exactly what it is. It was in the Convocation Records Room. Before the records all went digital they used to mark down any magic items that passed through Convocation hands before being dispersed to their rightful parties or stored for safe-keeping. Things like this."

He tilted the page and Kaylee saw written in neat script: Summoning Urn.

"That's from the djinn giant from the mall," Kaylee said.

"The record of the first time the Convocation had it."

"So what does this tell us?"

"Well, we know the Slayers aren't strong enough in number to launch an all-out attack without massive magical backup. That means if they want to do something big it needs to be via a rare, powerful item. Specifically, one of these."

Edwin flipped to a section in the back. This list had been decimated by thick, angry ink scratches.

"These particular items were recorded until the Convocation thought they were too dangerous to be kept on record. Lucky for me, when they decided to 'destroy' the evidence they probably used some lazy intern who didn't care enough to do it properly." Edwin shook his head. "I told my dad he should have made the internship paid. But at least it allowed me to do this."

He ran his fingers down the parchment, as if tickling the page. Where his fingertips brushed, the ink blots drained away and flowed to the bottom margin, clearly revealing the words beneath.

"I see Baba's been teaching you some seriously advanced magic," Kaylee said. "Redacted documents are powerless against you."

Edwin bumped her knee and Kaylee laughed.

"I *have* gotten better, believe it or not, and not just at reading."

He was still smiling as he turned back to the book. Kaylee perched her chin on his shoulder. She wasn't quite sure what compelled her to do it, but Edwin's breath only hitched for a moment before he started reading the items listed aloud.

"Seal of Solomon, Book of Kells, Drake's Drum, Smoking Mirror, Mjolnir—"

"Wait, you're telling me the Convocation had Thor's hammer *Mjolnir*? Really?"

"It's possible," Edwin said.

"Come on, Edwin."

"This disbelief coming from a girl who will one day be able to sprout wings and a dragon's tail."

"I've always wondered about that. When I shift my tail, is it going to…you know, where does it come out…"

Edwin burst out laughing, and Kaylee had to clamp her hand over his mouth, shooting a worried look toward the door. "Quiet! It was a legit question!"

Edwin finished chuckling into her hand until she pulled it away. "Sorry, sorry. I guess no one ever explained it to you. When a dragon-kin shifts parts of their body, yes, it causes an actual physical change that affects clothing and space. Appendages *off* the dragon-kin's physical body, like wings and a tail, aren't actually physical. They're made by magic so they don't follow the exact same properties as a physical shift."

"I'm...not sure I follow."

"If you remember next time you're with Randy, ask him to show you. Wings and a tail seem physical, but if you get a closer look they're actually almost intangible. They don't displace space, like the clothing you wear."

"Except when you need to hit someone with them, or fly."

"Yep, and because they're not wholly physical, that's why," he said, snickering again, "we don't see a bunch of trained dragon-kin running around with holes in the backs of their pants."

Kaylee smacked him. "Point made."

Still chuckling, Edwin pulled the book from her lap and flipped the page. This one was empty. "But after these rare items, I've hit a dead end again. The problem is there's no way of knowing which items the Convocation still has and which the Slayers still have access to. Just because the item is written down here doesn't mean it wasn't stolen or lost again."

"Maybe you could ask Alastair."

"He doesn't even know I went to the Convocation Records. He's okay with me reading from his library, but after last year he's still wary about us getting more involved than we have to."

Kaylee leaned back with a huff. "Clearly. He hasn't sent us on another mission in months."

Edwin drew his hand back from the page and all the crossed-out lines rushed back to their proper place. "I can't ask Alastair, or Baba..."

"Nononono, don't do that," Kaylee said. "I like my limbs attached, thanks."

"So I was thinking you could ask Randy. I know I mentioned it before, but I'm sure he wouldn't go telling my dad."

Kaylee thought about it. There was a chance Randy might have more insight, but he would definitely question what she was doing. Especially since he was still on her about the whole

Brendan thing. If he didn't think she was over that, there was no way he'd allow her to continue investigating the Slayers.

There was also the fact Kaylee didn't completely trust him.

"I can tell by your face that's a no," Edwin said. "I guess that means a trip to the Slag Heap."

Kaylee raised an eyebrow. "I'm still not sure Damian will let us back."

"Damian doesn't have a choice. We need info and we're going to get it."

Edwin's jaw was set, his eyes firmly planted on the cover of the book. His confidence caused a small flutter of admiration in her chest.

"You have changed," she muttered.

Edwin leaned toward her. "What'd you say?"

"Kaylee?"

Kaylee had all of three seconds to shove Edwin off the other side of the bed and leap back into her desk chair before Reese opened the door.

"Hey, Katy-did, dinner's—what are you doing?"

Kaylee slyly nudged Edwin's book beneath the bed with her foot and continued leaning back in her chair, keeping her lower body still on the bed.

"Uh, what are you doing?" Reese repeated.

"Relaxing. I'm combining the comfortableness of my bed with the ergonomics of my chair."

Reese blinked. "Oookay. I guess you haven't changed as much as I thought since I've been gone."

His eyes jumped to the open window. In a second, he'd crossed the room and closed it, staring out into the dark a second longer than necessary. He did a quick check around the room, as if something were amiss. Kaylee's heart briefly stopped when his gaze lingered beneath the bed, then moved on.

"You shouldn't leave it open like that," he chastised.

"What?" Kaylee said, trying to ignore how close he'd stopped next to where Edwin was hiding. "You think some big bad monster's going to come in and snatch me?"

"Yes," Reese said simply. "Now come on down, dinner's ready."

He paused at the door, his hand hooked on the frame.

"Kaylee, you know you can tell me anything, right?"

Kaylee was taken aback. Reese had always been nice to her, but never the kind of brother to get overly sentimental. That he was even offering to have a true heart-to-heart discussion was a far cry from the kid who'd left for school only last year.

"I…guess I knew that."

"I mean it. Anything."

"Okay. Thanks."

"Now hurry up, I'm starving."

Kaylee listened to the thump of his feet as he went back downstairs. She jumped when the window once again closed behind her as Edwin left.

CHAPTER TEN

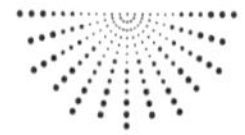

"I'm telling you, it's weird," Kaylee said. "She hasn't been here for two weeks."

Jade finished adding the last few lines to her English report. She chewed the end of her pen.

"Jade?"

"Huh? Did you say something?"

"Dani. She hasn't been to school in a while."

Jade picked her head up from writing and took a look around the quad, as if Dani would simply appear now that they were discussing her. "Dani's a human being, no matter how unnaturally happy she is. She probably got sick or something."

"But you told me she stopped hanging around the Convocation recently, too."

"Yeah, but again that could also be because she's sick."

"For two weeks?"

Jade made a non-committal grunt and scratched out something else on her paper.

Kaylee sighed. She knew when she was fighting a losing battle with Jade's concentration. "You realize you had, like, since Thanksgiving to do that, right?"

"Between Convocation meetings and extra practice, you mean."

Kaylee opened her mouth, then closed it again. Extra practice, as in the Tamer test Jade was still prepping for. The time since Christmas had been so chaotic Kaylee hadn't even had the chance to hang out with Jade and Maddox as much as she usually did.

"Here." Kaylee took the pen and paper. "And it's *Something Wicked This Way Comes*, not *Something Crooked.*"

"Thought that didn't sound right," Jade said, leaning back with a relieved sigh.

DESPITE JADE'S assurances that everything was fine with Dani, Kaylee found herself worrying about her through the rest of the day. It wasn't like it was anything she could put a finger on, either. Dani hadn't been in an accident (that Kaylee knew of). She actually *could* have been sick, but Dani's demeanor had been off even before now, and Kaylee knew she wasn't imagining that. Jade might not have believed her, but Kaylee couldn't let it alone.

So right after school, Kaylee found herself taking a long walk to the eastern side of Scarsdale where Dani lived. She'd been able to find her address from the staff credits in the Yearbook Club, one of the thousand school groups Dani was part of. Strangely, when Kaylee had asked the girls Dani usually hung out with, none of them could recall having ever actually visited her house.

Kaylee slowed as she reached Dani's house, tucked in the deep bend of a cul-de-sac. From where she stood, the front of the house looked pinched. All the shades were drawn. The grass was unkempt, and a car with a deflated tire and rust trailing down the sides sat unloved in the driveway.

Kaylee double-checked the address. This couldn't be right. Not that Kaylee had thought much about Dani's home up until now, but she had expected something brighter. Something more alive and similar to her neighbors on either side: Narrow stoops but with homely decorations, freshly tilled flowerbeds and blinds open to the world.

Feeling a bit intrusive, and with unease prickling at the back of her neck, Kaylee approached the front. She raised her hand to knock.

Someone sobbed faintly from inside.

Kaylee's hand hovered an inch from the door. "Dani?" Her voice wavered. She forced it steady. "Dani?"

Silence.

Kaylee tried to make her arm move, but a strange power held it back; a feeling she never in a million years would have associated with Dani: Fear.

Kaylee tried to dismiss the emotion. Dani was…Dani was sick, and Kaylee was here to see if she was okay, maybe fetch her something if she needed to feel better, as she had done a dozen times before for Jade.

There came a distant crash, followed by a cry of alarm, barely discernible through the door. Kaylee pounded on it.

"Dani!"

Waiting was agony. The next-door-neighbor's flag snapped in the wind. In the distance, a dog barked, but here, in front of Dani's, Kaylee felt as if she was in her own universe, composed only of whatever noise she heard next and whatever would happen when that door opened.

If it ever opened.

There was the thump of feet crossing tile. Kaylee exhaled as a bolt was scraped back and the door pulled open a crack.

"Dani?" Kaylee ventured.

It sure didn't look like it. The Dani Kaylee knew was a vibrant spirit; a ball of sunshine manifested in human form. The person who peered through the narrow space of wood and doorframe had red-ringed eyes and a haunted look, her face gaunt and tinged slightly gray. In an instant, Kaylee knew this was no normal sickness.

"Kaylee?" Dani's eyes widened as if she faced an oncoming train.

The door slammed shut.

"Dani! Open up!" Kaylee pounded again, but even that couldn't drown out the pained scream that came from the other side.

Screw this. Kaylee took a quick glance around to make sure nobody was coming, then focused on drawing her magic to her shoulder. She could feel the muscles tighten, the bones beneath her skin knitting together as scales interlocked over it.

Kaylee backed up and rammed against the door. Once. Twice. Another scream inside and Kaylee pounded again, more frantic this time. It occurred to her that this was insane. That what she was doing was beyond illegal, but also that something on the other side of the door was terribly, horribly wrong.

Kaylee backed up again and put more force behind the next push. The door popped inward, bouncing against the inside wall, but Kaylee was already moving.

The first thing she noticed was the blood. Teardrops of it splattered in a morbid trail on the tile, stark against the white. Kaylee forced down her welling horror and followed the trail to the back of the house, to another door.

"Dani!"

"Don't come in!" Dani screamed. There was another sob. With one turn of her claws, Kaylee broke the knob and rushed inside.

Things clicked into place very fast. The dark looks Dani had had at school, the result of a secret, unwelcome discovery; scratching her arms, missing her normal activities. Hiding. Afraid.

And now Dani, kneeling in the center of the floor in front of her, beautiful aqua blue scales littering the carpet like diamonds, mingled with blood as Dani desperately tried to rip them off.

CHAPTER ELEVEN

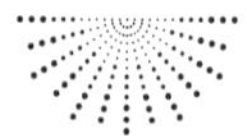

"Stop!"

A spray of water sluiced at Kaylee's head, but her instincts took over and she dodged aside, the attack instead making a dent in the wall behind her. Kaylee slid beside Dani and gripped her claws. Dani tried to throw her off but Kaylee held tight.

At least until Dani gave another screech and a second blast of water slammed Kaylee in the face. She was thrown back into the closet, her head hitting a vacuum with a painful thump. When she looked up, the other girl wore an expression of pure horror.

"Kaylee! Are you okay? I didn't mean to—"

Her eyes moved back to her arms and Kaylee fought a sudden wave of nausea. It seemed Dani had been picking away at her scales for some time. Most remained, but there were small chunks of them missing, blood pooling from the shallow holes and mixing with the aqua blue.

"I have to get them off, Kaylee. This can't be—I won't let it be."

"You won't get them to go away like that," Kaylee said. She crawled from the closet, one hand held reassuringly out in front, and kneeled across from Dani. Her heart was racing. Her mind whirled with a million different questions, but right now Dani needed her help.

"Watch." Kaylee held up her hand, shifted it to dragon scales, then back. "Just breathe. When you first get them, they come out when you're scared or get overly emotional."

Dani choked a sob. "Overly emotional. Story of my life."

"Breathe," Kaylee repeated. She shifted back and forth again. "Think of pulling the magic back into your arms like a rope. Bring it in. Coax the scales to go away."

Dani was still crying, but now her arms had gone limp in her lap. She took a shuddering breath. "It's not working!"

Kaylee gently placed her hands on Dani's arms. Dani winced and, for a moment, Kaylee flashed back to the first time she'd grown her own scales. That fear that somehow everyone knew what was happening to her and that they'd find out at any moment. That she was nothing but a hideous creature they would only ever see as a freak.

You're an abomination. You never should have existed.

"Focus," Kaylee said, as much to herself as to Dani. "Breathe, focus, and coax them back. It's your magic. Make it listen to you."

Kaylee matched breaths with Dani. She concentrated only on that. Not the warm blood seeping through her fingers or Dani's eyes darting from one covered window to the next.

"*Breathe,*" Kaylee commanded.

Dani closed her fluttering lashes. A moment later, the scales beneath Kaylee's fingers softened, then returned to skin. Kaylee sighed.

"There. That wasn't so hard, was it?"

Dani turned her arms over. Kaylee tried not to wince at the numerous shallow gouges where the scales had been. She'd have to talk to Alastair right away to see if a Merlin healer could do anything to fix those.

"Do you have a first aid kit? Band aids? Anything?"

Dani continued marveling at her skin, as if she'd never seen it before. Kaylee snapped her fingers. "Dani?"

"What?"

"First aid."

"Oh. Bathroom."

Kaylee found the bathroom in a narrow hallway and stepped inside. She tried to ignore the blood-stained towels stuffed into the trash can and instead dug under the sink until she found a store bought first aid-kit.

It wasn't until she tried opening the kit that she realized her hands were shaking. She gripped the sides of the sink to steady them and looked in the mirror. A terrified girl stared back.

Dani, a dragon-kin. Did Alastair know? Did he know what Dani was doing to herself?

Kaylee squeezed the sides of the sink harder until her shaking was reduced to nothing more than a slight tremble. Dani couldn't see how scared she was. She was supposed to be the strong one. She'd get her friend through this and then...then Alastair could figure things out.

"Come with me," Kaylee said when she returned to the other room. "We'll patch you up in the kitchen."

Dani, still in a daze, allowed Kaylee to lead her to the kitchen.

"This is going to hurt," Kaylee said, turning on the water. Dani nodded mutely. She didn't make a sound as Kaylee washed out the gouges the best she could, then dried them with a couple towels. At least a dozen times she wished Edwin were here. He was stupidly rational when it came to these sorts of surprises, plus he may have known some healing spells.

The cleaning done, Kaylee used up all the band aids, then finished with the rest of the gauze and tore the towels into strips to tie off the whole thing.

"There," she said when she was finished, stepping back to examine her handiwork. "It isn't Girl Scout worthy, but it should hold until we can get you some better help."

Dani took one look at the bandages and burst into tears. She threw her arms around Kaylee. "Th-thank you! I was s-s-so scared! I didn't know what to d-do!"

"You should have told me, or Jade or Maddox," Kaylee said gently, patting her back. "We could have helped you. Believe it or not, we kind of know about this stuff."

A flash of naked fear crossed Dani's face. Her fingers fumbled with the hem of her shirt Kaylee had rolled up to bandage her arms. Kaylee caught a glimpse of purple splotches before Dani tugged the sleeves down and wiped her eyes.

"I-I'm not as strong as you. I couldn't face it, so I thought..."

"You tried handling it yourself. I think that's pretty strong."

Dani gave her a watery smile. Then she glanced at the clock. Her eyes widened. "You have to go."

"I can't leave you—"

"You have to go now—"

"The Convocation—you're a dragon-kin, they need to know."

"Kaylee," Dani spun her around, gripping her arms so hard Kaylee could feel her claws re-emerging, digging into her skin.

"Breathe," Kaylee reassured her. "It takes a few times to get it under control. Alastair will—"

"You can't tell *anyone*," Dani said. She shook Kaylee. "Promise me!"

"Dani, you need their help. This is only shifting. Once you get more elemental magic you don't want that going off whenever."

"Promise. Me."

"No! I won't let you go through what I did."

Kaylee heard a car squeal into the driveway. If it was possible, Dani went even paler.

"Go!"

"I need my backpack."

But Dani grabbed Kaylee and nearly wrenched her to the front door. They had nearly reached it when a man walked into the family room. Time seemed to stop. He looked to be in his late fifties with graying hair going bald and wearing a rumpled suit. A messenger bag was slung over one shoulder. His stormy expression only grew worse as his gaze moved from the busted-in front door, to Kaylee, to Dani's wrapped arms.

Dani's mouth opened and closed like a choking fish. "Dad, this isn't—she was just leaving."

"What is this?" Dani's dad said in an eerily calm voice. "I thought I told you, a hundred times I thought I made it clear, no friends. No one. Period. And..." he refocused on Dani's arms. Then on Kaylee. Kaylee could almost hear an audible click as his mind made the connection.

"She knows."

"Daddy—"

"She's one of them dragon freaks. Just like I warned you about."

In a second, he'd thrown his bag to the side, advancing on Kaylee menacingly, and Kaylee forgot that he was an adult, that he was Dani's dad, just a normal man, not a Slayer, not a rogue, but still her magic surged, the temperature in the room stirring.

"You stay away from here. Get it?" Dani's dad said, spittle flying from his mouth. "No daughter of mine is going to be some —some beast. You come here again, you're dead."

He grabbed Kaylee's arm and hurled her out the door.

"Go, Kaylee!" Dani yelled from inside. "I'll be fine, go!"

"And you," Dani's dad said, turning on her. He slammed the door shut.

Bile rose in Kaylee's mouth as she sat on the sidewalk, her palms stinging from scraping the concrete, her arm throbbing from where Dani's father had grabbed her. She expected at any moment to hear screams from within, but the ensuing silence was almost worse.

She should...she couldn't.

But Dani...told her to leave. She would only make it worse.

And Alastair...she said she...

More than anything, Kaylee wanted to run back inside and pummel and punch every enemy she found there. But there was no enemy, only a father and his terrified daughter.

So, fighting every cell screaming at her, Kaylee stood, and fled back home.

~

KAYLEE DRIFTED like a phantom through her house. Her feet moved of their own accord, her mind still stuck, frozen on the still image of Dani's face as the door slammed on her.

Useless, Kaylee told herself. She'd been useless. She'd been helpless. Wasn't that the entire point of her training? So that others would never get hurt protecting her, but that she could instead protect those she cared about?

Kaylee punched the wall. A bump upstairs answered and the light in Reese's room flickered to life, causing Kaylee to blink.

"Kaylee?"

Reese was nothing but a silhouette at the top of the stairs. Kaylee's heart stuttered. For a moment—just a moment—she had seen something else. Something who was not her brother, but instead a person with blades and a hatred for her that could only be quenched by violence.

Then Reese stepped into the light and the sensation passed.

"Kaylee? Why are you standing in the dark? You okay?"

"Fine," Kaylee said. She dragged her feet the rest of the way upstairs. "Where is everyone?"

"Mom and Dad went out to dinner and Jeremey's at a friend's house."

"Okay."

"I thought you were at Randy's—is that blood?"

Kaylee looked down at the sleeve Reese had grabbed. Brown stains were dotted like pinpricks on her shirt. She hadn't even considered how she might look after leaving Dani's. Hopefully, the blood was the only sign that anything was wrong.

Reese pulled her into his room. "Where are you bleeding? If he hurt you I swear I'll kill him."

"Randy didn't do this."

Reese wouldn't be dissuaded. He sat Kaylee on his bed and began brushing aside stuff on his desk. Kaylee hadn't realized how much his room had changed since she'd last been in it. Before, it seemed as if there wasn't enough wall to hold all his posters, or enough shelf for his books. He and Edwin would have gotten along fantastically, Kaylee realized. She had forgotten how much Reese liked to read.

But all that was gone now. The extent of what Reese had returned home from college with included a single trunk and a pile of textbooks. This new space felt sterile. Sparse.

Another crash. A pair of running shoes fell off the desk as he went through the drawers.

"Out running?" she said, trying to talk about something that would help calm him down.

"New workout routine," Reese said absentmindedly. "Better than my last one."

Kaylee blinked. Since when did Reese like working out? Even she hadn't found exercise all that appealing before her dragon-kin training, and she'd still managed to move more than he had.

"Band-Aids, Band-Aids," Reese muttered.

"Reese," Kaylee said, realizing she'd better put a stop to him before he tore what little he had left apart. "The blood isn't mine."

Reese slammed the drawers shut. "Then whose is it?"

"Nobody you know."

"If you're in some kind of trouble..."

"Not me. A friend."

"Kaylee, I need to know—"

"Can you...not ask me what happened? Please. I just need to think."

Reese stared at her for a moment. Then he took a heavy seat down on the bed beside her. The beads on his wrist clacked as he played with them. He hadn't been lying. He actually *had* started working out. His arms were sinewy and strong, laced with a couple faint white scars.

"Where'd you get those?"

"Hm?" Reese turned his hands over. He chuckled. "Karate club. I was part of it until last semester."

"I didn't know Queensbury University had a karate club."

"Queensbury has many different clubs. There's even this one…" Reese paused. "No. Don't distract me. You don't want to tell me what happened, that's fine. But Kaylee?"

Kaylee turned to him. She was shocked to feel a warm tear run down her check. Reese gently brushed it away. "You know you can tell me anything."

"You said that already."

"I meant it. Anything. Even if no one else believes you, I will. Understand?"

"Sometimes…" Kaylee said before she could stop. "Sometimes I want to do something, but I don't know what. There's a hundred things I wished I'd done but I didn't, and I feel so useless. Why are there so many evil things? And why can't I stop them?"

Reese looked at the wall. One hand continued rubbing the beads.

"Reese?"

"There are some pretty twisted things in this world. And no, I don't know why it's such a broken place. Sometimes I wish…" he punched a fist into his open hand. "Sometimes I wish they were all something we could physically fight against. They're not, but I guess we each have to find ways to fight them somehow. You'll find a way to fight back, too."

"What if the evil thing isn't something you can fight?"

"There's always something to fight. There are always evils in this world, true monsters. Only a few of us are strong enough to stand between those who want to hurt others."

Kaylee felt vaguely as if she'd heard someone say that before, but her head was starting to hurt too much now to remember. Kaylee wanted to tell him about the Convocation right then, but Randy's warning flooded back to her. When she looked in Reese's eyes and saw the intensity there, directed at an unknown adversary she couldn't see, she could almost understand why he'd told her to wait.

Reese opened his arms. "Come here."

Kaylee leaned into him. It was just as she'd done when they were kids during a thunderstorm, or when Kaylee had heard a scary movie playing from the TV downstairs. She could still remember tip-toeing down the shadowed hallway, her breathless knocks, light as butterfly wings, on Reese's door. Yet still Reese heard them. He always heard them. He'd always answered, and although he acted annoyed, he had always let her curl up on the other side of the bed until whatever had been bothering her was gone.

But now storms didn't scare her. She was the storm. And now scary movies didn't scare her, because she'd faced those creatures in real life.

Now it was her turn to be the protector.

"I have to go," Kaylee said.

Reese slowly let her up. "Where?"

"To help a friend. There's always a way to fight, right?"

Reese nodded. Kaylee left him there in his room, hunched over and staring at nothing in particular at all.

CHAPTER TWELVE

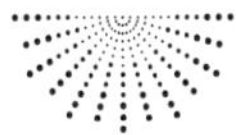

"You were right, I was wrong," Jade said. "To think it was in front of me the whole time..."

"You weren't *wrong*, Jade. There was nothing to be wrong about."

"But I'm a Tamer. I should have recognized the signs."

"And I'm an actual dragon-kin. If anyone should know something was different about Dani, it'd be me."

Jade let out a long breath. She kicked a pinecone out of her way, her feet scuffing the sidewalk up to Edwin's house. "Tell me again what happened?"

"I'll let Alastair. He's the one who called us."

"A dragon-kin," Jade said in disbelief. "We haven't had one around here—like, actually born here—in a while, and she was..." Jade lowered her voice. "She was pulling the scales *off* herself?"

Kaylee felt nauseous at the memory. "Yes."

"Oh, Dani," Jade said sadly.

Kaylee was grateful the conversation was put on pause when they reached Alastair's front door and Tibbs let them in.

"Alastair will meet you in the lounge," Tibbs said. "And I believe Master Edwin will be joining you shortly."

"Only if he manages to unstick his face from whatever book he's currently reading," Jade said.

Tibbs gave a low bow. "You have an uncanny understanding of my young master's personality."

Kaylee stepped into the lounge and froze.

Dani sat rigid on one of the couches. Despite the fire going in the fireplace, the sheer chill as she turned to them could have summoned ice more powerful than anything Kaylee could.

"Dani—" Kaylee started. But no sooner had she opened her mouth than Dani stood and slapped her with one bandage-covered arm.

"Hey!" Jade stepped between them, pushing Dani away as she jabbed a finger at Kaylee.

"You lied."

Kaylee let the sting settle on her cheek. She tried not to be mad. This wasn't Dani talking, this was fear. "I didn't lie."

"You promised you wouldn't tell."

"No, I didn't."

"Dani!" Jade said sharply as Dani threw her off. Kaylee noticed her arms were wrapped with new bandages. Alastair must have had a healer look at them.

"You ruined my life!" Dani shouted.

Kaylee ducked as Dani made another swipe. Her earlier fear at how Dani would react was gone now, replaced by annoyance, then anger.

"It looked like your life was already pretty ruined to me."

Dani let out a growl. She flexed her hands like she wanted to rip Kaylee's face off. Jade tensed, but Dani's fingers remained fingers.

"You said you wouldn't tell anyone," Dani seethed.

"You needed help, Dani."

"I had my powers under control."

"Not just with that."

"He's my family."

"We're your family now, too," Jade said.

"He was hurting you, Dani," Kaylee said softly.

Dani blinked away tears. "He was just scared of me. *I'm* scared of me. He wanted to make sure I didn't hurt anyone."

"By hurting you?"

Dani's cheeks splotched with red. Her voice rose. "Don't pretend like you have any idea what I've—"

"Been through?" Kaylee said, holding up one shifted arm. "You mean like being hated, hunted, feared, reviled, called any number of horrible things and made to feel like, just because of what you are, you're lesser than dirt, lower than the most disgusting thing on the planet? Of course not. How could I possibly know how that feels?"

"My whole life—"

"Is still there. That's what it took me a little while to figure out, and now I'm saving you the trouble of figuring it out for yourself. This isn't the end, Dani."

Dani looked between the two of them, then sank to the floor, her shoulders heaving with sobs. In her, Kaylee saw her own struggle. Maybe not physically, but the torment that had raged through her for most of her first year: that black horizon of uncertainty in the future, and moving further toward it no matter how hard she resisted.

But she hadn't been alone. She'd had Jade and the Convocation. Friends and family by her side the whole way.

Kaylee knelt beside Dani. After a brief hesitation, she put her arms around the other girl's heaving shoulders and allowed her to finish crying herself out. Dani wiped her tears with the palm of her hand.

"I'm sorry," she said. "For slapping you, I mean."

"I've had worse."

Dani gave a hiccupy chuckle. "I believe it. You know…" She wiped her eyes again. "You know…." she said again, but the sentence didn't sound like she knew what she was going to say.

"I had to tell, Dani," Kaylee said.

Dani stayed silent.

"I don't expect you to forgive me, but—"

"You know what the worst part about it was, about…that?" Dani said. "It was putting the mask on every day, pretending I had this perfect life all the time. Being away from home, and being truly—*truly*—happy, but knowing in the back of my mind that I had to go back, and that those brief bits of happiness were all I was going to get. And you know what? I told myself I could live with that. I was okay with that. But then," she said, holding up her arms and let them flop down again, "then this happened."

"It'll get better," Kaylee said. "Both of these things will."

"Better?" Dani shrugged out of her grip. "Can you look me in the eye and promise me that?"

Kaylee couldn't meet her eyes. "No, I can't. I'm sorry."

"That's what I thought."

There was a soft knock and Alastair entered. He took in the scene immediately, then gestured for Kaylee and Jade to leave the room.

"Miss Richards, Miss Azuma, if you please. Miss Fairfax and I have a few things to discuss."

Amelia passed them as they left, carrying a tray of hot chocolate. Alastair held the door for her, then closed it softly behind him. He sighed.

"I apologize. I had not filled Tibbs in on the situation and didn't realize he'd put you both in the same room." He sighed again. "The things that girl has been through…it just proves that dragon-kin are far from the biggest monsters in our world. Kaylee, I want to thank you for telling me about her."

"She hates me."

"For now, yes. But hate like hers is a fluid emotion. She will move beyond it."

"You have to promise she'll be taken care of, no matter what kind of dragon-kin she is," Kaylee said. "She can't be sent back there."

Jade was giving her a funny look, but Alastair's expression told her he knew exactly what she was referring to.

"You've talked to Zaria, I assume."

"What if I have? Is that wrong?"

Alastair shook his head. "No. We are not such a dictatorship that we don't allow the influx of new perceptions, no matter how, er, skewed they might be."

"Dani *can't* end up like them."

"And she won't." He stood up straighter, his figure imposing. "Have I ever given you any reason to doubt my word on that?"

"No..."

"Kaylee, I want you to know that resentment tends to distort the truth. What you have is her side of certain events, however true or false they may be. My side is what I show you in how I act and perform my duties for the Convocation every day. I won't pretend like it's the same everywhere, but it's the same in enough places. I'll leave you with that, and you can decide how you want to believe."

He gently patted her shoulder. "But I also want to tell you that what you did for Dani took a lot of bravery."

"It sure didn't feel like it."

"Being brave never feels like being brave. It's the act of acting regardless of a good friend's desire that you do not. That's why when you were being 'brave' last year and trying to find the Slayers, I got so upset. That was derived more from the selfish desire to be right than anything benefiting the greater good of dragon-kin kind."

"We thought we were helping," Jade muttered.

"Nevertheless," Alastair said with a chuckle, "I'll speak with you on it later. Oh, and Kaylee?"

Kaylee held back for a moment while Jade went ahead. "How is your training with Randy going?"

Kaylee thought back to the last couple weeks: another unexplained absence by Randy; her powers growing steadily stronger, but still a sense of distance between them.

"Has he helped you at all?" Alastair said. "You can be honest."

"He has," Kaylee said. She just wasn't quite sure how much yet.

"Good. If you ever need to talk to me, I'm here."

If you ever need to tell me anything...

"Thanks, Alastair."

Jade and Edwin were waiting in the foyer. Before Kaylee could even say hello, Edwin had wrapped her in a tight hug.

"What was that for?" she asked, slightly breathless, when he released her.

"For helping Dani," Edwin said. He nodded behind Kaylee. "That was also a—"

"Thank you from me."

Kaylee barely had time to catch her breath before Maddox ambushed her with a bone-crushing hug from behind.

"Thankyouthankyouthankyouthankyou," Maddox said.

"Seeing. Spots," Kaylee wheezed.

"Oops." Maddox gently let her feet touch the floor and Kaylee gulped in air.

"Maddox told me what happened," Edwin said.

"I only hate that I didn't step in sooner," Maddox said.

"You know about...about her father?" Kaylee said in disbelief. "How?"

"Dani and I have known each other since kindergarten. We used to hang out a lot more than we do now. Back in middle school, after her mom died, her whole attitude went crazy different. She became this, like, super happy person. And she is, really. But I always thought things were a little rough back home. Jade told me you'd noticed she seemed off, and I did too. But I never expected...well, that."

"Or that she'd be a dragon-kin," Edwin said.

"Do you know what kind?" Jade said. The three of them

looked expectantly at Kaylee, who struggled to recall the color of Dani's scales through the swirling torrent of memory from that afternoon.

"Light blue. I think they were light blue. And she hit me with water."

"Water dragon-kin then," Edwin said. "Or sea dragon. We won't know until she starts her training."

"Which she probably won't do," Kaylee said.

"She has to," Maddox said. "All dragon-kin have to learn to control their elemental powers."

"She was—she didn't want her scales. I'm telling you, she won't start training now. Maybe not ever."

"That's okay," Edwin said before Maddox could insist again. "Convocation rules do require dragon-kin, especially late ones, to go through training to control their powers. But Dani's powers aren't Kaylee's. Water dragon-kin are pretty common, and their magic isn't as volatile. That's probably how she could hide it for so long. I think Alastair will give her some time to adjust before she starts."

"Maybe not," Jade said. She was picking at something at the bottom of her shoe, but her expression was deep in thought. "He'll want her starting ASAP. Once the Slayers learn of this, they'll be here."

Edwin and Maddox were both silent.

"What does Dani getting her powers have to do with them?" Kaylee asked. "She's not a storm dragon-kin. She should be pretty safe, right?"

"Just being a storm dragon-kin wasn't the only reason the Slayers were in Scarsdale. It was just the biggest," Jade said. "A new dragon-kin's power is stronger than normal for a short time. Plus, dragon-kin who haven't been completely inducted into the Convocation have a better chance of being swayed to the Slayers' side."

Edwin crossed his arms. "The Merlins and Protectors of the

Scarsdale Convocation are already working to make sure word doesn't get out about Dani. They'll have to tell the Northern Scarsdale Convocation, but hopefully they'll keep her discovery a secret."

"It'll get out," Maddox said darkly. "I bet it already has. In fact, I bet when we go to the Slag Heap, Damian won't be surprised at all."

"He's right," Jade said with a sigh. "The Slayers are coming. It's only a matter of time."

OUT OF ALL Dani's strengths, Kaylee had to admit perseverance had to be her biggest. Not two days after their meeting at Alastair's, Dani was back in school. Kaylee caught glimpses of her in the hallway between classes, chatting with her friends. She learned Dani was telling everyone her arms were bandaged as a result of a horrible baking accident, and whenever someone asked Kaylee what had happened to Dani, that's what she passed on.

But for all her outward show of normality, there was a shroud over Dani's usual bright mood that Kaylee now saw whenever she looked her way. That, and it was clear Dani wasn't even close to forgiving her yet. The few times Kaylee tried to approach her in the hall, she'd always mysteriously vanish before Kaylee could reach her. Or she'd come up with a convenient excuse to be somewhere else, always hurrying off with a quick goodbye, without even a glance Kaylee's way.

Kaylee tried not to let it sting. And so, even though it hurt, she stayed away. She tried to content herself with the fact that, although the nicest girl in Scarsdale blamed her for ruining her life, at least said girl wasn't sprouting dragon scales in the middle of English, or returning home to a place of sadness and pain.

Kaylee's lessons with Randy continued, and she was happy to

have more time to hang out with Jade, Edwin, and Maddox afterwards now that the days were staying brighter longer. The bitter chill of deep winter still thawed in the back of their minds, but bright mornings promised warmer days on the way. School drudged on as it usually did. Edwin kept his ear to the ground for news of the Slayers, until finally…

"Edwin says tonight," Kaylee said. She checked her phone again. "And he thinks…we should bring Dani."

Jade stretched out further on the courtyard bench, soaking up a rare glimpse of sunshine that had broken through the clouds, shining like a spotlight into the courtyard. Other students, eager to linger for any last taste of fresh air, were finishing up lunch around them.

"Does it have to be tonight?" Jade said. "I have a big test tomorrow and I finally have the time to study for it."

Kaylee checked the text again.

"He said Damian's keeping the Slag Heap closed for some reason. It's our best bet to talk to him without anyone else around. And if there aren't any Merlins or dragon-kins there that'd probably make it easier…"

"For Dani," Jade finished. "If she decides to go at all."

"I could ask..."

"And have her scamper away like you forgot deodorant? We'll have Maddox do it."

"Because she doesn't hate Maddox."

"She doesn't hate you either, Kaylee." Jade turned so that she was poised sideways on the bench like a swimsuit model. "Dani's entire life has just changed. Through no fault of your own," she emphasized. "How would you react? How *did* you react?"

"I had you. You showed me your Power Ranger fighting skills and told me that what I believed the world to be like up to that point was basically a lie."

"Exactly," Jade said cheerfully. She pointed to Dani, who was clustered with a group of friends at another table. "And she has them. Give her time. I promise she'll come through."

Kaylee slowly nodded. "Fine. But the Slag Heap's still tonight, test or not."

Jade groaned and rolled over. Mrs. Monroe, the lunch monitor, snapped and jabbed her finger at Jade. Jade reluctantly sat up and plopped down next to Kaylee.

"I would normally ask him to change it," Kaylee said, "but Edwin thinks he's onto something."

"He *always* thinks he's onto something. Your boy's a regular nerdy Indiana Jones. With magic."

"He's not *my* boy."

"Uh-huh."

"Listen," Kaylee sputtered, trying to divert the conversation before it entered dangerous waters, "I can help you study. Randy's going to ramp up the training soon, but right now I might be able to help you get over all this work."

"It's not just the homework. I've been...trying to figure some things out."

Kaylee waited for her to elaborate. When she didn't, Kaylee said, "Maddox told me you've been talking to the guidance counselor about careers."

"He told you that?"

"Well you didn't."

It was a feeling alien to Kaylee: learning something about Jade that Jade hadn't directly told her. But it'd been happening more frequently this past year, and though she didn't feel quite comfortable with this change in dynamics, she understood it more now. Their lives were beginning to diverge, and Kaylee couldn't fight it.

But as long as Jade was still with her for a little longer, she'd make the most of it.

"I've been thinking of what to do after high school," Jade said. "I mean, other than becoming a fully-trained Tamer. I'd still take the test next year, but at least I'd have options after."

"That's great," Kaylee said. "Any ideas?"

Jade shook her head. "It could be nothing."

"You can tell me, Jade. I promise not to laugh unless it involves becoming a professional clown."

This pulled a smile from Jade. "I'll let you know what I decide to do. Promise."

She suddenly waved. Maddox had emerged from the cafeteria. He spotted them and hurried over.

"Slag Heap tonight." Jade pointed to the group of girls across from them. "Tell Dani she's coming."

"What am I, your dog?" Maddox complained.

But he didn't look upset as he swiveled back around and strode to Dani's table. A couple girls brushed their hair back when the saw him coming. A couple more giggled when he cracked a joke. He leaned down and whispered in Dani's ear. Kaylee saw her eyes flicker to Kaylee. She said something. Maddox tried again. Kaylee held her breath.

Finally, Dani gave a curt nod. Maddox beamed and gave the other girls a wink as he walked away. A couple let out loud sighs.

"Suave devil," Jade muttered.

"We're good to go, captain," Maddox said when he rejoined them. He rubbed his hands together. "Let's see what kind of trouble we can get into tonight."

KAYLEE WAS NEARLY THROWN FORWARD into the front seat as Maddox slammed on the brakes, grinding his van to a halt.

"What the heck!" Jade said, rubbing her forehead where she'd smacked it on the seat in front of her. "A little warning next time, Maddox!"

Maddox continued peering intently into the headlight-illuminated gravel road leading into the trees. The Slag Heap was just ahead, just out of sight around the bend.

"Maddox?" Edwin said from the passenger's seat. "Problems?"

"Maybe." Maddox shut off the van. "Let's walk from here."

"Is this how you guys usually hang out?" Dani muttered to Jade as they slid open the doors and piled out.

"No," Jade admitted. "Usually there's at least one monster involved. And magic. Lots of magic."

Dani pursed her lips, as if she couldn't tell whether Jade was joking or not. Maddox and Edwin had already walked ahead of them. Maddox was still squinting into the woods, but other than the lack of people and bone-jarring music that usually accompanied their approach to the Slag Heap, Kaylee couldn't see what the matter was.

"I thought I saw…" Maddox said. He shook his head at the surrounding trees. "Never mind."

They continued down the gravel road. The woods closed on them again, then opened to reveal the Slag Heap in all its glory.

"*This* is what you guys keep talking about?" Dani said in barely contained disbelief. "This is…nice, I guess."

"It's not usually like this," Edwin promised. "Right now it's like a completely different place."

The only time Kaylee had been to the Slag Heap, a party had been in full swing. Music, spotlights, Merlins, even some dragonkin, had been spread across a multi-acre space that had once been an old gas plant. Without the usual light or noise, the place now oozed an eerie vibe; the metal gas tanks, network of pipes, and crisscrossing stairways standing tall and silent in the dark.

"Next time you come here we'll have to get you some mead," Jade said. "It's amazing."

"Next time. Of course," Dani said. She stared at the bulldozer that was normally used as a bar to hand out magic-laced drinks and a staging point for bartering charmed goods. To her credit, she was trying to be optimistic about it, but even Kaylee had to admit that without the flash, noise, and people, the Slag Heap was...a heap.

"Damian's probably at the warehouse," Edwin said. He started toward it, but Maddox put a hand against his chest. His spear was suddenly in his hand. In an instant, Jade had drawn her sword.

"Behind me," Kaylee said to Dani.

Maddox's eyes narrowed at the darkness. Then he leveled his spear. "Get back to the van—"

There was the hiss of blades slicing air as knives shot right toward them.

CHAPTER THIRTEEN

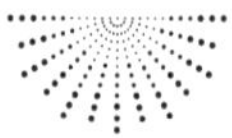

Kaylee brought up her scaled arms, deflecting the first of the blades as they reached her. More sprung from their right, but by now Edwin had conjured a shield and the rest bounced harmlessly away from Maddox and Jade.

Slayers leapt from the shadowy overhang of the nearest boiler, clothed head to toe in black body armor, armed with numerous sharp objects Kaylee was sure were meant just for her.

The lead Slayer pointed to his three companions, then to Jade. "Kill them. The dragon-kin is mine."

The Slayers charged, but Jade, Maddox and Edwin were already moving, drawing the brunt of the attack toward them. Kaylee grabbed Dani's hand and yanked her up the rusting stairs wrapping the nearest boiler. Her foot came down hard on the next step. The beam beneath crinkled, nearly throwing her off the side. Kaylee felt the beginning sensation of weightlessness just before Dani pulled her back.

"Thanks," Kaylee muttered, steadying herself.

"Next step's just as bad," Dani said. She had somehow remained calm through all this.

The top of the boiler gave them nowhere to hide. In the Slag Heap grounds below, Kaylee spied the intermittent flash of Edwin's magic. Blurry shapes moved back and forth in the darkness as Jade and Maddox traded blows with the Slayers. Kaylee's stomach clenched in fear.

Relax. They know what they're doing.

"Kaylee?" Dani said uncertainly. "Kaylee, he's coming!"

The metal shook with the pursuing Slayer's footsteps. Kaylee looked for a way out. It wasn't that she was particularly scared of a single Slayer, but she'd been hoping to get Dani to a safer place before taking this guy out. Her eyes fell on a thick pipe bridging the gap to the next boiler.

"Across. Now."

Dani backed up when she saw what Kaylee was pointing at. "That has to be a fifteen-foot drop!"

A sting of pain raced across Kaylee's cheek. She turned as the Slayer reeled his arm back, returning a blade connected to a thin metal thread to his hand.

"Come here, little dragon-kin," he jeered. "If you don't make me work to get you, maybe I'll let your pretty friend live."

Kaylee backed up, pressing Dani onto the pipe.

"I'll hold him back until you get across. Then I'll follow."

"Kaylee—"

"Time's up!" the Slayer snapped. He flicked his hand and whipped the knife at Kaylee. Kaylee shoved Dani onto the pipe and caught the string around a scaled arm, wrapping it tight. She pulled. The Slayer was yanked forward, but dug his feet in at the last second. Kaylee tugged again and this time the Slayer relented, plunging for her and swiping at her head. Kaylee ducked and swiped back, her claws slicing ribbons off his body armor. His fist clubbed her across the cheek. Copper exploded in Kaylee's mouth. She crouched, feeling the warm taste coat her tongue. The Slayer cracked his knuckles.

"Thought a storm dragon-kin would be a bit more of a challenge. Guess Lesuvius was wrong."

Magic sang in her ears, begging for release. Kaylee focused her thoughts, prayed she wouldn't lose control, then let it go.

"That's because I haven't started trying yet."

A gust of wind blasted the Slayer sideways. A sheet of ice frosted the metal beneath their feet, making him slide. He growled and dug a knife into the metal just before falling off the edge, jerking him to a halt. Thunder rumbled overhead. Kaylee's body thrummed with power. She focused on embracing it, on keeping it in her control.

Hot pain lanced through her left calf. The Slayer drew back his knife.

Move your feet! Randy's voice yelled.

Kaylee leapt as the Slayer struck again. When she came down, she slammed her hands to the metal, forcing the Slayer to roll aside as a thin bolt of lightning skittered across the metal toward him.

Move your feet. Duck. Attack.

The Slayer rolled up to a crouch. He pulled out a metal jar.

"Now you've made me use this."

Kaylee didn't wait to see what 'this' was. She brought her claws together, then drew them apart. A network of spider-webbing electricity formed between them. She lobbed it at the Slayer. His eyes widened in surprise a second before it caught him in the chest, sending him hurtling back and off the—

His knife caught the lip. The Slayer let out an angry roar as he scrambled to climb back on top of the boiler.

Definitely time to get away from here.

Dani had made it all the way across the pipe and was now frantically gesturing for her to follow.

"Hurry!" She squealed.

"Trying to, Dani!"

Kaylee stepped onto the pipe. The metal groaned. Another step—was it shifting beneath her? She wouldn't look down. She wouldn't—crap! The ground was much farther away than she'd first thought.

Eyes up and ahead. Focus on Dani.

Kaylee placed one foot in front of the other. She ignored the crumbling bits her shoes scuffed off. Or the swaying metal.

Or the vibrations as the Slayer behind her clambered to the top of the boiler again.

"Look out!" Dani cried.

Kaylee instinctively crouched, keeping her center of gravity low. A black mass of buzzing insects flew just over her head. She twisted around.

The Slayer had opened the jar. Scarabs poured out of the top, forming a tight mass of black above his outstretched hand. A ring glowed on one of his fingers. Magic. He had to be controlling them with magic.

The Slayer spread his hands toward her and the scarabs re-formed into a glittering black wall.

Screw being careful.

Kaylee ran, her feet barely touching the narrow metal. Her breath tore at her throat. The sound failed to drown out the buzz of the scarabs gaining on her. Dani was just ahead, reaching out a hand—

Then they were on her.

A thousand tiny feet pierced her clothes. A thousand mandibles bit at her exposed skin and snipped at her hair. Kaylee screamed and dropped to the pipe, pulling her magic close. The insects continued biting up until Kaylee released a blast of electricity through her skin.

The black cloud surrounding her vanished. The pinpricks of pain all over ceased. When Kaylee opened her eyes, tiny beetle bodies fell from the sky, tinging off the metal like a hailstorm.

Then she was falling.

Her feet scrambled to grip nothing. Dani's outstretched hand slipped away. Kaylee felt the air at her back as she picked up speed. Then she felt something else at her back. A slight tugging in her shoulder blades. The agonizingly wonderful feeling of stretching a muscle that had been tight for too long.

But still, as she twisted, the ground came up fast.

Storms can do far more than summon lightning. You're only using a fraction of your power.

Kaylee called on a torrent of wind. Her ears filled with a void of sound. Her breath raced out of her as a cushion of air swept beneath her body, slowing her just enough so that she merely stumbled when her feet hit the ground.

She clenched the cool grass beneath her fingers, never happier to feel the ground. The tightness in her shoulders was gone. What had that been? Had she imagined it?

The thump of feet pounding metal snapped her back to the fight. The Slayer was rappelling down the boiler's siding. He kicked off and Kaylee had a moment to scramble back and try to absorb the blow as his fist met her stomach.

"Those scarabs cost me a fortune, girl," the Slayer snarled. He whipped his foot around. Kaylee caught it, but the man twisted and kicked again and Kaylee barely managed to re-direct it before it hit her face. The man sneered.

"If you think one of Lesuvius' hand-picked officers is going to be beaten by one lousy dragon-kin then you're dead wrong."

"How about two dragon-kin?" Dani said.

A gush of water slammed into the Slayer's side, tossing him against the boiler. He sputtered, looking at the stairway across from him in disbelief.

Dani held her arms out, looking furious. She swayed slightly when she began to walk down, holding herself against the railing. Kaylee wondered how much energy that attack had cost her.

"Don't. Touch. My friends."

The Slayer laughed.

"A two-fer! You just made my day, girl. Didn't think finding the new dragon-kin would be so easy."

He snapped his hand out. His knife line shot across and nearly sliced Dani's side, sticking into the metal just beside her head. Dani let out a squeak of alarm. She stumbled again, nearly losing her balance.

Kaylee drew one claw down her opposite arm. Ice solidified over it, creating a short blade which she used to slice through the Slayer's line.

"Dani, get back to the—"

She grunted as the Slayer caught her in the side with another kick. Dani had begun making a break down the boiler stairs.

"Not this time, monster," the Slayer barked.

He fired a second knife. The line it was attached to wrapped around the staircase's rusted support beam. He pulled. The stairs screeched as they tore away from the boiler's side. Dani gripped the handrail for dear life.

Kaylee saw the moment as if in slow motion. Watched as Dani's grip failed and she went flying.

Kaylee dove, summoning a burst of icy wind to jet her forward the last few feet. Dani landed on Kaylee as she hit, and it took all Kaylee had to keep her scales shifted along her back, cushioning the blow. They skidded the last ten feet before grinding to a halt.

"You break anything?" Kaylee groaned.

"No, I-I think I'm good." Dani's eyes were wide in shock. "I was—I thought I was dead—but you—Thank you!"

"Welcome to the Convocation," Kaylee said. "Get back to the van. I'll handle this g—"

Dani's arms moved before Kaylee realized the Slayer was behind her. A blast of water jetted from her outstretched palms, sending him hurling back. Dani gaped at the space where the man had been.

"He was about to stab you!"

"Yep, that's what they do," Kaylee said. "Don't think too much about it."

A chilling laugh made Kaylee spin around. The Slayer had pulled himself to his feet. Another pair of wicked knives were angled at them. *What* would it take to make this guy give up?

"I guess capturing just won't do with you two," he said. "It's time to stop holding back."

He took a step toward them. Kaylee readied herself for a fight. She was beat, but she could hold him off long enough for Dani to get away.

Thunk.

The Slayer froze. Teetered. Then collapsed, out cold.

Damian raised a hand and caught the metal boomerang as it whirled back to his hand. He pressed another button and it collapsed. He glared at the Slayer. Then at Kaylee.

"Correct me if I'm wrong, but didn't you bring Slayers here the last time you came around my place?"

"Technically those were Stymphalian birds."

"Sent by the Slayers."

"Well, yeah, if you want to get specific."

"Oh, I do. See, you're becoming a problem that I—is your friend okay?"

Dani had stayed kneeling on the ground, her arms splayed on either side of her in exhaustion. Her scales were vibrant in the low light and she was staring at them; not with fear, Kaylee realized, but not quite with admiration, either. It was as if she didn't know whether to be horrified or ecstatic at what she had just done.

Kaylee heard Damian suck in a sharp breath when he got closer.

"Great. Another bloody dragon-kin. You better have a good explanation for this one, Kaylee."

"I don't," Kaylee said. She crouched beside Dani. She put a gentle hand on the other girl's shoulder.

"Good job. That Slayer was levels beyond the others I've fought. I don't think I could have gotten out of that one without you."

Dani slowly nodded. "Did you see how I hit him?"

"I did."

"And all that water. *I* did that."

"Yep."

Damian gave Dani a funny look. "Yeah...you did. Is she in shock or something? Here." He dug deep into the pockets of his tattered jeans and pulled out a few brightly colored discs with runic markings on them. These he tossed into Dani's lap.

"Pain subduing charms. Ingestible. Pawned 'em off a Merlin here a week ago so I'm pretty sure they're still good."

"No." Dani held up her claws. "I'm not hurt. I just need to..."

Kaylee caught her as she almost slumped over.

"S-sorry. Just really tired."

"You used a lot of magic you weren't ready for," Kaylee said. "Adrenaline will do that."

Dani breathed in. Once. Twice. The scales on her arms receded. The claws shrank to fingernails.

"Nice," Damian said, clearly impressed. He stuck out a hand and helped them both up. "I would have remembered if we'd met. I'm Damian."

"Dani."

"Dani...You seemed pretty shook up there—not that you did bad, but how new are you to this whole dragon-kin thing? I think I would know if another one was hanging around Scarsdale."

"I've been one for a little while, but I've officially been one for about a week."

Damian whistled. "Even more impressive."

Dani blushed.

"There were more Slayers around here," Kaylee said. "Are my friends okay?"

"They're fine," an unfortunately familiar voice said. Zaria emerged from the darkness, surrounded by a few rogue dragonkin. She grinned at Kaylee. "You can thank us for that."

CHAPTER FOURTEEN

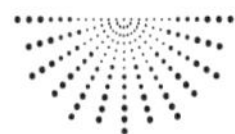

Kaylee kept Zaria in her sight at all times as the group made their way over to Damian's warehouse. It was more habit than helpful, as Zaria's goons surrounded her on all sides. Kaylee tried to resist rolling her eyes. She found it hard to be too intimidated by kids who looked like they'd just been let out of elementary school, dragon-kins or not.

"Sure you don't need any pain charms?" Damian asked Dani for what had to be the fourth time.

"Positive," Dani said.

"That was pretty incredible. What you did back there."

A faint smile ghosted across Dani's lips. "Thanks."

Damian nodded. He looked befuddled, as if he couldn't decipher her, this newest addition to their mix. And Kaylee could understand. *She* still didn't know how to feel about this new, slightly more aggressive, Dani.

Rather than going through the front, Damian pointed them around the back to a padlocked door.

"You'd be surprised how many Merlins and dragon-kin can't even undo this," he said proudly. Zaria held up one metal-covered arm.

"Bet I could."

Damian's expression soured. "Yeah, bet you could."

He unlocked it. They went up a narrow staircase to what might have been a foreman's office. Damian had shoved couches and a flat screen TV in here. Against one wall was a fridge and a pinball machine.

Jade sprang up from the couch where she'd been wrapping Maddox's arm.

"Kaylee! You're all right—"

Zaria stepped into the room. There was a flash of steel. When Kaylee blinked, Jade had Zaria pinned against the wall, a blade at her throat. Maddox and Edwin faced off against the rest of the rogues as both sides began summoning magic.

"Hey!" Damian barked. "My place, my rules! Weapons away! And magic!"

Jade didn't move the knife. "Kaylee told me you kidnapped her," Jade snarled. "Tell me what you're doing here."

"Same as you, darling," Zaria drawled, unfazed. "You aren't the only one who uses Damian for information. Now," she said, gripping the blade with a metaled hand and bending it away from her. "Why don't we talk?"

"Put it away, Edwin," Kaylee said. "They actually did help us."

Edwin reluctantly squelched the ball of magic in his hand. Maddox slowly uncurled from his attack stance. Jade backed off Zaria who brushed herself off, grinning.

"Oh, I *like* these guys, Damian. You didn't tell me you had such violent people frequent here."

"That's because they're not *supposed* to be violent," Damian said. "But every time they come over they bring unwanted guests."

Zaria gave Damian a significant look. "Unwanted, but not unsurprising." She snapped her fingers. "Billy, Claire. What's happening with the Slayers?"

A skinny boy with a slight overbite said, "I think Kim and Danny are helping the others take care of them, Zar."

"*Danny*?" a stubby girl said. "He couldn't 'take care' of a cactus."

"Like *you* could?"

"My group, out!" Zaria said, rubbing her forehead. "You're giving me a headache! Take care of the Slayers, then scout. Chances are those were the only ones, but we need to be sure."

"You three go help, too," Damian said to Jade, Maddox, and Dani. "We're crowded enough already."

"You don't tell us what to do," Jade said. "And if you think I'm leaving Kaylee with her, you must think I'm an idiot."

"I'll be here," Edwin said. "We'll be fine."

"Really, Jade," Kaylee added.

"And while you're out there, please don't maim any of my rogues," Zaria said. "They have a lot of bark but they're harmless. Mostly."

"Are not!" Billy said, straightening up his skinny figure.

"It's all right, Jade," Kaylee said again.

Jade shot one last death glare at Zaria, then followed the flow of people out the door. Damian closed it behind them with a satisfying click. He eyed Zaria.

"I hope 'take care' of the Slayers doesn't mean what I think it does. I won't have murder on my grounds."

"Aw, is someone concerned?" Zaria flopped onto one of the couches, hooking her legs over the armrest.

Damian leveled his gaze at her. "Zaria…"

"Relax, Damian, of course I don't mean kill them. You think I'm gonna let those kids commit first degree murder? We're rogues, not monsters. They'll take them somewhere else and alert the Convocation. What happens when *they* get them isn't my issue. And you're welcome for cleaning up your mess."

"Sounds like you've done it before," Edwin said.

"I've done it enough. When you don't have petty rules holding you back from where you can and can't go, you tend to run into problems more than usual."

"But you have no problem using the Convocation as your garbage crew," Kaylee said. Zaria grinned.

"If they're there, might as well make 'em useful. Speaking of the Convocation, that offer still stands, Kaylee."

"What offer?" Edwin said, giving Kaylee a questioning look.

"To join our little group, of course," Zaria said. "She didn't tell you? I thought she told you *everything* about our meeting."

"The answer's still no," Kaylee said.

Zaria shrugged. "Pity. I'll keep trying. You might change your mind after what I tell you."

"And what's that?"

Zaria gave a Cheshire grin, and Kaylee had the strong urge to punch her teeth in.

Damian opened the fridge, snagged some Cokes, and tossed one to each of them. He popped the tab and sank into the leather armchair. Kaylee and Edwin sat on the couch beside him, Edwin facing Zaria in case she tried anything. But despite the other girl's attitude, Kaylee trusted her. At least enough to know she probably really was here for information from Damian. Plus, Zaria had the type of crude personality that didn't lend itself to deception. She was brutally honest, whether you wanted to hear it or not.

"First thing," Damian said, pointing at the door, "that new girl. The water dragon-kin. What were you thinking bringing her out here? And tonight, of all nights, when the Slag Heap wasn't happening and the Merlin protection charms were down."

"We were thinking the same thing as when *I* came out here," Kaylee said.

"So, absolutely nothing."

"To *relax* and get to see the world she's entering into, Damian.

You have no idea what Dani's been through. She just found out about her magic this week. She needed support from others like her. She needed to see she wasn't alone."

Damian gave a dark laugh. "I'd say she knows now. She had any training?"

"Not yet."

"Hm...pretty good without it. But you guys are still idiots. You realize the Slayers will be—"

"Flocking here because another dragon-kin has appeared. We know," Edwin said. "Though, as Zaria alluded, that's not the only reason they're coming to Scarsdale, is it?"

Zaria stopped flicking the tab on her can and looked up at them. "Pretty sharp, nerd boy. They told me you'd be on the ball, unlike that old man Alastair of yours."

Edwin started to get up, but Kaylee put a hand on his arm.

"Easy."

"What does my dad have to do with this?" Edwin demanded.

"You tell me. It wasn't my negligence that led to the Slayers almost killing Kaylee last year."

"My dad's not perfect, but at least he stands for something."

"Oh, dear, the classic *honorable* excuse. Don't make me puke. You know, Damian, I'm not thinking I want to share my very special information anymore."

"Don't be a jerk about it, Zaria," Damian said with a long sigh. He rubbed the bridge of his nose in frustration, as if he was mediating between two groups of warring toddlers. "You insulted the dude's dad, what did you expect?"

"A man who has done more for Merlins and dragon-kin than you ever could hope to," Edwin said.

"You mean like letting dragon-kin slip through the cracks like that girl out there?" Zaria said.

"He's not perfect," Kaylee said.

"I'll agree with you on that. Far from it. I wonder how many dragon-kin have been overlooked or abandoned by men like him over the years. The ones who think bringing everyone into their club brings unity, when really it just abandons others."

"We didn't come here to listen to your sob story," Kaylee said. "Whatever your problem with Alastair is, get over it."

Zaria laughed, flopping back on the couch. "I knew there was a reason I liked you! Not afraid to call me out. Good, good. Fine, I'll leave Alastair alone as long as he does the same to me. But..." At this she met Kaylee's eyes. "I'd take a hard look at the other people you choose to associate with."

A flash of memory crossed Kaylee's mind. An unknown girl's picture. An empty shed. Randy's tight grip on any and all secrets he was carrying.

"If you're talking about my Uncle Randy, he hasn't given me any reason to question him," Kaylee said, smoothly enough that she almost believed it.

"Then you haven't looked close enough. Anyway." Zaria crumpled her empty can in one fist and tossed it into the trash. "My personal beefs aren't why I'm here."

"I sure hope not," Damian said. "You're already making my head hurt."

"Kaylee," Zaria said. "I mentioned I wanted your help with something."

"But you wouldn't say what."

"Well I am now. I came to Scarsdale because I heard rumors of an extremely powerful magic item in the area. A large area, but still in the area."

"Wait, you don't mean—?" Damian said. "Zaria, how can you even begin to guess *this* is where it'll end up?"

"Outside information," Zaria said. "My own sources. And it's not *here* in Scarsdale. But definitely in one of the big cities nearby. Maybe within a museum."

"What is this 'it' you keep talking about?" Kaylee said.

"It's one of the lost items, isn't it?" Edwin said slowly. Zaria winked at him.

"Nailed it. Cute and smart. Yep, it's an ancient book of spells called the Book of Kells."

Kaylee smothered a laugh. First it was Mjolnir, now this. At this rate, she should just start reading fairy tales to gather factual information on what she might face next. "Um, the Book of Kells is in Ireland. Also, it's not a book of spells."

"*That* one is fake, and a very good one, too. The true Book of Kells, as told in ancient lore, was the combined knowledge of some of the most powerful Merlins from the Order of St. George, the order the Slayers broke from."

"But if they've found the real Book of Kells, then what's the one in Ireland?" Damian said.

"It's something called a Merlin's Codex," Edwin said. "Another collection of spells, but not nearly as dangerous. The real Book of Kells is on a whole other level."

"The last volume of only a few in existence," Zaria agreed.

Kaylee scooted to the edge of the couch. "What does it do?"

"A lot of things. I'm sure many of the spells are useless to most Merlins. Merlins nowadays haven't spent every waking hour of their lives steeped in learning and the magic arts. They wouldn't be strong enough to use half the spells." Zaria held up a finger. "But there is one. One has the Slayers *mucho* interested. Called the Horn of the Hunt. Also known as the Dragon's Curse."

A shiver ran through Kaylee. Her throat had suddenly gone dry and she took a steadying sip of Coke. Nobody else seemed to have experienced the same effect from the name except for Zaria, who was staring intently at her.

"Yeah, you should be scared. The Horn of the Hunt spell can summon the Herald of the Hunt. One bad dude. Made of magic. Maybe even a fairy, I don't know. What we do know is that if he gets out, he can then summon the true Hunt."

"Like, from the King Arthur legends?" Edwin said.

"Like from your nightmares," Zaria said. "The Hunt is led by

St. George himself. And that, my friends, is bad news for all of us."

Damian folded his hands across his lap. He was staring through the window at the darkened interior of the warehouse.

"What do you want me to do about it, Zaria?"

Zaria crinkled her nose. "*Do*? I don't want you to do anything. I just want info. Last time I was here your intel helped me stop the Slayers' raid in Canada. Lot more people would have gotten hurt without it."

"When was this?" Edwin said.

"Couple years ago. The Slayers tried for another magical item, Drake's Drum. Can inspire mad fervor in all their followers, and that's a pretty sweet deal for a brainwashing cult. The Convocation near where it was didn't believe us, so we took matters into our own hands."

"Sounds familiar," Kaylee muttered to Edwin. His jaw tightened but he nodded.

"Unfortunately, I don't know who has the Book of Kells now," Damian said. "Those kinds of items are far beyond anything that passes through here. Even the wandering traders I usually get my tidbits from wouldn't know. It's too far out of their reach for them to care."

"You must know something," Kaylee said.

"About the same as you," Damian said with a wave of his hand. "Nothing but flits and whispers that the real book has been discovered, and that the organization who found it plans to put it on display around here soon."

"In a museum?" Edwin said.

"Yeah."

"There must be a dozen museums in the bigger cities around here," Kaylee said.

"And the group that found it is keeping the whole thing close to the vest," Zaria grumbled. "If I didn't know any better, I'd say they were doing that to throw the Slayers off."

"Except they're planning to display it in public," Edwin said.

"And the Slayers are already here," Damian added.

Zaria suddenly stood. Edwin tensed, but Kaylee held his arm reassuringly. She wasn't quite sure what his deal was. She didn't trust Zaria either, but that didn't mean she actively mistrusted everything about her as well.

"What are you going to do now?" Damian said.

"Wait it out," Zaria said. "Keep our eyes and ears open." She fixed Kaylee with a stare. "I'm hoping to get a few allies to join the fight."

"Absolutely not," Edwin said immediately.

Kaylee held Zaria's gaze. "What were you thinking?"

"Kaylee! You can't seriously want to *help* them?"

"If it means stopping the Slayers, then yeah, I do."

"She attacked you—"

"I think you'll find little Miss Storm Dragon-kin is more than capable of taking care of herself," Zaria said.

Edwin was up in an instant, his fists glowing. But before either could move, Kaylee stepped between them.

"Enough! Both of you! Edwin, what is your problem? Zaria, we'll think about what you're asking. No promises."

Zaria scoffed. "Don't need any promises, just results. As long as we stop the Slayers from getting that book I don't care about your allegiances."

"That's fine. Right, Edwin?" Kaylee added.

Edwin clenched his fists.

"*Right*, Edwin?"

"Right, but it'll be on our terms."

Zaria chuckled. "Now you're thinking like a rogue."

"And if Kaylee—if any of us—gets hurt because we helped you and you didn't come through for us..."

Zaria's eyebrows raised. "Oh. I see it now." She shrugged and went to the door. "We'll be in touch the next few weeks, until this whole thing blows over. And Edwin?"

"What?" Edwin snapped.

"Believe what you want about me, but I promise I'm not the enemy. Because if the Slayers manage to summon the Hunt, we're all royally screwed."

CHAPTER FIFTEEN

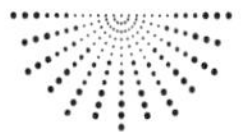

Randy's house was deathly quiet. The latest spring rain had transformed the dirt and splotchy sod of the front yard to a mess of mud and sodden grass. Each step Kaylee took squelched beneath her feet until she hit the porch where the boards began to creak.

Randy still didn't appear.

Kaylee didn't even need to look inside. She immediately went to the shed. It was empty.

Except…

She crouched. In the mess of mud, motorcycle tread drew a path out into the driveway and down the road. Kaylee could taste just the barest whiff of exhaust on her tongue. She could almost imagine the heat rising from the ground in waves where she'd crouched. He'd been here recently.

But where was he now? And why? Randy keeping secrets from her was nothing new. Up until this point, his secrets had just been something that annoyed her, but she'd never challenged him on them, assuming he'd either tell her anything she needed to know eventually, or she'd confront him on it when she was ready.

She was ready.

It was too much of a coincidence, really. Zaria brought news of the Book of Kells, which the rogues had been tracking for some time. Randy knew about the rogues—who knew how *much* he knew?—but he knew, and now he was gone. And Kaylee wanted—no, needed—to find out where.

She pulled out her phone and dialed. Jade picked up on the first ring.

"Kaylee? I thought you were supposed to be with Randy?"

"He's not here."

Jade swore loudly. "And after we just ran into some Slayers. Is the guy an idiot, or does he just have the worst timing in the universe?"

"He didn't know."

"Timing, then. Look, Randy has to have had a Convocation Merlin put charms up around the house or something. Stay inside until I get there—"

"Actually, can you bring Edwin when you come? Do you think he could get out of training with Baba?"

Kaylee could hear Jade letting air out between her teeth. "Uh, maybe. But why would he need to be there?"

Kaylee walked outside, her eyes trailing the vanishing motorcycle tread until it hit the road.

"Just tell him to come too. And have him bring a car."

"Do you think you can still do it?" Kaylee said.

Edwin paced around the empty shed, every now and then holding up a hand as though feeling for some invisible energy.

"Maybe, but a simple Seeking Spell works best when I have an actual object from the person. Or the person in question has been to wherever they are now before."

Jade, leaning against one of the wooden beams, nodded to the workbench. "Maybe one of those tools was used on his motorcycle."

Edwin picked up a couple of them and balanced them in his hands. He put them both back and systematically began running a hand just above the rest. He paused.

"Bingo," he said, twirling a socket wrench in his fingers. "It's always the socket wrench."

"How do you know?" Kaylee said.

"Magical energy signature. It's kind of like…think of it like…maybe…"

"You don't have to explain it to me, I believe you," Kaylee said, completely understanding. She was a dragon-kin who was still learning to control her own magic, and he was a Merlin who had only recently learned to use his; neither of them were particularly qualified to understand the detailed intricacies of how the others' magic worked, just as long as it did.

Edwin crouched. He placed the socket wrench on a clear space and began drawing a number of symbols around it in the mud.

"Chalk works best for these kind of charms, but I should get a decent lock. Give me a minute."

"Not that I don't trust your reasons," Jade said to Kaylee as Edwin began muttering to himself, "but why are we tracking your uncle, anyway?"

"I think…I'm not sure, but I think he's up to something."

"Of course he is. He's *Randy*. Even Alastair wants to keep him on a tight leash. Does this have to do with what you told me about the other night? What Zaria said about the Book?"

Kaylee listened to Edwin's chanting as it grew louder. The scrawled circle had begun to glow. "Maybe. I don't know yet."

"He could be on a Convocation mission, you know," Jade said. "I'm sure Alastair has been sending him to do stuff and just isn't telling us."

"Look, you don't have to come if you don't want to," Kaylee snapped.

Jade jerked back as if struck. "I never said I didn't want to go."

"There's just—I need to know what he's doing. You don't have to follow me if you don't want."

"I'm your Tamer, and your friend. I'll always be there if you need me. Even if I don't..."

Kaylee glanced at her. Jade was staring out the shed.

"Even if you don't take the Tamer test," Kaylee finished. "And if you don't, you won't be my Tamer anymore."

"Right."

"Have you thought more about it?"

"A little." She sighed. "A lot."

"And?"

"And I think—"

"Got it!"

Edwin was clutching the socket wrench in his hand. It was emitting a glow nearly as bright as his smile. "Let's ride."

THE FACT that they didn't have to go too far from Scarsdale to find Randy's magic trail was both very good and very bad.

After about ten minutes on the highway, Edwin pulled off to a rural farm road. The town of Lariet was to their left. To the right was rural land much like that which surrounded Scarsdale.

Edwin went left.

"Almost there," he muttered. He'd been following some internal GPS given off from the spell he'd performed. "And Jade, for the last time, *please* stop fiddling with your knife. I puncture this leather and my dad'll kill me. I was barely able to convince him to let me drive it."

Jade let her knife drop into her lap. She sank further into the plush seats. "It isn't like you don't have three more cars."

"My *dad* has three more cars. I have this one."

"You shouldn't even need your knife," Kaylee said, twisting back to look at Jade. "We're just going to find Randy to see what he's up to. No fighting at all."

"Kaylee, in what alternate universe do you live in where *that's ever* happened to us?"

Kaylee grimaced. "I thought maybe saying it aloud would give it a better chance of coming true."

"We're here," Edwin said.

After taking another ten minutes to parallel park, ("Just use the stupid rear camera, Edwin," Kaylee snapped. "That's cheating and you know it," Edwin snapped right back.) he turned the ignition off. They had ended up down the street from a business complex. The white, windowless building fronts stared at them, as if questioning what they were doing here. Edwin nodded to what had once been a bowling alley. The front doors had been plastered over with wax paper. The handles had a ridiculously oversized padlock on it.

"There's our place," Edwin said.

"I don't see Randy's motorcycle," Kaylee said.

"He's probably hidden it."

Kaylee unbuckled her seat belt. "Okay, here's what we'll do. You two stay alert, and I'll go take a peek."

"*Ha*!" Jade and Edwin said at the same time.

After checking that the coast was clear, the three of them strolled casually across the street. The other buildings had vacant parking lots, save for the few cars of those staying behind to work late. An air conditioner hummed to life nearby, cutting through the end-of-day silence.

"To the back," Jade whispered. She took the lead and gestured for them to follow her through an alleyway to a loading bay at the rear. A single door marked Employees Only was firmly locked and sealed with another padlock.

"There has to be a less obvious way in," Kaylee said as they crouched along a chain link fence. It'd be suicide to simply waltz inside. Just because there were no obvious signs of Slayers definitely didn't mean they weren't here.

Edwin pointed to the lip of the roof hanging not too far over their heads.

"I can get you up there."

"How?" Jade said.

After some searching, Edwin produced the dented lid of a trash can. Kaylee, knowing exactly what he was going to do, immediately stepped onto it. Edwin closed his eyes. A moment later, the lid levitated her to the roof line where she hopped off. Edwin lowered it again. He put his hands on his knees the second the lid settled on the ground.

"Don't you dare say I'm too heavy!" Kaylee hissed down to him.

Edwin grinned at her, straightening up. "I don't have a death wish. Jade?"

Jade was a little more hesitant, but after some joking that she couldn't possibly be heavier than Kaylee, ("Edwin!") she joined Kaylee on the roof.

Edwin closed his eyes once more. "You're all clear," he said after a pause. "I don't sense any protective charms. I'll keep watch out here."

"We'll only be a minute, right?" Jade asked Kaylee.

"Right," Kaylee agreed, reluctantly leaving Edwin and slipping across the rooftop. Jade found an air vent and managed to pry the rusted grate loose with her knife. They peered into the dark. The smell of stale air and something potentially dead greeted Kaylee's nose.

"By all means, dragon-kin first," Jade said, stepping aside.

"Some Tamer you are."

"When it comes to smells, I'm a self-preservationist."

The air duct was cramped but manageable. Kaylee dropped in feet-first and curled her body tight. After some maneuvering, she began shuffling in one direction, trying to make as little noise as possible every time her knees hit the metal.

After what might have been a hundred yards, or only ten, Jade made a barely audible warning sound. Kaylee froze.

Voices. A few of them directly below. A couple more just ahead.

"Look for a vent we can see out of," Jade whispered.

Kaylee began sliding forward again. The panel beneath her bowed and she jerked to a halt. Her heart stopped almost as fast as the voices did. Or maybe that was her imagination.

A man laughed. Kaylee could suddenly breathe again.

The two shuffled along a little farther until Kaylee's eyes picked up pasty yellow light leaking in from another vent. After some contorting, she and Jade managed to press their faces against it to see.

Slayers below. At least ten, though Kaylee couldn't crane her neck far enough to the side to see beyond the twenty-foot segment directly in front of her. The tables and chairs at the head of each bowling lane were relatively intact. Discarded bowling balls, even some pins, were tossed carelessly around. A spot had been cleared away by the snack bar for the Slayers to lay down cots. Kaylee suppressed a snort. The Slayers might have been a deadly ancient organization, but glamorous they were not.

"Hear anything?" Kaylee whispered.

"No. Can't really see much either. A few at the popcorn machine. A couple—"

There was the crash of pins. "—actually *bowling*. Are you serious? The machine doesn't even work, you numbskulls."

"Focus, Jade. Do you see Randy?"

Jade shifted, nudging Kaylee over a bit.

"No, I don't. Maybe he isn't here?"

"He has to be. This is where Edwin's charm led us."

"That means he came by at least once before, but maybe not right now."

Kaylee couldn't believe that. They couldn't have come out here and found the Slayers without Randy. Because if they were in this den of Slayers without Randy around…

"Wait, there's some more people." Jade pressed her cheek more firmly against the grate so that small squares popped from her skin. "At a far table. I can't get a good look, but it looks like they're holding a meeting. Seems important."

"Can you tell what they're talking about?"

"If you're asking if I can read lips from thirty feet away the answer is no. All but one is facing away from me. One's wearing a hood, too."

Kaylee tried to get a better look. "A hood?"

"Ouch! Watch your elbow. I can't get a good look—especially *with that elbow of yours*!"

"Sorry. Just…scooch."

"Kaylee…" Jade's eyes narrowed on the scene below. "We can't see Randy. But that hooded one…you don't think…he wouldn't be…"

"No," Kaylee said, refusing to let her finish voicing the thought.

"But you said he goes out a lot, and he just kind of showed up and nobody knew where he'd been for a while."

"No, Jade. Randy's not a Slayer. He can't be."

The half of Jade's face that was awash in light gave her a pitying look.

"You sure?"

"Positive. You don't know him like I do."

That was the thing, though, wasn't it? That was what she had wanted to find out. She didn't know Randy. At least not well enough for her voice not to hitch when she denied that he was a Slayer. Or enough to say with absolute confidence that it wasn't him down there.

But it *couldn't* be. Randy was rough. He was curt, and rude, and mean, and his training was grueling, but he was fair, never cruel. Even though Edwin had said there were some dragon-kin with the Slayers, Randy couldn't be one of them.

Believing it's true doesn't make it so, a nasty voice inside her cooed. *What allegiance does he have to anyone? What loyalty does he have to you?*

But what about to his family? He had to care about them—

The picture! The picture of the girl Kaylee had found in Randy's room. No Slayer would be that sentimental. They weren't capable of it. They were monsters. Evil and single-minded and—

Horrified. Resignation writ across his face as he looked up into the beams crashing toward him. As he looked up at his death.

Had Brendan been that, too? A complete monster? Incapable of love or caring?

Kaylee wanted to scream that he was, that they all were, but the scream locked in her throat. Brendan had been someone with his own hopes, dreams, aspirations. But they were all gone now, crushed into nothing at the instant he had been.

"Kaylee!"

Kaylee's eyes flew open.

"Steady!" Jade hissed. "Where'd you go?"

"Let me try to get a look at the table," Kaylee said.

"Okay, let me just—hold *on,* Kaylee. I can't move—"

"Watch it! The screen. The screen is—"

Kaylee heard the sound of wrenching metal a second before the grate popped off. Time held its breath as the grate disappeared from view, suspended before the moment of impact.

There was a loud bang below. Kaylee's breath stopped. Every Slayer's eyes went to the floor. Then traveled up to them.

"Oh, crap," Jade muttered.

CHAPTER SIXTEEN

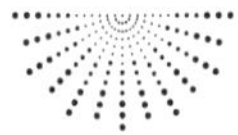

Oh crap indeed.

Before anyone could move, Kaylee's hand slipped on the lip of the air duct. The metal gave a torturous squeal as the entire duct collapsed, followed close behind by a chunk of the ceiling, spitting them out onto the floor in a heavy cloud of plaster and dust.

"Get them!" someone shouted. Kaylee was already up, tugging Jade to her feet. The Slayers' murky shadows were closing in on all sides.

Kaylee pulled her lightning to her and sliced through the haze, creating a protective, sparking field around them, and splitting the Slayers' ring in two. The pair plunged through. Jade grabbed her arm and pointed to another break in the Slayer's line. "The exit's just to the right once we get through."

There was a high-pitched whirring at their backs. Before Kaylee could register the source of the noise, Jade threw herself in front of her and brought up her knife. A spinning bladed disc shattered at their feet. Kaylee ducked as more discs buzzed overhead. Jade slashed two more down. Bits of twisted metal scattered across the floor.

"Go, Kaylee!"

Kaylee drew the lightning to herself and blasted it forward, creating a singed scar of black on the floor to lead their charge through. The nearest Slayers shouted. Kaylee pulled Jade behind an overturned table. There was a dull *thunk* as more discs bit into the wood.

People were shouting now, mobilizing as the dust settled and their vision cleared. At least three Slayers were advancing on their hiding place. Kaylee threw herself onto her back. She drew her magic to her feet. She felt her bones hardening, the skin knitting together tighter, the muscles swelling.

She kicked. The table launched forward and pummeled those in the front of the group. Their comrades leapt over them and continued the charge.

That...hadn't been as effective as she thought it would be.

Exit. They needed the exit.

As Kaylee looked, her eyes brushed over the group that had been sitting apart at the table in the corner. Two of the Slayers, the leaders, she assumed, were standing and staring fixedly right at her. The third had pulled his hood farther around his face.

"Kaylee!"

The nearest Slayers reached them. Kaylee rolled away as a sword cut the tile where she'd been. She blocked the next strike with her scaled arm and whipped to standing, spinning an air current around herself as she did. Debris leapt from the ground and smacked her assailants away.

"Duck!" Jade yelled. Kaylee obeyed a second before a buzzing disc would have cleaved her head off. Seemed these Slayers, whether they knew she was a storm dragon-kin or not, wanted her dead.

Kaylee broke the blade of the nearest Slayer and Jade delivered a crunching blow to another's nose. Her eyes widened.

"Behind—"

The whistle of a projectile, then the sensation of the skin of her exposed back splitting as something sliced across it.

Without thinking, Kaylee conjured another torrent of wind. There was a clatter as a half-dozen arrows were blown off course and hit the far wall. Kaylee scoured for the source of the attack. Crossbowmen. At least five taking shelter behind the front counter. Kaylee shot a bolt of lightning at them but they simply ducked and her blast toasted the popcorn machine behind them.

Jade grabbed her collar and yanked her behind another upturned table as they fired a second volley. Vicious arrowheads punctured through the wood, their points reaching for her.

"Turn around," Jade demanded. Kaylee let her prod the tender cut, biting her tongue to keep from crying out.

"Bad?"

Jade flattened the remains of the fabric on it. "Not your worst. We'll have Edwin look at it once we get out of this." She peered over the table. "They're cutting off our escape."

"And *they're* getting away," Kaylee growled.

The three Slayers that had been at the table were beating a hasty retreat now that Kaylee and Jade had been contained. They'd stuffed a sheaf of paper into a small bag and were hurrying toward the only available exit.

"Can you hit them?" Jade asked.

"I'm pretty drained." She nudged her head toward the cross-bowmen. "Need to save it for these guys."

Another volley nearly took Kaylee's head off as she looked again. And then…she barely had time to duck before—and she had to blink twice to make sure she wasn't seeing things—an electrified bowling ball exploded against the front desk, blasting apart the Slayers' cover.

Where Randy had come from, Kaylee didn't know. She only knew he was suddenly *there*.

And he was pissed.

Kaylee had only seen snippets of how annoyed he could be

during their training sessions, often when she was being lazy or obstinate or just didn't agree with him in general.

But she had never seen his fury. And if this was it, then Kaylee could believe that whatever stories Alastair had heard about Randy were true.

Randy gripped the nearest Slayer by the throat and hurled him across the room, his body slamming against the exit and stopping the three fleeing Slayers dead in their tracks.

The remaining Slayers sensed that Randy was the more imminent danger and switched all their attacks to him. Randy moved like a lightning bolt. First one place, then in a blink another, swiping out with claws bared and sending Slayers flying every direction. Electricity enveloped him, knocking away arrows and discs and hurling them back at his attackers. Sparks from the lights rained down, coating his head and shoulders in a shimmer of destructive force.

Kaylee could only gape in wondrous horror. This was what a dragon-kin in full control of his power could do. This seamless melding of man and beast, of magic and brutal, beautiful ferocity.

Kaylee's eyes fell on the three figures, still standing stunned in place.

"Hey!"

The three turned as she charged them. The one in the hood shrank back from the ball of lightning Kaylee had conjured in her hand.

"You were stupid to come here, girl," the lead Slayer sneered. "This pathetic attack hasn't accomplished anything."

He thrust out an arm. Kaylee ducked as needles shot toward her face. She slammed the lightning into the ground and the nearest Slayer yelped as the electricity shocked him unconscious. The other two leapt to safety on top of a table.

"Don't just stand there!" the lead Slayer said, shoving the hooded one toward Kaylee. "You want to truly be useful then take care of her!"

The hooded one hesitated. Kaylee didn't. She attacked, trying to mimic the same ferocity she'd seen in Randy. Though her elemental magic was almost drained, she still had enough energy to take these clowns down.

Despite his initial hesitation, the hooded one dipped and dodged, easily flowing away from each of her attacks. Kaylee whipped up a sudden burst of wind, rotating her wrists to direct the attack at him.

The Slayer lunged forward and grabbed her arms. Kaylee swore she could feel his penetrating gaze on her—right before he released her arm.

Kaylee didn't question why. She sliced, tearing at every spot she could reach, tattering his cloak, tearing at his arms.

"Are you an idiot?" the lead Slayer atop the table bellowed. "Use your weapon!"

Kaylee drove a punch into the hooded one's stomach, sending him stumbling back toward the exit. She dropped to the ground, shifting one foot to talons and swiping clean through the table's legs with one kick, dropping the other Slayer to the floor. Kaylee heard a soft cry behind her. She whirled around, but Randy had already dropped the first Slayer Kaylee had thought was unconscious. A crossbow the man had been aiming at her back clattered to the ground.

Randy's eyes flickered. "Get him—"

But by the time Kaylee turned, the hooded figure had already pushed his way out the exit.

Randy knelt by the man who'd been on the table. Out cold. His eyes narrowed on something in the rubble Kaylee couldn't see. He picked it up, glared at it, clenched his fist around it.

Jade was kicking weapons away from any of the other downed Slayers. Edwin had somehow made it inside and was surveying the surrounding carnage with a semi-shocked expression.

Kaylee went to try to help Jade, but suddenly Randy was blocking her way. Her stomach dropped.

"Oh, hey, Uncle..."

Kaylee's quip died on her tongue. Randy didn't look upset. He looked furious, made all the worse by the white-hot snarls of electricity snapping off him and nipping at Kaylee until she was forced to back away.

"Why don't you explain to me what you're doing here," Randy said.

"F-following you."

"Following me. Following me straight into a den of Slayers?"

"Yes...?"

Randy gave a mocking laugh, running a shaking hand through his hair. "Alastair told me you were reckless. Reckless I can deal with. Stupid I can't. So what he meant to say was stupid."

"You'd disappeared again," Kaylee shot back. "I wanted to know where you went. What was I supposed to do?"

"I was on a job for the Convocation! You know, that organization in Scarsdale that clearly fails at teaching any of their members *common sense*?" At this, a bolt of electricity shot from one of his hands and exploded against the pinsetter. Kaylee tried to stop her own from shaking. She'd seen her mom and dad truly angry before, but it was nothing compared to this. This frightened her. This was more than anger, more than Kaylee simply disobeying the rules, though she couldn't imagine what it was.

"You were gone again," Kaylee said in a steadying voice.

"On *missions*, Kaylee. It's what I do."

"I didn't know that! And then we find out you're headed toward more Slayers and—what was I supposed to think?"

"You thought..." Randy said, putting the pieces together. "You thought I was one of them? That's your grand deduction? Not any of the other two dozen options?"

"N-no."

"Haven't I earned your trust yet?" Kaylee was shocked to hear real hurt in his voice.

"You have…"

"Clearly not. Alastair not trusting me I can understand. Even the Convocation, and your mother, too. But you? Have I ever put you in harm's way or given you any reason to doubt me?"

He hadn't. Not at all. But for some reason those words of reassurance didn't help. Because while he hadn't given her a reason to mistrust him, he hadn't given her a reason to trust him either.

Randy waved a disgusted hand to the mess around them. "Now look what you've done."

A flare of anger ignited in Kaylee. "I know what I'm doing, Randy."

"Obviously, which is why this little raid or whatever you want to call it went so smoothly. One got away to go warn his friends and the rest, who were giving me plenty of intel, by the way, won't be giving anyone much of anything for a while."

"You're not the only one who's dealt with them before! While you were out running around all over the country I was protecting myself!"

"Not well enough."

The sure way he said it infuriated her. It was as if he thought she was completely incapable of anything except staying put and behaving herself like a good little dragon-kin. Because he was Randall Conners, the great electric dragon-kin of which a hundred stories had been told, each more incredible than the last. Randy, who even Alastair had admitted was a force to be reckoned with. Randy, who could take out an entire group of Slayers as if it were nothing but a warmup. In his eyes, she was just an overeager newbie who was way out of her depth, and always would be.

"So I messed up this time," Kaylee said. "At least I was trying to help somebody else besides myself."

"Stop talking before you sound like an even bigger fool," Randy said.

"Just because I can't fight as well as you doesn't mean I'm useless. I can help—"

"When you're older and stronger we can talk about—"

"You can't hide me like Alastair did! You can't hide me like—like that girl!"

She hadn't meant to say it. In her anger, the knowledge had sort of slipped out.

Randy looked confused. "Girl? What girl?"

Kaylee wanted to take it back, but there was no stopping now. "The girl you have a picture of. Is she…is she someone you lost? Because I get it, and…"

As she spoke, Randy's expression darkened with understanding. His mouth turned to a snarl.

"If you want to talk to me about her—" Kaylee continued.

"You had no right to look through my things."

"I know, I'm sorry—"

"Kaylee…"

"But I get it now, why you're so worried about me—"

"Enough!" A small bolt of electricity slammed into Kaylee's chest, punching the air from her lungs. She gasped for breath, but Randy was already storming toward the exit.

"Our training is done. Good luck facing the Slayers without me next time."

"Hey! What about all these guys?" Edwin said to Randy's retreating back.

Randy didn't even slow. "You're adults now, right? Figure it out. But I'd make it quick."

He pushed his way through the exit and was gone. A second later, the sound of a motorcycle revving to life came from the alleyway, then faded down the street, soon replaced by sirens.

Kaylee met Jade and Edwin's terrified faces.

"Let's get out of here."

CHAPTER SEVENTEEN

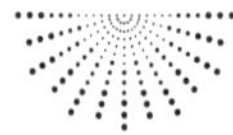

Edwin eased the car to a stop. His lips were pursed so hard they were a thin line in the darkness. He wouldn't look at her, but Kaylee knew it wasn't her he was mad at.

"I don't think this is a good idea."

"I know you don't. You've only said it about ten times on the drive over here."

"Well, then I *really* don't think it's a good idea."

"He's my uncle, Edwin. He's not going to hurt me."

"You sure about that?" Jade said.

"I *know* he won't hurt me." Kaylee looked at Randy's house at the end of the drive, draped in night. She knew Randy was angry —beyond angry—at her. But she had sensed something else behind the anger. A deep sadness that hinted at something more than what she had done today.

And…she kind of did have to apologize. As much as the word made her mouth taste like chalk, and her mind resisted it with every fiber of her being.

Jade unlocked her door. "I'm coming too."

"No, you're not," Kaylee said. She unbuckled her seatbelt. "I need to do this. Alone."

When Jade hesitated, Kaylee patted her arm reassuringly. "I'll survive. Promise."

"I'll kill you if he kills you."

Kaylee smiled. "Noted."

She slid out, but one of her hands stayed behind. She looked back to find Edwin gripping it. He gave it a gentle squeeze. "Be careful."

She squeezed it back. "I will."

Kaylee waited until they'd driven off before making her way to the front porch. Her mind seesawed back and forth. This *was* dumb. But necessary. But dumb. She should have never brought up the girl. But she'd been angry, and Randy had been wrong. She wasn't a child.

But maybe *don't* bring her up. Because who was she, really? Until she knew that, it was best to keep her mouth shut about it because she didn't know. She didn't know anything about Randy.

And there lay the crux of the problem. Short of everything Alastair had told her about him (which wasn't much), and her mom had told her about him (which also wasn't much), Kaylee hardly knew anything about the man. And she'd kept it that way. Maybe not intentionally, but in her actions. She'd snuck around him instead of simply asking. She'd never tried to get to know the man who was training her, the man who had been absent from her life for so long. Not *really* tried.

The door creaked when she opened it. Kaylee paused. There was a heaviness in the house, but no one was rushing at her, demanding that she get out.

She dropped her backpack by the stairs and checked the kitchen. The refrigerator door hung open. She closed it.

"Randy?" She kept her voice barely above a whisper. Her first thought was to check his study, but after today that was the last place she wanted to run into him.

Instead she went to the living room. "Ran—?"

He was sitting on the couch in the dark. His arms were

thrown over the back. His legs were kicked up on the table in front of him, scattering brown glass bottles. More than five of them.

"Um…need some light?" Kaylee tried the switches. They didn't work.

"Fuses are blown," Randy said. "Bulbs are burned out, too."

He took a drink from the bottle in his hand. His words were a bit slow, not slurred, but his eyes were fixed straight ahead. "S'what happens when I get a little…upset."

"Oh."

Kaylee eased herself into the chair next to him. Still Randy didn't move. He had acknowledged her presence without kicking her out. That was a start. Kaylee tried to come up with a way to continue the conversation, but Randy did it for her.

"You dealt with the cops, I assume."

"Er…not exactly. We ran. Before they got there."

Randy snorted. "Classic. Running." He raised the bottle. "You're more like me than I thought."

"What's that supposed to mean?"

Randy tossed the bottle onto the table and produced another one from between the cushions of the couch. Kaylee wondered how many of them he had stashed away there. She tucked her arms between her legs, suddenly feeling much more out of her depth than she had when she first resolved to speak with him. She'd imagined storming in and, after a brief apology, brazenly demanding answers. But now Randy was so…vulnerable, that all of her earlier bravado fell to the floor like the bottles at his feet.

"What I mean," Randy said, "is you like running away from your problems. I'm not saying that to be mean, I just say it as fact. I physically do it. You do it mentally."

"No, I don't."

"You sure about that?"

"I…"

"The boy you sometimes see. The one you killed. You can't

face what you did so you fight and run instead of facing your actions. You still can't fully control your storm powers all the time because of what happens when they get out of control, so you settle for med-medio-ah, heck." Randy tapped his forehead with the lip of the bottle. "Mediocrity. There we go. You train and train in order to protect others from a pain you can't bear to watch them take, even though you have no control over it. That's still running, it just looks a little different."

"And I suppose you don't do that."

"'Course I do. Worse than you. I don't just turn away from problems, I leave. Poof, gone."

"Is that...what you did at the bowling alley?"

Randy snorted. "No. No, I won't take credit for that. That was purely your stupidity."

"But you left us."

"Yeah, I did."

The clouds parted outside. Moonlight crept along the floorboards and reflected off Randy's watery eyes. Before he blinked, Kaylee swore a tear had trickled down his cheek. She didn't like asking when he was like this, but she couldn't back out now.

"Who was...? You know..."

"The girl in the picture. The girl you snooped to find."

Kaylee sunk lower in her chair, face burning. Randy held up two fingers. The girl's picture was caught between them.

"She's the biggest thing I've ever run from. And for once, it wasn't by choice. Her name is Claire, and she's probably about your age right about now."

"Is she—"

"My daughter. Yeah."

Kaylee blinked. She thought that might have been true, yet her mind still rebelled against the truth when she heard it. Randy was so completely opposite the kind of person she thought would ever have a kid. But then again, maybe once, not so long ago, he had been in love and dreamed of having a family.

And based on the anguish on his face as he peered down at the picture, Kaylee realized that was the truth.

"I see a lot of her in you," Randy said. "At least, you're how I assume she'd act."

"I'm sorry."

Randy gave her a lopsided look. "For what?"

"For what happened to her."

His confused expression deepened. "Nothing's happened to her. Not yet."

"You mean she's not…she isn't…?"

Randy laughed. He laughed until he coughed and then smothered the cough with another drink. "She's alive, girl. And the best part about that? She's alive 'cause I'm not there. See, I tried the 'normal' thing. I tried facing my problems head on at first. It only attracted trouble. Threats on my life and hers. I couldn't do that to my girl so I ran. I've been running ever since.

"I've told you before we all have our own curses to break, and it's true. This is mine. A daughter I love, but I can't see her, can't even get near her without hurting her, so I stay away. Always close enough to see, but never close enough to be. That's my curse."

"If you faced it and couldn't beat it, then how am I supposed to beat mine?"

"By being better than me. I expect it of you. You have what I never did. Friends. Family. The Convocation. There's no excuse to fail."

"And if I still do?" Kaylee said in a small voice.

Randy turned his watery eyes on her and, for a moment, they were as clear and sober as could be. "You won't. We all have our curses. That boy, your powers, this Slayer thing. Break yours. Break it like I know you can."

He took one final sip, then leaned over, kicking up a plume of dust as he thumped onto the cushions.

Kaylee stood in alarm. "Uncle Randy?"

A large snore answered.

Sighing, Kaylee pulled a ratty blanket from the hall closet. She draped it over Randy, being careful not to smother him. The idiot was out so cold he could die and sleep right through it.

Satisfied he was comfortable, Kaylee grabbed her backpack and went upstairs.

Kaylee awoke to the heavenly smell of bacon. Her stomach screamed with desire as she rolled to sitting, rubbing her eyes. She'd collapsed atop one of the spare beds upstairs, still dressed in yesterday's clothes. Her skin felt caked with a layer of sweat and debris from the fight yesterday. She considered taking a shower, but her stomach practically tugged her out of bed toward the kitchen.

Randy was at the stove, a frying pan in each hand. He flicked his wrists and bacon soared in a glorious arc onto a plate. Another flick and pancakes landed on another. Randy half turned and shot Kaylee a grin.

"Claire loved it when I did that."

Kaylee gave a small clap and sat down while Randy brought the plates over. "I'm impressed," she said. "Fighting and cooking skills. Hard to find that in a man."

"Don't you forget it," Randy said. He sat and tossed Kaylee her cell phone.

"You left it down here. Been going off all morning. I told your parents where you were so it's probably your friends seeing if you're dead."

Sure enough:

Edwin: *Kaylee, ARE YOU DEAD?*

Jade: *He better not have killed you <3*

Maddox: *Um no idea whts goin on but jade said to check on ur wellbeing???*

Kaylee assured them all that she was very much alive before digging into the food. It was probably the most delicious breakfast she'd ever tasted, and she made a mental note that, whatever Randy's faults, the man could cook.

Randy leaned back in his chair. He sipped his coffee. Every so often, she would catch him glancing at her, though it could have been because of how much food she was stuffing in her face.

"You gonna eat?" Kaylee said through a mouthful of pancakes. Randy chuckled and raised his coffee.

"I ate earlier. Now I drink the elixir of life to take the edge off…well, you know."

Kaylee gulped more water. "Last night. About that. I'm—"

"Forget it."

"I don't want to."

"Kaylee, I was drunk, I talked too much, and I have a pretty good idea of what I told you which you will *not repeat to anyone else.*"

Kaylee nodded quickly.

"Good." Randy leaned back in his chair again. Kaylee put her fork down. "And…about not training me? Did you mean that?"

Randy raised an eyebrow. "Maybe. Depends very much on whether you want to be trained."

"Of course I do!"

"And whether you're willing to do what I *definitely did not say* last night and own this dragon-kin thing. Own your curse."

Kaylee pushed her fork away. She still wasn't sure what Randy meant about the curses, or whether she actually had one. But her situation was now the same as Dani's; she couldn't do this alone. And if dealing with a curse would make Randy help her out, then she'd do it.

"I want to," Kaylee said.

"Then I'll think about training you again."

Randy snagged a couple pieces of bacon from Kaylee's plate. "Sometimes I think no matter how much training a dragon-kin has, they have limits on their elemental magic until they get older. I didn't fully control my electricity until I was twenty. Sometimes it just takes a little more life experience. You reach a point where your powers aren't swayed by the ups and downs of the teenage mind."

"Excuse me?" Kaylee growled.

"Oh, cool your jets." Randy bit into the bacon. "I was stupid when I was your age, too."

"Some would argue you still are."

"Not as dumb as you, jumping into the Slayers' den. Seriously, *what* did you think you were going to accomplish?"

"I thought I'd find out where you were going."

"Well you did. Congrats. Scouting mission for the Convocation. Just wanted to keep tabs on where the Slayers are. Or were, I guess."

"You sure it wasn't to find out where the Book of Kells is?"

Randy inhaled a chunk of bacon and immediately coughed. He grabbed his coffee and downed the next hack with a giant gulp.

"Where," he gasped, wiping off his mouth, "did you learn about that?"

Kaylee smugly sat back in her chair. "You know, Alastair made the same mistake you did, thinking we were just clueless kids."

"I never said you were…"

"You implied it."

Randy slowly nodded. "You're more like me than I thought. Which isn't exactly a good thing. Yeah, I was looking for some intel on the Book of Kells, and no, neither the Convocation nor Alastair knows about it. Yet. I'm assuming you know what the Book does?"

"It's a spell book and can…summon…stuff."

"Very precise," Randy said dryly. "I see Damian's information is as vague as ever. And don't gape at me like that, of course I've met Damian. Been by the Slag Heap a few times, too, to see if what he knew was any good. Don't know what you kids see in a place like that."

Kaylee closed her mouth, then said, "So if you're looking for it too then you must have a better idea of where it is. Or what it does."

"Wrong, but I'm getting there." Randy pushed himself up and started clearing the table. Kaylee grabbed her own dishes and brought them to the sink.

"I'm sure you think I should just forget about it," Kaylee said glumly.

"Don't be an idiot, of course I don't," Randy said. "The Slayers are trying to kill you. Again. You should be worried about it. Just don't go throwing yourself into fights without a plan. Know your enemies first. Have that nerdy boyfriend of yours do more digging through the archives. He'll come up with something."

"Edwin's not—"

She was interrupted by a loud knock on the front door. Randy let the dishes fall into the sink with a loud clink.

"Too early for visitors." He shifted a couple fingers to claws behind his back as he approached the front door and opened it.

"Reese!"

Her older brother was glaring at Randy, but his gaze softened when he saw her. "Hey, Katy bug."

Kaylee hugged him. Reese tensed, then relaxed, wrapping one arm around her. "What's this for? You act like you haven't seen me in forever."

"What are you doing here?"

"Mom and Dad told me you stayed the night. I came to pick you up. We need to leave soon."

"Leave for what?"

Reese gently prodded her forehead a couple times. "You must have had some serious mid-terms. The beach? Spring Break?"

Kaylee had completely forgotten. And though mid-terms

weren't to blame, a slew of training, sneaking around, and trying not to die had made the last few weeks blur together.

"Go grab your stuff," Reese said.

Kaylee hurried upstairs. When she came back down, Randy and Reese were standing so close to one another they looked like they were about to go to blows any second. Randy, for his part, seemed unperturbed. Reese looked like he'd barely managed to contain his anger at some unknown slight.

"I'll meet you in the car," Reese said. "I have to talk to Randy for a bit."

Randy picked something out of his teeth. "That's cute, playing at being grownup."

Reese's fists clenched.

Kaylee placed a gentle hand on Reese's shoulder. "Reese, if this is about me doing chores for Randy then it's really no big deal."

He shrugged her hand off. "It's not."

"Then what's it about?"

"Nothing you need to worry about right now."

"Whatever your problem is with him, just drop it."

She tried to put a hand on his arm again but he flinched back, like he couldn't bear to be touched by her. It was only for a second, but Kaylee felt like she'd been kicked in the gut.

"Just go to the car. Please."

"Fine. Whatever."

Kaylee stomped outside to the car and slammed the door shut. Through the glass and distance, she was unable to hear what they were saying, but a minute later Reese slid into the driver's seat.

"You're acting like an idiot," Kaylee said. "I've gotten over what he did. Why can't you?"

"And you sound like you don't know what you're talking about," Reese retorted, throwing the car in reverse.

They didn't speak the entire way home.

CHAPTER EIGHTEEN

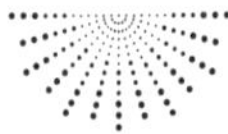

Whoever's idea it had been to go to the beach over Spring Break had been an idiot.

Kaylee had even worn a new swimsuit Jade had helped her pick out, but it didn't make a difference since she covered it with her hoodie to protect herself from the lingering bursts of chilly air. The others, too, weren't keen on taking off more clothes than necessary, all except Maddox, who was apparently part polar bear. But despite all his boasting that he didn't feel the cold, the goose pimples covering his arms were a dead giveaway. Fifteen minutes after they hit the beach, he looked almost as miserable as Reese, who had been grouching alone on his own towel, placed away from the group.

"Did he get food poisoning or something?" Jade said. She was studying Reese, shielding her eyes from the weak sunlight. "The gas station food wasn't *that* bad."

"I don't think that's it," Kaylee said. "He and my uncle got into an argument."

"About what?"

Kaylee held up her hands. "Search me."

Jade's gaze swept across the rest of the beach, lingering for a moment longer than usual on Maddox as he attempted to goad Edwin into the chilly water. Further down the beach, Damian and Dani were walking close together, eyes down in the sand. Every now and then, Dani would pick something up to show Damian. To say Kaylee was surprised Damian had decided to tag along with them would have been an understatement. The guy looked pitifully—happily—uneasy. Every time Dani handed him something Damian would pick up a find of his own and show her right back. When she smiled, he smiled too, a hesitant, awkward thing.

"I'm going back to the house."

Kaylee hadn't heard Reese walk up. He'd tucked his towel beneath his arm.

"You can sit with us." Kaylee gestured to the spot next to her.

"Thanks, but no."

"Are you…okay?" Kaylee lowered her voice. "I'm sorry about getting mad at you. Let's forget it and enjoy ourselves."

"I'm just tired. See you guys later."

Kaylee watched him thread his way through the mass of kids and families, duck beneath a Frisbee, and disappear into the parking lot.

"Something's definitely up with him," Jade said. "The guy looks lost."

Kaylee cocked an eyebrow. "Right…and you would know that because…?"

Jade shrugged. "I'm just saying. I remember when we were kids, Reese always…he always knew what he wanted. And when he set his sights on something, nothing stood in his way. But I've never seen him so shaken before. Gives me hope."

There came a shout of alarm from the ocean. Maddox had thrown Edwin in.

"Hope?" Kaylee repeated. "That's a little sadistic."

"Well…" Jade curled her arms around her knees. "If someone

as sure as Reese can have doubts about something, it makes me feel better about what I want to do."

"Which is not take the Tamer test."

"I never said that."

"Jade." Kaylee forced Jade to look at her. "If the thought of being a fully-trained Tamer for the Convocation makes you unhappy, then you're the last person I want as my Tamer."

"Wow...tell me what you really think."

"I mean it."

Jade let out a breath. "I know. And thanks, but I'll still take the test. I've trained so much already, and it'd make my parents happy. But after that then..."

"Tell me."

"Tell you what?"

Kaylee nudged her. "I know that look. You've decided something and you want to tell me."

Jade smirked. "We can't hide anything from each other, can we? Yeah, I—and don't take this the wrong way or anything—but seeing what you did for Dani, how you helped her, it got me thinking about doing stuff like that. Outreach. Social work. That sort of thing."

"For the Convocation?" Kaylee said. "Don't they have people like that who go looking for new dragon-kin?"

"They do." Jade rested her chin on her arms, gazing at Damian and Dani. "But I'm not exactly sure about doing it for them."

"I still think it's a great idea." Kaylee threw an arm around Jade. "You'd be perfect at it."

"You think so?"

"Definitely. Besides, any outreach you do can't be much worse than mine. Dani hates me now."

"No, she doesn't. Dani's personality makes it literally impossible for her to hate anyone. I bet if she ran into another Slayer she'd try to get them to join the decorations committee for the spring formal."

Kaylee laughed, but it tasted bitter. "You clearly haven't been paying attention to her the last month or so. She barely looks at me."

"Have you actually talked to her?"

Kaylee dug her toes into the cool sand, thinking back to the times she and Dani had interacted since the incident. "A little bit...?"

"That night the Slayers attacked us at the Slag Heap doesn't count."

"Oh. Then no, not really."

"I'd recommend that."

Kaylee felt a flush of embarrassment. She'd made sure Dani was doing okay since joining the Convocation, checking in with Maddox and Alastair to see how she was faring. Part of the reason for doing that had been because she couldn't ask Dani directly, but part, Kaylee hated to admit, had been because she didn't want to. It was as if, by avoiding the other girl, the problem would simply fix itself on its own and they could go back to how things had been before.

"Dunk time!"

Kaylee looked up to see Maddox and Edwin rushing toward them, teeth chattering, faces blue. "No more sitting in the sand!" Maddox said.

In a flash, the tip of Jade's knife was jutting out of the sleeve of her jacket. "Sure about that?"

The boys screeched to a halt. They began backing up, hands in front.

"Maybe later," Maddox amended.

"Thought so," Jade said sweetly.

Kaylee grinned as Jade tucked the knife back into her sleeve.

KAYLEE JERKED AWAKE. She didn't remember falling asleep, but her neck ached and her body felt heavy and sluggish, as if she'd been out for a while. That was unexpected. She'd had so many thoughts rushing through her mind when they'd all turned in for the night that she'd lain wide awake, staring at the ceiling for hours, while Jade breathed evenly beside her.

Kaylee carefully pulled the covers off and slipped out of bed. Jade mumbled something but slept on.

The rest of the house was quiet. The gentle lull of the ocean surf came through the window in Dani's room. Kaylee stood in the hallway, letting the soothing sound wrap around her like a cocoon. That lasted for a whole five seconds until a jarring snore rumbled from the game room at the end of the hall. Kaylee glanced inside. Maddox was sprawled across the leather couch. Both Edwin and Reese had taken over opposite corners, curled beneath blankets they'd found in the hall closet. Damian had headed home earlier.

Maddox let out another snore and Kaylee quietly closed the door. She was surprised she hadn't awakened sooner with that much noise. She was also surprised she was the one up walking around and not Reese with the way he'd acted earlier. Jade had been right. He seemed more strained than usual. She knew he was still doing whatever latest workout program he was on, so maybe he was overdoing it? Or perhaps Mom and Dad were pressuring him to figure out what his plans were next now that he'd taken a break from college.

And *that* was the weirdest thing.

Kaylee went to the kitchen, poured herself a glass of water, and perched on the island, letting the cool granite countertop soothe her muscles.

Jade was right, Reese had *always* known what he wanted, and had a tendency to go after it with a zealousness that bordered on stupidity. Wasn't it just last year that he was talking about all the great groups he was getting involved with at his college? He'd seemed so vibrant, boundless with expectation for the coming year. Not that Kaylee was any expert at college stuff, but something had happened to him since then. Or maybe he was at the same crossroads of choice Jade was; both deciding their purpose and place in the wider world. Kaylee only wished, like Jade had, Reese would tell her what his was.

Something *snapped*. In an instant, Kaylee was crouched on the kitchen floor, eyes peering into the darkness, pulse racing through her body. The Slayers couldn't be here. There was no way they'd know how to use Airbnb—

Snap!

Kaylee crept around the island and let out a sigh. The ocean breeze was picking up the blinds hanging from the living room door and dropping them again. She put her water down and went to close the window.

The door was open.

Kaylee stared, her mind trying to make sense of it. Their group had come in late. They'd been tired. One of them simply hadn't closed it hard enough, that was all.

The blinds rapped on the glass again.

Kaylee began to close it when her eyes caught something on the porch: Footprints in the sand starting off the edge of the concrete. A dozen pairs heading toward the house, and one heading out.

Kaylee stood frozen as the wind chimes tinkled. Then she stepped out, shutting the door firmly behind her. It was a clear, cloudless night, easy to see in, and the footprints led from the back of the porch over the next swell of sand and disappeared.

Something wasn't clicking. Something in her sluggish mind wasn't putting the pieces together. Everyone was in the house. They were all sleeping. She'd seen them.

All except for Dani. She'd assumed she was in her room.

Terror seized Kaylee's throat and propelled her legs to move. She didn't run. Running would only confirm that this was real and not just a symptom of her tired imagination. She tried to dampen the panic and focus only on following the footprints. There was nothing to worry about. Dani was still inside and these were from earlier. Or maybe Dani was on a walk. Dani…

Was right there.

Ahead, the sandy beach ran straight into a mound of smoothed brown rock. Here, the sand shifted to pebbles before changing to large stones, which then collided with boulders, stacked atop one another. There were no other houses beyond this. They'd purposefully picked this Airbnb beach house at the end of a long line for some extra privacy.

Kaylee could see Dani's lone figure at the edge of the sea cliff, staring out into the ocean. Kaylee's heart stuttered into overdrive. Her body moved on its own, unsure of what Dani was going to do—if she was even doing anything—but dreading it all the same.

Kaylee's bare feet gripped the porous rock as she clambered up the smooth side. She stopped twenty yards behind Dani. Dani simply stood there. It was hard to tell from behind, but she didn't appear to be doing anything other than gazing at the ocean, the moon, then back again.

Kaylee crouched and crept forward.

Just as Dani stepped off the cliff.

Kaylee didn't have time to cry out. A half-whisper was whisked from her lips and taken away by the wind. Then she was scrambling over the rocks to where Dani had stood. She wouldn't—she couldn't—

Kaylee reached the edge and peered down, bracing herself for a gruesome sight below. She didn't see Dani sprawled at the bottom. Or any sign she'd been there at all.

Kaylee stepped back. That's when she saw the path. A narrow trail hugged the cliff side, leading down to a crevice of rock below.

Kaylee hurried along it slowly enough to ensure she wouldn't go flying off the edge herself. For not the first time she wished she could shift to dragon wings. Forget running, she could be soaring after Dani right now.

Kaylee reached the end of the trail and slid between some rocks. After another slight squeeze, the path opened up to a slot canyon. It was hard to see her feet so Kaylee used the scar of open sky above to guide her down a couple twists and turns until she came out at a lagoon.

The lagoon was enclosed on all sides except for a lone inlet carved into the rock wall on the other side. Small waves lapped against a rocky shore. Kaylee let her eyes adjust to the new brightness and spotted Dani.

She crouched at the shore like she was about to take off running for one of her soccer games. Her arms were out in front, shifted to dragon scales, and she was pushing and pulling the still water ahead of her. The faint glow of magic, a light aqua blue, was emanating from her.

Kaylee could only watch, impressed. She had only seen Dani shift the one day she'd been tearing off her scales and at the Slag Heap. Since then, it'd seemed the other girl had avoided having anything to do with shifting except by accident or in desperation.

Kaylee came closer. Dani finished moving the water toward her again, then raised one hand and flicked it. The water gurgled and spat. Dani huffed and tried again. This time the water rose in a small vortex. It twirled together in a braid, hanging suspended in a long thread like a snake poised to strike. Dani held it there until her arms began shaking, then dropped it.

"You're doing really good," Kaylee said.

Dani whipped around. Kaylee barely caught the flicker of her arm before a spray of water hurled itself straight toward her. She instinctively ducked and forced a gust of air to explode upward, creating a wall of current that dispelled the attack.

"Kaylee!" Dani gasped, clutching her chest. "Don't *do* that! I could have hurt you!"

Kaylee felt the fine, gentle spray misting her skin. “I think I would have been okay.”

“What are you doing here?”

“I—” Kaylee’s mind went blank. Her original goal to find Dani was over, and actually approaching her to talk had been more an impulse than anything she’d planned.

“Uh…what are *you* doing here? How’d you find this place?”

Dani frowned at her evasion. “My family came to this beach a lot when I was a kid. My dad showed me this lagoon. He—”

She stopped. Her eyes dared Kaylee to say anything about her family, but Kaylee picked up a smooth rock from the shore and tried to skip it. It sank the second it hit the water.

“I saw you practicing,” Kaylee offered. “You were doing good. Really good. Have you started taking lessons?”

“No.”

“Oh. ‘Cause it looked like you had. You’re way better than I was when I first started.”

“That’s because you’re a storm dragon and I’m…” She pulled her arm farther back behind her. “Never mind.”

“Have you thought about starting lessons?”

“No.”

Kaylee sighed. “Dani, I know you’ve been avoiding me, and if you don’t want to talk, I get it.”

Dani’s eyes were stuck at the ground at Kaylee’s feet, so Kaylee plunged on, “I know you think I ruined your life and I suck, and this is terrible, but I hope you know you’re still the same person you were, and if you ever want someone to listen, I’m here, and I’ll stop talking now because I’m rambling.”

Kaylee forced her mouth closed before she blurted out anything else. Dani gave a small smile. “I don’t think you ruined my life. It was ruined long before you came along. And…I’m sorry I’ve been avoiding you. If it makes you feel any better, I’ve been avoiding a lot of people.”

“Is it because…?”

Dani shook her head. "It's because of me, because I haven't accepted this yet. I just need to learn to deal with it."

When Dani said that, some sense of understanding came to Kaylee; something she'd had bonking around in her head for a while, ever since Randy had spoken to her the first time about it. "We...all have our curses. That's what my uncle said. Maybe not actual magical curses, but things we think hold us back. You and being a dragon-kin, me with..."

Kaylee's throat caught on the words.

"Jade told me what happened," Dani said quietly. "About the boy. I'm sorry you had to go through that."

"Don't be. I couldn't do anything about it, I didn't want it, just like you didn't want this. But it happened, and it's part of us now whether we want it to be or not. But we don't have to 'suck it up.' It's not something we get over. We live with it and move on. We don't let it define us."

Dani was quiet for a long time. "You really believe that?"

"I have to. Because I won't believe that you and I have to deal with this the same way for the rest of our lives."

"Huh." Dani had her hand up and was staring at it. She tilted it this way and that. Then she shifted it, then back again. "I guess I could try looking at it like that."

"I think we both have to. Otherwise things aren't going to change."

And in her mind, Kaylee knew it was true. As much as she hated to admit it, Randy was right. Already, she could feel a weight lifting from her shoulders and fluttering away. It didn't mean her problems were gone—she knew that Brendan would probably always haunt her in one way or another, as would anybody else she was forced to hurt—but maybe, just maybe, she could handle it now.

"You think you could show me what you were doing earlier?" Kaylee said.

"Right now?"

Kaylee spun in a circle. "I don't see anybody here to judge us."

Dani, too, had looked around as though an entire procession had somehow followed them to the lagoon. Then she held her arms up, raising them so they were parallel with the water. A moment later, bubbles appeared on the surface. A twenty-foot strip of water pulled itself up and hung suspended in the air.

"Hold it there." Kaylee pulled her hands back and thrust them forward, drawing the heat from the water, sucking it out. The suspended water froze into a bridge of ice, which promptly collapsed beneath its own weight and hit the lagoon with a loud *slap*!

Both of them stared at it. Then they burst out laughing.

THE SUN WAS JUST COLORING the horizon by the time the two of them left the lagoon. They were still some distance from the house when Kaylee heard someone calling her name. They started jogging until Kaylee spotted Jade at the back door, hands around her mouth, shouting for her.

"What? What is it?" Kaylee panted, sliding to a stop in front of her.

"*Where* were you?" Jade demanded. She turned to the beach. "Maddox!"

Maddox's head popped over the nearest sand dune. Jade waved. "They're here! Tell Edwin!"

"Jade, what's going on?" Dani said.

"We have to go home," Jade said. "Kaylee, your brother already took his own car back, but he doesn't know."

"Doesn't know what?" Kaylee said as Edwin and Maddox hurried over.

"The Book of Kells," Jade said. "They've found it."

CHAPTER NINETEEN

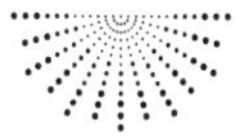

"Well look who decided to show up."

Kaylee briefly hesitated in the doorway before entering Alastair's study. Zaria was plopped in an armchair, drink in hand. Judging by her tone, she wanted a reaction. Kaylee was determined not to give her one since the other girl clearly felt the need to show up whenever Kaylee least expected her.

"You?" Jade said, filing in behind Kaylee.

"What's she doing here, Alastair?" Maddox demanded.

"*I'm* the reason you're all here," Zaria said.

"Hurry up, all of you. That includes you, please, Miss Fairfax." Alastair gestured for Dani to step inside.

"M-me?" Dani said.

"This concerns you as well."

Dani hesitated, then took a seat in the corner. Edwin followed her in and gently shut the door. His eyes briefly widened when he saw Zaria. Like Kaylee, he had clearly grown used to her random appearances.

"Zaria's the one who found the Book, Alastair?" Jade said. "We had Kaylee speed all the way back—"

"Safely, of course," Kaylee hurriedly added.

"—because of her?"

"As much as I hate to admit it, Zaria helped us last time," Edwin said. "I think we should hear what she has to say."

"Agreed," Alastair said. "Are the rest of you okay with that?"

His tone made it clear he didn't care one way or the other whether they were okay with it or not. There were mixed affirmations from the others. Alastair resumed his spot on the edge of his desk. "Zaria came to me with information concerning the whereabouts of the Book of Kells, which, based on your lack of surprise, you've already heard about."

"We might have heard something about it," Kaylee admitted.

Alastair frowned. "I'm sure. If I remember from last year, there were quite a few things you 'heard something about,' whether you were supposed to or not."

Edwin opened his mouth, but Alastair went on, "Regardless of what you did, I admitted I was wrong in not listening to you. And so," he said, opening a hand to Zaria, "when Zaria desired to meet to discuss a mutual concern, I decided it best to listen."

"Where's Randy?" Kaylee said. "Shouldn't he be here?"

"That tool?" Zaria said.

"That *tool* could whip you in a fight," Kaylee shot back.

"You think so, don't you?"

"Enough, girls!" Alastair said. He looked to already be regretting his decision to bring them together. "Zaria, we waited for them like you asked, but I still think I should alert my actual Convocation team—"

"You can tell them later." Zaria threw her legs up on the table, making Alastair wince. She turned to the others. "Remember our little talk earlier about the Book of Kells?"

"Of course," Edwin said.

"Is this the Herald of the Hunt guy you were telling us about, Edwin?" Jade said.

"Wait, I didn't hear that," Maddox said.

"You kept falling asleep," Jade said.

Maddox mumbled something about lacrosse practice while Kaylee gestured for Zaria to go on.

"We remember. What about it?"

"We found it."

"We know, that's why we're here. What else?"

Zaria looked chagrined. "Someone's impatient."

"Zaria, please," Alastair said.

Zaria picked at her nails. "The National Historic Society has it. They must've had it longer than we thought 'cause it just showed up without warning, and we would've heard of them discovering it any time recently."

"What's the National Historic Society?" Dani said in a quiet voice behind Kaylee, making her jump. She had forgotten the other girl was still there.

"They're part of an organization run by many of the top universities in the country," Alastair said. "They also happen to house many magical items, though the Society believes them to be merely artifacts of great historical significance. Many of our Convocations go to great lengths to ensure it stays that way."

"How do we know this is the real Book of Kells and not another fake?" Edwin said.

Zaria's eyes flickered up from her nails. "You'll just have to trust me, won't you?"

Jade's fists clenched. "Guess we will."

"We do," Kaylee said. About as much as they'd have to, anyway.

Alastair reached across his desk and pulled up a map of their surrounding area. "Edwin, if you please."

Edwin chanted a few words under his breath. The map tugged free from Alastair's hands and affixed itself to the air in front of them. Zaria stood and started pointing at each of the major cities around Scarsdale.

"Syracuse, Rome, Albany, Rothsburg. Cities with museums big enough for the Historic Society to put the Book on display."

"Why would they do that?" Jade demanded.

"To gloat," Maddox grumbled.

"Ignorance," Alastair corrected. "The Society has no idea what they've picked up, and their goal is to preserve historical objects for the public to enjoy. That means displaying them in museums."

"Which I know they'll do soon." Zaria had snagged a sharpie from Alastair's desk and was drawing circles around the cities. "The second they put that book on display, that's when I can grab it."

"You mean *we* can grab it," Maddox said. "It belongs to the Convocation."

A low growl escaped Zaria's throat. Her arm thickened beneath her sleeve, metal coating her fingers. "The *Convocation* lost the Book years ago. That's why we're in this mess now."

"All of you stop!" Alastair said. Kaylee hadn't realized Jade and Maddox had pulled their weapons. Even Dani had stepped forward, ready to attack.

"Typical thanks I get," Zaria spat. "I came to you with this information out of the goodness of my heart, even after all the nothing the Convocation gave me."

"I'm sorry for any wrongs other Convocations may have committed against you," Alastair said. "However, the Book would be safer with our protection. For now, let's focus on the bigger issue."

Zaria reluctantly withdrew her arms. The others dropped their weapons. "Fine. We'll discuss ownership once we get the Book. Which is going to be the fun part. You can bet if I know the Book's whereabouts, every Slayer in New York will too. Maybe even that Lesuvius guy I keep hearing about."

"He's in New York?" Jade said abruptly.

"We don't know," Alastair said. "And until we know, he's not our main concern."

He went to the map and tapped a couple of the circles. "We have small clusters of Convocation members and safe houses in some of these cities. I can move supplies and people if necessary to whichever one the Book pops up in."

"So can I."

They all gave Zaria a skeptical look.

"What?" She fluttered her eyelashes at them. "You didn't think my little gang 'o misfits were the only ones who listened to me, did you?"

"Yeah, we actually did," Maddox said.

"Then I'm just full of surprises. There you go, Alastair. I did my part and filled you in with what I know. I recommend you don't forget this. And that you keep some ears—"

"I know how to do my job, young lady—"

"—and eyes on these guys." Zaria indicated to Kaylee and the others. "Word is they have a knack for taking things into their own hands." She pressed a mocking hand to her chest. "Kids after my own heart."

Alastair looked at them, weighing the possibility of what Zaria said. "I think they need to be part of this, too. I'm sure even if we were to exclude them they would come along regardless. Isn't that right?"

Kaylee nodded her head so fast it felt like it'd fall off her neck.

Alastair sighed. "Very well. Zaria, your help is greatly appreciated. I'll be in touch if we hear anything about the Book. Now, we should prepare for whatever the Slayers use to retrieve it."

"Quite a lot, then," Zaria said matter-a-factly. "The Book of Kells isn't the *final* final chance they have at using any spooky ancient magic to kill us, but it's definitely one of their best shots."

Alastair held the door open for Zaria and the two of them walked out of the study.

"Are we...really going after it?" Dani said.

"If we have to," Kaylee said. "But we usually end up having to."

Dani nodded slowly.

"You don't need to come along," Jade added. "We'd be the ones getting it. You haven't had combat training like us."

"I think she should come," Kaylee said.

"I'm not sure that's a good idea."

"I think I should too," Dani agreed. "I'm part of this now, aren't I?"

Jade looked at Maddox. He shrugged. "She's part of this," he agreed.

"Okay, then."

"I'm gonna go start unpacking the car," Maddox said. "You coming, Edwin?" He looked back. "Edwin?"

Edwin was up at the still floating map, muttering to himself.

"I'll get him. You guys go ahead," Kaylee said.

The others trickled out, Jade gushing to Dani about some kick-butt fighting moves she could teach her. Kaylee joined Edwin.

"Let's hear what you've come up with."

"How do you know I've come up with anything?"

"Because I know you. When you're deep in thought you go into this vegetative state where you only respond to the promise of food and verbal threats."

Edwin chuckled. "My two greatest weaknesses." He placed a finger on one of the cities Zaria had nearly blacked out with a sharpie circle. Rothsburg.

"I checked the Historical Society's website while we were talking. There's no announcement of when or where their next exhibit would be. My guess is the Book will be put on display at an existing exhibit, so they probably wouldn't make a big deal out of it. Then I did another search and Rothsburg is the only city with a museum with a Celtic display. It matches."

"You did all that while we were talking?"

"Impressed?"

Kaylee bumped him with her hip. "That I can't find answers that fast in school? Yes."

Edwin laughed and bumped her back. His fingers brushed the circle around the city. Again. Again. Again. "Isn't there a spring formal at your school or something?" he blurted.

Kaylee cocked an eyebrow.

"Maddox told me," Edwin said quickly. "Not that I was asking —he just told me there was one in a couple weeks and—you were gonna go, right?"

"I hadn't really thought about it. I've kind of had other things on my mind."

"Right. Of course."

"And you're homeschooled, so a public school formal..."

"Yeah, but it's not like they would *know* I didn't go there if I showed up. Especially if I went with—"

Kaylee didn't hear what he said next. Her eyes had caught something on Alastair's desk behind Edwin, peeking out from beneath a stack of papers. It was a half-hearted attempt to hide it, as though Alastair had wanted her to discover it herself rather than be forced to explain it to her face-to-face.

"Kaylee?" Edwin said as she brushed past him. Kaylee pushed aside the papers and picked up the bead bracelet. She didn't have to look closely to know whose it was. But why?

You know why. You've known for a while, haven't you?

Reese, picking at the beads as he drove her angrily home from Randy's house.

The hooded figure's reluctance to attack her at the bowling alley.

Randy, scooping something up from the rubble after all the Slayers had fled.

No. NO. *NO.*

"Kaylee?"

It was Alastair. Kaylee realized her hand was shaking, causing the beads to clack together. Sparks of electricity buzzed from the tips of her fingers. This time she didn't try to dim them.

Kaylee held up the bracelet. "You want to explain what these are doing here?"

When she turned, Alastair hadn't moved from the doorway. He didn't look sorry, or surprised, which confirmed Kaylee's suspicions that he'd *wanted* her to see them. And if he had them, he'd known for a little while; at least since they'd been with Randy at the bowling alley, which meant Randy had told him and not her.

The coward.

"What's going on, Dad?" Edwin said.

"How long?" Kaylee said.

"Only a little while. I was informed last week," Alastair said.

"No, how long has Reese—how long has he been with them?" She could barely get the words out. Imagining her brother, the one who comforted her, loved her, doing *that*.

Alastair's shoulders sagged. He took a step forward, but Kaylee held the beads out like a weapon. "How. Long?"

"We're not completely sure. Maybe a year or more. We think he may have run into some Slayers through a group at school and got caught up with them. We don't think he knew exactly what he was doing."

"We, we, we. You mean Randy."

"Yes."

Kaylee swore, nearly tossing the beads down in disgust. Just when she thought she could trust him he went and did this to her. "Why didn't he tell me himself when he found out?"

"Frankly? Because he thought you would react like this." Alastair indicated to the room.

But Kaylee didn't care if the wind had picked up or the temperature had dropped. She didn't care if the ceiling lights had dimmed, as if a dark cloud had swallowed them whole. She didn't even care that, for the first time she could remember, she felt perfectly in control of the storm she was summoning. It was like having a single focal point of anger to aim toward had brought her powers under her control more than any training ever had.

Randy, who'd lied. Randy, who'd sat there and told her a sob story about his daughter while knowing about Reese and not really caring at all about how that knowledge could destroy her family.

"I need to go," Kaylee said.

"Not like this," Alastair said. "I understand you're upset—"

"Upset? I just found out my brother's probably been killing dragon-kin. Yeah, I'm *upset*."

"We've found no evidence he's killed anyone, or even gone on missions for them."

"Kaylee, please calm down," Edwin begged. "You know this isn't going to help. We'll find Randy and ask him."

"No, I'll find Randy. Right now."

Kaylee tried to move, but her feet were caught. Thick roots had emerged from the ground and were wrapping their way around her ankles. The potted plants in the corner had grown three times as big, their enormous branches flailing around, mirroring Alastair's arms.

"I'm sorry I have to do this," Alastair said, his claws growing, his eyes now green slits.

Kaylee let more of her magic out. The storm growled. "So am I."

She ducked as one of the plants tried to grab her arms. In two slices she'd freed her ankles, sending the roots withering back into the ground. More burst forth to try to hold her but she froze the floor solid to slow them down.

That left only Alastair in her way.

He moved in a blur. First he was at the door, then he was in front of her. But as he reached to hold her in place, magic tugged at Kaylee's gut. The windows exploded inward. Edwin cried out and covered his face. Alastair was momentarily distracted and

Kaylee used it to barrel past him, sending him flying into one of his plants with a loud crash.

"Kaylee!" Edwin yelled after her. But Kaylee was moving so fast it was as if the wind had kicked up her heels, as if she had wings.

She only slowed a bit when she reached the sidewalk out front and took off toward home.

CHAPTER TWENTY

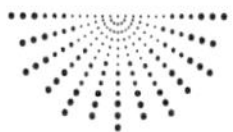

Reese's car wasn't at their house. Kaylee wasn't surprised. She doubted he'd come home at all. He'd known. Their whole trip he'd known. The darting looks he'd given her following that night with the Slayers he'd known.

Kaylee was forced to walk as she made her way down Scarsdale's main road. She ignored the traffic and people passing by her, her focus lasered ahead, the rhythm of her feet staying consistent with the pounding in her chest. Each beat was like a chant.

Wrong.

Wrong.

Wrong.

This was wrong. She was being dumb. She was overreacting. She'd get there and nothing would be the matter. Randy and Reese would just be talking and they'd both laugh at how upset she looked.

The second Kaylee felt she was out of sight of any bystanders, she took off down the farm to market road, drawing on her magic to speed her up as it'd done before. The grass whipped by in a blur. Gravel kicked out of her way. The rocks picked through the soles of her shoes and made her feet feel like she'd stepped on a field of marbles, but she didn't stop until she reached the end of Randy's driveway.

Kaylee stood there panting, letting her tired, magic-drained muscles recover. Then she began walking toward the house. All was quiet. A loose panel from the roof of the shed slapped in the breeze. Reese's car sat in front. The engine still clicked, cooling down. He hadn't been here long.

This time Kaylee went around the back. Twice she peered in the side windows, hoping to catch a glimpse of something. Anything. The kitchen was empty. One of the bottom floor bedrooms was bare. The living room was as clean as she'd ever seen it.

Kaylee sucked in a breath before yanking the screen door open and going inside.

"Randy? Reese?"

Sudden movement upstairs startled her; the sound of scuffling coming to an abrupt halt.

Kaylee took the stairs two at a time. The office door at the end of the hall was ajar. She pushed it open.

"What are you doing here, Kaylee?"

Randy stood leaned against his desk, hands clamped on the edge. The wood beneath his fingers was blackened, his face grim and facing Reese across the room. The air smelled charred.

"Go wait in the car, Kaylee," Reese managed to say. He stood across from Randy, casually leaning against the closet wall, one hand behind his back.

"No," Kaylee said.

"Kaylee—"

"I know, Reese. I know what Randy found."

They both winced.

"How long?" Reese said quietly.

"Did I suspect? A little while. Did I know for sure? Just now."

Reese shifted uncomfortably, his arm never leaving his back. "How?"

"Alastair. Or really, Randy."

"Found the bracelet, did you?" Randy grunted. "Yeah, that one, boy," he added when Reese glanced down at his naked wrist on his exposed arm. "Took you both long enough to put two and two together. Never wear anything distinguishable, boy. First rule of doing something illicit."

"I wanted to tell her," Reese snarled.

"No, you wanted to kill her. It's what your little fan club likes to do, get it?"

"I would never—"

"When were you going to tell me, Reese?" Kaylee said.

Reese continued glaring at Randy.

"Reese?"

"I didn't know they were—when they recruited me they promised I could make a difference."

"Oh, you could. For them," Randy said.

"Shut up!" Reese roared. He took a menacing step toward him but still didn't remove his arm from behind his back. "This is all ruined because of you. All I had to do was stay in Scarsdale and let them know if I found out anything about the Book. Then you were here and wouldn't leave. You wrecked everything."

"I'd say you did a pretty good job of that yourself. Maybe next time, when you join a group, you read the fine print instead of ingesting word-for-word the BS they spoon-feed you."

"*I'm* making the world safer. *I'm* making a difference. How can someone like you possibly understand?"

"Someone like me? And what am I?"

Reese sneered. "A nobody. A pathetic low-life just out for himself. I know the things you've done, Randall Conners. The Slayers kept me well-informed of all those dark little secrets. A daughter? Really?"

The desk groaned as Randy clenched it harder. "Keep her out of this. She has nothing to do with our world."

"You go through all this trouble to keep your own flesh and blood out of harm's way, but when it comes to my little sister you drag her into this like it's just a big joke."

Kaylee shifted one of her arms. She held the scales up to the glittering light. "Look at me, Reese."

"Leave, Kaylee," Reese said gruffly. "Go outside."

"Please, Reese."

"Kaylee—"

"Don't have the guts to even face what they want you to kill, do you?" Randy said.

"Reese."

Reese's eyes must have been tethered to a thousand-pound weight, because it took him forever to drag them up from the floor and affix on her arm.

"Oh God, Kaylee. You—"

"I'm the same person I was," Kaylee said. "I'm still your little sister. At first, I didn't want this either, but it's a part of me now. It's my blessing and my curse."

"And Jeremy?" Reese said. "Is he…is he like…?"

"He's normal," Kaylee said. "At least as normal as Jeremy can be." She gave a small smile. Reese didn't return it.

"I don't know what the Slayers told you, but they're lying," Kaylee said. "Not everyone in the Convocation is bad. Not all dragon-kin are monsters."

Reese was silent, save for a few labored breaths. Kaylee let her arm fall. "You can help us," she added. "The Slayers are planning something with the Book of Kells."

"Trust me, he knows all about that," Randy said. "Like he said, he didn't come home to see you or the folks. I knew that the day he arrived. He's been gathering as much info on that book as he could get his grubby hands on."

"Shut up," Reese growled. "Shut up right now."

"Aw, did somebody decide to grow a conscience?"

"If they get that book they're going to kill all the dragon-kin," Kaylee said. "They'll kill me."

"No." Reese shook his head. "No, that's not it at all. That book's going to save us. Lesuvius said that book—"

"Get your head out of the sand and think for yourself, boy!" Randy barked.

"Shut *up*!" Reese produced a black gauntlet from behind his back. Runic symbols were carved into the palm. "You're the reason she's involved in the first place!"

Reese splayed his fingers and a glowing light appeared beneath Randy's desk. He leapt aside a second before it ignited, sending shards of wood spraying every which way. Kaylee felt Randy's body pummel into her and wrap her tight. Felt the jarring thump as they were tossed into the wall. Randy pulled her up. "Get out of here!"

"Don't hurt him!"

Reese had summoned a glowing circle in front of him. Shards of dagger-like light were gathering within it. Randy grimaced at it. "Don't hurt him? He's trying to kill us, Kaylee."

"He wouldn't. He—"

They dove again as the daggers sliced toward Randy. With one swipe, he shot an arc of electricity and snapped them away. Reese was already readying another volley.

"Stop!"

Reese didn't have time to turn before Kaylee plowed into him. She found his wrists and held tight as they hit the wall, pinning him there. "Stop this, Reese!"

Reese struggled but Kaylee dug her claws into the wood behind him. Her feet were shifting to talons, digging into the ground. "This isn't you. You wouldn't hurt Randy and you won't hurt me."

For just a second, Reese's struggling slackened.

"I'm doing this for the good of everyone," he murmured.

Kaylee ducked as a bolt of light cut across her cheek. Reese thrust out his palm. It connected with Kaylee's stomach, there was a *push,* and she was thrown through the doorway.

Kaylee's world spun as she tumbled. She barely remembered to shift her back to scales in time before she collided with the stair railing and splintered through it. There was a weightlessness, then a sudden stop as she hit the ground. Kaylee gasped for breath. The pain was dulled by the shift, but the air had been knocked from her lungs.

"Kaylee!" Randy's cry sounded far away. Kaylee was aware of another crash, this time of glass. Then shouting outside. She rolled to her feet just as Reese's car roared out of the driveway and down the road.

Randy thudded down the stairs. He paused beside her. "You okay?"

"Y-Yeah."

Randy held her steady with one hand. "You sure?"

Kaylee waved a hand, too winded to answer more. All she wanted was for the world to stop spinning. Randy looked at her a moment longer, then threw open the front door and rushed outside. Kaylee didn't have to guess where he was going.

Her lungs felt seared, her back a pulping mass of bruises, but still Kaylee limped to the shed. By the time she arrived, Randy had already strapped about a dozen weapons on the back of his motorcycle. He was pulling down others, moving with practiced efficiency. The leather bags slung over the back were filled with traps, swords, daggers. More gear than he'd ever need for a simple Convocation mission, or to train her.

"What is all this?" Kaylee croaked. "What are all these weapons?"

Randy finished stuffing a particularly nasty contraption with barbs at the end into his motorcycle's saddle bag. "This is my big secret. Happy now?"

"I don't understand."

"Of course you don't, but you should. I'm sure you've heard plenty of stories about me by now. These," he said, gesturing to the weapons on the back, "these are the tools I use for the good of all dragon-kin. I lie, I kill, I make the world safer for us." He chuckled, but there was no humor in it. "I guess I sound like a regular Slayer, don't I?"

Once again, Kaylee's world started spinning. "Randy, you won't…what do you plan to do with all this?"

"What does it look like?"

"You can't hurt him. He doesn't know what he's doing!"

Randy let out a barking laugh. "I'd expect that excuse from a three-year-old. Your brother knows exactly what he signed up for."

He tightened the final strap. Kaylee pulled her magic to her claws as Randy straddled the bike and kicked the ignition. A searing bolt of pain shot into her tender skull as the engine noise filled the shed, rattling the panels. Kaylee stumbled back.

"You can't hurt him!" she shouted.

"Go home!" Randy said. "Tell Alastair I've found what I came here for and I won't be coming back."

"What are you talking about?"

Randy's eyes were shadowed as he pulled goggles on. "I'm going after the Book of Kells. That's why I came to Scarsdale. Consider your training over."

CHAPTER TWENTY-ONE

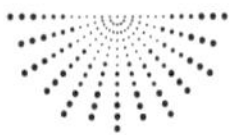

The rumble of his engine still shook her bones long after Randy had left; until her legs actually were shaking and she collapsed.

When she woke, someone was calling her name. Kaylee forced herself to stand and limped outside, every muscle protesting. Jade, Edwin, and Maddox were spread out around the house and surrounding yard. When Jade spotted her, she let out a small gasp and helped Kaylee into Edwin's car. Kaylee expected them to bombard her with a million questions, but Alastair must have filled them in on what had happened in the office. Or they saw Randy's motorcycle was missing and the result of her fight and figured it out.

Either way, Kaylee was grateful for their silence.

The next couple days passed in a haze, and Kaylee avoided everyone. She barely left her room. Even Jeremy, who loved tormenting her in some form or fashion whenever he passed her room, gave her an odd sort of distance.

A few times her parents came up to see how she was doing, and Kaylee simply said that she was swamped with school. After making sure she was all right, her mother would hover at the doorframe for a brief moment, and Kaylee fought the urge to say *Did you know Randy had a daughter? Did you know why he was really here? Know he never really cared about any of us?*

Because maybe he never had. She didn't know what was true about him anymore. One thing she did know, though, was that she'd been stupid enough to believe him in the first place.

Her parents had asked her where Reese was, but Kaylee had made up some excuse about one of his crazy training exercises and left it at that. Because what did it matter? When it came to him and Randy, one lie was as good as another.

KAYLEE MADE sure the window didn't squeak as she pushed it the rest of the way up. She lowered herself as much as she possibly could toward the ground and dropped into the bushes. Her still-sore body screamed in protest. Wishing she had Edwin's levitating board, Kaylee brushed twigs and leaves off her clothes and hurried across the front yard, not worried about being spotted by her family. Everyone was asleep, and her mom had already checked on her that night.

Once she reached the street, Kaylee traced the familiar route Edwin had shown her the previous year. Kaylee had been down this way a couple times since. Once more with Edwin, once alone.

She checked her phone. Speaking of Edwin…he'd texted her a few minutes ago, asking if she was awake. Kaylee had debated whether to answer, or whether to ignore her friends again. That didn't seem fair. None of this was their fault, and she did miss them.

Her fingers hovered over the reply, then pressed it.

Out right now. See u tomorrow.

There. Already she felt less guilty about closing them off the last few days.

The street dead-ended and Kaylee turned up a squiggly gravel lane. The wrought iron gates of the Scarsdale cemetery came into view a second later. Kaylee hopped the fence where it was lowest and used the gnarled oak tree on the other side to climb down. She didn't have to look hard to find the mausoleum. It was by far the biggest structure around, a clean-cut design of marble and granite rising above the jumble of headstones.

The second Kaylee went inside, she could feel the tension draining out of her body. She imagined all her problems from the last few days thudding against the mausoleum walls outside, failing to reach her quiet space.

Kaylee ran her hand over the engraved plaques. The second time she and Edwin had come here she'd finally thought to ask whose space they were invading.

"Convocation members," Edwin had said.

"Oh," Kaylee had answered, suddenly embarrassed they were there. "Then maybe we should go…"

"Some of them died from old age," Edwin said. "Others were killed by the Slayers. But it's no big deal we're here, if that's what you're worried about. They need to be remembered, you know? Even if it's just by us."

Just by them. Kaylee sat on the floor now. She stared at the far wall and simply let the silence take her.

Footsteps crunched outside.

She was up in an instant. *No one* came to this cemetery, and especially not at night.

Kaylee shifted her claws as the footsteps stopped outside the mausoleum. If they were Slayers, they'd really picked the wrong night to mess with her. Manipulating her brother into joining them had assured that any future Slayers would get a one-way ticket to Painville.

"Kaylee?"

Edwin's voice sounded hesitant. Kaylee swallowed her surprise and poked her head out. He was peering curiously at the mausoleum entrance. He glanced at her claws when she emerged and chuckled.

"I had a feeling it'd be a bad idea to sneak up on you. Dealing with your wrath once this week is enough for me."

"What are you doing here?" Kaylee said. "How'd you find me?"

Edwin held up his cell phone. "You said you were out. At two in the morning. I figured there weren't many other places you'd go."

He grinned, and Kaylee saw narrow scabs on his cheek; nicks from the glass in Alastair's office that had cut across his face. Edwin must have realized what she was staring at because he put a finger to them.

"This is nothing. You know that. Didn't even hurt."

"I'm sorry anyways."

"Don't be. You were kind of awesome, actually."

Kaylee gave him an incredulous look. "I attacked your dad. I'm surprised he hasn't locked me up by now."

Edwin laughed again, hands now stuffed in his pockets. "Yeah, about that. I talked to him after it happened. He wasn't mad at all. He was more impressed than anything. I'm not sure how much you know about my dad, but he's no pushover when it comes to a fight. He was proud to see how far you've come. Randy will be happy to hear—"

He cut off. "Sorry. But, yeah, he doesn't blame you for reacting the way you did. *I* don't blame you either. That was the worst way to find out."

Kaylee shivered, overcome by a sudden chill. "I think I've known for a little while and just didn't want to accept it. With both Reese and Randy. Randy was never here for me. It's so obvious now that he only showed up after all these years just when the Book was found. I'm such an idiot."

"You're not an idiot," Edwin said fiercely. "And Randy did—does—care about you."

Kaylee met his defiant gaze. "How do you know?"

"You have any idea how many times Randy came ranting to my dad about how stubborn you were, how slowly you were progressing, how you fought him on everything? He sounded frustrated and proud. Nobody does that if they don't care. And that night at the bowling alley? You can't fake fear like that.

"Look," Edwin went on. "Randy…I don't know a lot about his past 'cause my dad won't tell me, but he's complicated. And Reese…" Edwin sighed. "He screwed up, I'll admit. We don't get to choose our family, but they *are* our family."

"You're saying I should go after them?"

"I'm saying, at the very least, you should find them and give them a piece of your mind."

"And how do you suggest I do that? I haven't heard from Randy in days."

"You haven't heard from anyone in days," Edwin muttered. Kaylee glared at him and he cleared his throat.

"And…" Kaylee added. "I have no idea where Reese went."

"Reese and Randy both went to the same place. I was right about Rothsburg. A display containing the Book of Kells showed up in the Rothsburg Museum of Natural Science and Ancient History a couple days ago. My dad and some of the Convocation left to get it yesterday. I guarantee your brother and uncle will be there too."

"Then it's too late," Kaylee said. "The Slayers will have gotten it by now."

Edwin shook his head. "Not yet. At least, not since a few hours ago."

Just then, Maddox's minivan pulled up to the front gates and honked. Edwin waved and turned back to Kaylee. "What do you say? Want to go help save the Convocation again?"

He offered her a hand.

Kaylee could feel a smile spreading across her face. "So romantic," she said as she took it. "Let's do this."

~

"I THINK that guy's tailing us."

Maddox hunched farther over the steering wheel, glancing in the rearview mirror for what had to be the tenth time. "I'm not making this up, guys."

"We're on a one-lane highway, Maddox," Jade huffed. She banged the GPS on the dashboard again. "Maybe, just maybe, they're going to the same place we are."

"What idiot would be driving around at four in the morning?"

"We are."

"Exactly."

"Here, Jade." Dani reached across Kaylee and gently plucked the GPS unit from Jade's hands. "I think it needs a little more tender approach."

"All this magic is screwing the stupid thing up," Jade said. Dani pressed a few buttons. A clipped British voice creaked, "Rothsburg, five miles."

"There!" Dani said brightly.

Kaylee was simultaneously happy to see Dani with them, and also a little terrified she was with them. Sure, she'd harnessed and used her elemental magic faster than Kaylee had thought possible, but one encounter with the Slayers didn't mean she was ready for the intensity of a true battle. Kaylee wasn't sure *she* was ready, but they were almost there. It was too late to stop now.

Edwin zoomed in on the GPS. "Once we enter Rothsburg we need to find the safe house my dad set up. It's on a commercial street above a hardware store."

"The Convocation run it?" Maddox said.

"Yes, but last time my dad talked to me he said some of the rogues were there too."

"Seriously?" Jade groaned.

"They're on our side, Jade," Kaylee said. "Can't you just accept their help?"

Jade clenched her jaw. "This once. But the second that book is in our hands it's back to severely disliking them again."

"Fair enough."

"Oh! I printed these out for us," Dani said. She pulled out a thin stack of papers and began handing one to each of them. It was a full color map of the inside of the museum. There were even little scribbles to mark the entrances and exits. A gallery on the second floor, marked Celtic History, had little stars and rainbows drawn around it with the words, 'Book of Kells!'

"Wow," Edwin said, clearly impressed.

"I figured the better we know the layout, the better chance we have," Dani said. She pointed to the first floor on the map. She'd drawn a chubby giant sloth waving its claws at them.

"The exhibits are kind of mixed together, but bottom floor is mostly natural history. There's the main entrance hall, auditorium of science, and a planetarium. The ways in are the main entrance and a side entrance from the street out back that I think the employees use."

"Any way to get into the lowest level?" Edwin said.

"Here." Jade put a finger on it. "There's one entrance that goes straight into Griffon theatre."

"But we don't care about the lower level," Kaylee said.

"We'll still probably have Merlins and Protectors stationed there," Maddox said. "To keep the Slayers off our back while we grab the Book."

"Which is here," Dani tapped the entire second floor, labeled Ancient History (complete with chubby Vikings, Scots, Greeks and even, strangely enough, a T. rex. Kaylee was beginning to question how seriously Dani was taking this). "The book is in the Celtic History gallery."

There was no outside access to the second floor, short of a terrace on the south end they could scale, which meant the Slayers could too. There were also two main staircases. One was at the far end of Norse hall, past Ancient Asia; the other linked directly with the Grand Hall, currently labeled 'Rotating Exhibit.' That explained the oddly-placed T. rex.

"Alastair will want to see this, if he hasn't already," Jade said. "We can organize teams—watch it, Maddox!"

Maddox had taken a sharp left turn down a deserted street. At some point, they'd entered Rothsburg. A stubby skyline was haloed in the distance. Spotlights of streetlamps guided their way through streets of brick storefronts.

"Lost him," Maddox said triumphantly into the rearview mirror. "The guy was giving me the creeps."

Jade glanced back. "Good job. You probably 'lost' some baffled commuter."

"Better safe than sorry."

"Safe house should be just up one more street on the right," Edwin said.

"And we'll arrive tail-less, thanks to me," Maddox said. "You're welcome—"

Kaylee barely had time to shout a warning before a black SUV came barreling out of the alleyway ahead and cut them off. Maddox slammed on the brakes a second before another one blocked their retreat behind them.

"Everybody bail!" Jade yelled.

Kaylee hit the concrete at a run, barreling in the direction the others were going.

"Leave it, Maddox!" Jade yelled.

Maddox gave his mini-van one final, pained look, then followed after them.

Slayers dressed in black body armor had exited the other vehicles and were trying to close off their escape. A couple had crossbows, but others wore magic gauntlets. Just like—

Kaylee's stomach lurched as she drew on her magic. She swung around, clawed hand raised to the sky. A bolt of lightning seared down and collected there before she pounded it against the ground, knocking the nearest Slayers off their feet.

"We have to lose them before we reach the safe house," Jade said beside her. She knocked aside a few crossbow bolts. "Follow the others."

Maddox was leading Edwin and Dani down another narrow alley. The next street over was clear. Edwin gestured to the map when they stopped.

"One more up. Keep moving that way. I'm laying a trap."

He began flicking his hands in a complicated fashion across the mouth of the alleyway. He noticed Kaylee still beside him.

"Go, Kaylee! I'll be right there!"

But Kaylee stuck around until he'd finished and the nearest Slayers rounded the corner. They pointed at her and shouted. Edwin tugged her arm.

"That'll slow them down."

"What did you do?"

Kaylee's question was answered once the Slayers tried to follow them through the alley. The lead ones suddenly jerked to a stop as if stuck in a giant web. The rest clogged up those behind until half a dozen were bottlenecked, weapons caught in now-visible threads of orange.

"Always wanted to try that," Edwin said happily.

They caught up with the others on the next street.

"Where now?" Maddox said.

Edwin spun in a circle. "Hardware, hardware…"

"Watch out!"

Dani plowed into Kaylee. There was a monstrous roar and another black SUV zoomed past, kicking up grit and concrete. The SUV swerved around and faced them. Its headlights blinded Kaylee as she struggled to stand and help Dani up. She could barely make out a couple figures leaning out the side, weapons aimed at them.

"On the rooftops, too," Maddox said, slowly raising his hands.

Sure enough, at least a half dozen more Slayers had assembled above them, closing off any chance they had at escaping the street.

"On my mark," Kaylee said.

"They'll kill us before we can move, Kaylee," Jade said.

"They'll kill us if we don't. One...Two—"

A low thump, like the concussion of a firework, sounded from behind the nearest building. A ball of light slammed into the side of the SUV, careening it into the brick wall across the street.

The distraction was enough. Kaylee unleashed a blast of ice at the nearest Slayer above them just as Edwin cast a protective charm around the group. A dome of light enveloped them, deflecting the slew of crossbow bolts and throwing knives.

"Drop it...now, Edwin!" Kaylee yelled.

Edwin did. Kaylee unleashed another torrent of ice toward the next Slayer before he brought the shield up again.

"I can't keep the charm up while moving, "Edwin said. "We need to make a break for the next street."

"There!"

Maddox pointed to a woman who had just appeared in the alleyway across from them, wielding a ball of magic in one hand.

"Hurry up!" she yelled.

"Go!" Edwin dropped the shield. Kaylee spun to buy them time to get to cover, but the Slayers above were all gone. In their place, thick vines curled over the lip of the building, like snakes seeking prey.

They nearly ran into Alastair when they stopped, panting, in the alleyway. His sleeves were rolled up, exposing glittering emerald scales. An aura of power emanated off him as his slitted eyes took them in.

"I see you all made it in one piece."

"We're not safe yet," the woman said. She double-checked the street was clear, then joined their group. She had a couple more people behind her now. One was Zaria, grinning at them.

"You guys finally decided to join the party."

"Chat later," the woman snapped, clearly not happy at having Zaria with them. "Alastair, we should move. My men are still scouring for any stragglers."

"So are mine," Zaria added.

The woman ground her teeth.

"Take them the rest of the way, Stephanie," Alastair said to her. "I'll round up the remainders and join you there."

Stephanie gave a small salute. "Yes, sir." Zaria rolled her eyes and gave a mocking salute of her own.

"Of course, your majesty."

Stephanie looked ready to punch her.

Alastair took one big step, then was airborne, lifted to the rooftop above in two flaps of massive, semi-transparent magic wings that had sprung from the back of his suit.

Stephanie beckoned them. "This way. Hurry."

They crossed the next street and took another series of turns until Stephanie pointed to a nearly hidden staircase attached to the side of a building. At the top was a single door lit by a dim bulb. They ascended and Stephanie rapped on the door. There was the scuffle of someone moving on the other side.

"There's no one here," a voice said.

"Because we don't exist," Stephanie promptly answered.

A deadbolt was pulled back and a middle-aged man ushered them in.

"In the back." He pointed, shutting the door and locking it as soon as they were all through.

Kaylee and the others squeezed through the hallway into a gratefully large living room. Already, the thrill of the fight was trickling out of her, leaving her arms and legs heavy. The others, too, looked exhausted. Any one of the numerous plush couches or chairs looked good enough to crash on.

"Well."

Stephanie brushed past Zaria and planted her hands on her hips. "Welcome to Rothsburg. You've made quite the mess."

CHAPTER TWENTY-TWO

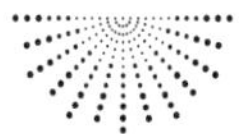

Kaylee wished she could reach into the sky and pull down the sun. It was too risky to make any move for the Book in the daytime, so the group was resigned to lying around the apartment until dark, while members of the Convocation and the occasional rogue from Zaria bustled in and out, eating lunch at the cramped table and then taking off for another round of patrols. It was clear the Convocation only tolerated Zaria's group grudgingly, no doubt on Alastair's orders. More than one disgruntled glance was shot their way whenever Zaria and her older rogues came in. It wasn't until Edwin got up and talked to one of the older rogues about what was happening with securing the Book that the two groups began to relax.

By the afternoon, Kaylee had grown too jittery to stay put. She paced around the apartment and managed to catch Stephanie's sleeve before she went out again.

"What's happening?"

"Nothing," Stephanie replied. "Museum's open as usual. We've got alternating watches on the Book."

"Then just grab it when they're not looking!" Kaylee said.

Stephanie gave her a look that immediately made Kaylee feel

childish. "I can guarantee that for every Protector and Merlin we have there, they have a Slayer just waiting for us to try something like that. There will be chaos the moment one of us goes for the Book, and I for one don't want unnecessary civilian casualties."

Kaylee didn't either, but she also didn't want to lose the Book. It was odd, however, that the Slayers were being so cautious. She remembered the djinn giant the Slayers had released in the mall the previous year. They hadn't cared about innocent casualties then, and it was only by a small miracle there hadn't been any. Now, despite nearly killing each other the night before, it seemed the Slayers and Convocation were treating the daytime in Rothsburg as a cease-fire of sorts, rather than the chance to avenge their ancient blood feud.

"Relax, Kaylee," Zaria said as Stephanie tugged her arm free and left with her group. "You'll see action soon enough."

"I'm surprised you haven't tried for the Book yourself." Kaylee didn't intend the retort to be mean, just fact. And apparently Zaria saw it that way too, because she shrugged.

"Alastair and I have an understanding. Priority numero uno is getting the Book away from the Slayers. Then we can quibble over the details. Like how and when he's going to deliver it to me."

She finished off the rest of an apple and popped the core into her mouth. There was a crunching sound, almost like metal grinding metal. Zaria nodded to her.

"See ya soon."

After more hours spent whittling away time watching Jade and Maddox sharpen their weapons, and Dani trying to teach them a modified form of gin rummy she'd learned on the debate team, Stephanie returned. She didn't look tired at all, despite spending all day scouting.

"Almost time," she assured them. "Alastair should be here any moment and we can—ah, there he is."

The man at the front door opened it and Alastair and Zaria

came in. Alastair accepted a water bottle from one of the Protectors.

"We're all ready to go," he said to Stephanie. "Zaria will be with me. The rest of you have your assignments. We'll begin in..." He checked his watch. "Half an hour. A little before the museum closes."

"It'll still be light out," Stephanie warned.

"For a bit, but that's a risk I'm willing to take. I have a feeling there were more Slayers there than we originally thought."

"How many?"

"At least thirty."

Stephanie paled. A couple of the Merlins nearby let out hisses of disdain. Zaria merely rolled her eyes and said, "We can take 'em."

"You all know your jobs and you're good at them," Alastair said. "There're more adversaries than we thought, but that just proves this book is more at the crux of whatever plan they have than we thought. Once we get it, we'll deal them a severe blow."

"Once *I* get it," Zaria corrected, earning the glares from other Convocation members. "Our deal, Alastair."

"Has not been fully discussed, and now is not the time," Alastair said.

"We await your signal," Stephanie said. She gave Alastair another small salute, then motioned to the other Convocation members to follow her.

"Where's our position?" Kaylee asked.

Alastair gave her a level look. "Before I tell you that, I want your assurance that whatever familial ties you have invested in this won't cloud your judgement. At least, cloud it no more than it usually is."

"I promise—"

"This isn't just about your brother, or Randy. A lot of good men and women are putting their lives on the line for the safety of the Convocation. If your focus on seeking out or getting back at somebody is going to hinder that, then you need to stay here."

Kaylee felt hot embarrassment flush through her, along with the sensation of every eye in the room.

"I promise. But if we find either of them—"

"Then either I or Stephanie will determine what to do at that time." Alastair paused to let that sink in. Then, "Edwin, if you please."

Edwin flicked his hand. A large map of the museum flew off the table and hovered in front of them.

"We're approaching from multiple points," Alastair said. "Our main objective is to hold off the Slayers long enough for us to disarm whatever electronic and magical alarms the Book may have and extract it safely. I will be leading the main team to the second floor where the Book is. We'll have four more groups spread out. Two on the third floor, and two on the first floor."

Alastair tapped the lower level, consisting of storage, Griffon theatre, and one lonely display of navigational instruments from the 1800's.

"I'm assigning Kaylee, Jade, Edwin, and Maddox here. Dani, since you're so new at this, I'm inclined to keep you here in the safe house."

Dani stuck out her chin. "I'm part of this. I should be there, too."

Alastair nodded with approval, as if that was exactly the answer he wanted to hear. "Agreed. However, since you haven't had as much training as the others I'm placing you with an outer perimeter squad. Your job is to keep your eyes open and alert us of any changes outside the museum."

"Like Slayers going in?"

"Precisely."

Maddox raised his hand. "Um, there's nothing on the lower level. I don't think the Slayers are going to actually care about it."

Alastair quirked an eyebrow. "That's exactly why I'm putting you there."

"You can't keep us out of the fight!" Kaylee said. "I thought we were as much a part of this as anyone else!"

"Miss Richards, I think you misunderstand me. Although I agree it's time you contribute more to the Convocation, don't think for a moment that means I'm going to be stupid about it. There's a big difference between allowing you on this mission and throwing you into the heart of the fray alongside Merlins and Protectors with years of experience and an enemy composed of trained killers."

"But—"

"If this doesn't sound good, you can always stay here," Alastair added.

"We're fine with it, Alastair," Jade said while Kaylee bit her tongue.

"Good choice." Alastair pulled the map from the air and rolled it up.

"There will come a time where you will be on the front line, Miss Richards." He slapped the map into his open palm, his voice taking on a deadly serious edge. "And at that time, I promise it will be the last place in the world you'll want to be."

THE MUSEUM GROUNDS WERE SILENT. The dark tint of the sky settled an oppressive weight in the air, creating the sensation of something big about to begin.

Maddox checked the watch Alastair had given him. Their cell phones had long since started acting up with all the excess magic in the air.

"The other teams should be heading in."

"Then we should too," Kaylee said.

She tried focusing her magic to her eyes. The Eyes of Dragon were one of the more advanced shifting techniques. Despite her eyes naturally changing when she shifted, Kaylee wouldn't actually get any benefit from it unless she knew how to harness the sudden flood of new information it provided. She usually didn't, and, much like shifting her ears, harnessing that information was difficult.

When she pushed her magic through her eyes, the grounds came into sharper focus. Color became richer. Supposedly, when she got really good at it, she'd be able to see as well in the dark as she did in the light, and even through walls, but right now the only thing she could make out near the museum was a murky haze. Certainly not a glimpse of Slayers or Randy like she'd hoped.

"I've got nothing," Kaylee said.

"Me neither," Jade said. "We're clear."

Kaylee shook her head to clear her vision, then followed the others.

They ran through a small rock garden and between some hedges until they came to a loading area where Kaylee guessed the latest exhibits were delivered. Maddox stepped up to the key pad at the door and held out a small charm. The charm frizzed and sparked where it touched the metal. The keypad beeped green.

"Wait." Maddox blocked their way inside. "I want to know if what you said to Alastair was true, Kaylee. That this isn't some revenge against your brother or Randy."

Kaylee tried to push past but he held his ground. She sighed. "This isn't the time, Maddox."

"This is the perfect time. This is different than other things we've done. We've done some pretty stupid stuff, but no one would have gotten hurt except us if we'd screwed up. Now other people could be hurt. *Especially* us."

"This isn't about Randy or Reese," Kaylee said firmly. "But I wouldn't be against running into them, either."

"Let's go, Maddox," Jade said. "She said what you wanted to hear. Get inside before some Slayers come along."

"Dani will let us know before that happens," Edwin said. He glanced at the surrounding gardens, as though he knew exactly where Dani was, crouched along with the other perimeter scouts.

Maddox finally nodded and pushed the rest of the way inside.

They entered a low-ceilinged basement, lit only by the faint glow of after-hours security lights. Stacks of irregularly shaped wood boxes were laid out in an indecipherable order in front of metal racks piled with unpacking tools.

Jade put a finger up and they paused. After a moment, she motioned them forward.

"We're the first ones here," she said.

"At least in the lower level," Edwin added. "I'm not sensing any magic charms."

They moved slowly, Jade and Maddox always keeping one step ahead of them despite Kaylee trying to nudge her way forward. They found a door marked 'Gallery.' Through this was the navigational instruments display, and at the end, stairs to the first floor.

"Now what?" Kaylee whispered into the dim.

"We wait," Jade answered. "Edwin, you should probably set alarm charms back in the unloading room. That's the only entrance down here. Kaylee and I—"

A loud thump from the floor above cut her off. They waited, but only silence followed.

"Are you *sure* the Convocation's the only one in here?" Kaylee said.

"We should be," Maddox said, but he didn't sound so confident anymore. "The scouts haven't reported any Slayer movement."

"The Slayers should have approached by now," Edwin muttered. "They've got the cover of darkness. What are they waiting for?"

"Maybe they don't need to break in," Maddox said.

The thought made Kaylee shiver. "I'm going to check upstairs."

She made it to the foot of the stairs before Jade caught her arm.

"We stay down here!" she hissed.

"There's no one down here. I'm just taking a look. What if Alastair and the others need help? What if we could be doing something?"

"Then Alastair would have asked us. Like he said, just because we're on this mission doesn't mean we have to be in the thick of—Maddox!"

"Just taking a peek," Maddox said, slipping past them. "Edwin's setting the charms to cover our back."

Kaylee hurried up after him, Jade following with some truly murderous muttering under her breath.

The first-floor entrance was shadowed and silent. A statue of a giant sloth sat on a habitat re-creation in the center. The second-floor balcony ringed above, while across and catty-corner were the stairway entrances to the Ancient Sea Creatures and Ancient Weapons halls.

"We're all clear," Maddox whispered.

Kaylee held up a hand. In a moment, she'd shifted her ear, amplifying the quiet around her. The sounds of the sleeping museum echoed in her head. The gentle creak of the strained lines holding the displays up; the whirr of the air conditioning.

There. Kaylee cocked her ear. Above to her left. The sound of pattering feet on tile. A soft cry of pain, quickly swallowed by the eerie silence. The more Kaylee listened, the more she got the impression that an entire silent battle was being fought all around them.

Then she saw the body.

The security guard's prostrate form stuck out to her once her eyes had completely adjusted. He lay face down in front of the giant sloth statue, covered in blood.

"Cover me."

In a second, Kaylee had slid in quietly next to the man and placed her finger on his pulse. Alive. Barely. A single large gash on his head oozed blood.

Jade slipped beside her, eyes narrowed darkly on the wound. "Our guys would never do this."

"Grab his other arm," Kaylee said. Jade did. Together they tugged him over to a frantically waving Maddox still at the stairs.

"Are you crazy? I just wanted to look, not stick our heads out!"

"See if Edwin can heal him," Kaylee said.

She sensed the movement before she saw it; felt the spark of magic running up her spine a second before an orange blaze of light erupted toward them.

"Found some!" a man shouted.

Kaylee didn't have time to shout a warning. On instinct, she dragged her arm up, pulling together a burst of lightning that sliced the orb hurtling toward her in two.

It wasn't enough.

Half the orb struck the ground near Kaylee and blew her back into the center of the hall. Her feet skittered for grip on the tile, her eyes searching for her attackers. Four shadows stood out on the railing above her. One of the figures pointed and another orange glow began to swell in his hand. But he didn't aim it at her.

"Jade!"

Jade still hadn't recovered from the first attack. The next attack flew toward her.

Kaylee leapt in front of her and managed to knock it away. The orb slammed into the giant sloth, exploding with a brilliant light and sending shockwaves of sound thundering throughout the entire museum.

There was a pause.

Then a battle erupted from every direction. It was as if Kaylee had fired the starting gun to begin the secret fight in earnest.

"Move!"

Jade pulled Kaylee to the opposite stairway as the Slayers on the second floor were attacked by members of the Convocation. Down the north hall, more shouting rose above the clang of metal on metal and shouted spells.

Jade caught Kaylee as she stumbled again. Her arm felt heavy and burned, the scales buzzing with unpleasant magic. The air smelled charred. Deflecting the blast had taken more out of her than she'd thought.

"Stay with me!" Jade hissed as footsteps pounded down the stairs toward them. Kaylee followed her, shaking her arm every few seconds to get the feeling back. They passed through the Ancient Sea Creatures exhibit; around a display case of Megaladon teeth and through the rib cage of a Liopleurodon. The exit bisected the planetarium and narrower Ancient Tribes exhibit. This part of the museum seemed empty.

"In there."

Jade paused to check around the corner, then waved them into the Ancient Tribes exhibit. When they finally slowed to a walk, Kaylee could barely make out the distant thumps and bangs of the battle overhead.

"How does it feel?" Jade said.

Kaylee shook her arm again. The singed sensation was still there, but at least she could move it.

"It's my job to protect you, not the other way around," Jade said.

"Darn. Guess you'll have to start keeping track."

"Can't. I left the score cards at home."

Another prickling feeling started at the base of Kaylee's neck. They'd just passed through the atrium of the Ancient Tribes exhibit and entered a half circular room. Against one wall was a scene of three cavemen fending off a pair of saber-tooth cats. The rest of the walls were glass displays filled with arrowheads, spears, and something called an unbreakable knife. Prehistoric birds hung on thin metal wires overhead.

"Let's get back to the others," Jade was saying. "I'm sure the Slayers are running their own interference while they go for the Book. We just need to stay out of their way long enough to get back to our position."

Kaylee whipped around. The prickling sensation had grown, sending more shivers down her arms. She didn't see any Slayers. The sounds of battle were still as muffled and distant as ever.

"Trouble?" Jade said.

"I'm not sure," Kaylee said.

"You still have Dani's map? I think this hall connects—"

One of the saber-tooths moved. Its glass eyes glinted their direction as its powerful body stepped off the display toward them.

Kaylee's voice had lodged in her throat. "Jade—"

"Hold on. I've almost got the map out—"

"Run!"

The saber-tooth pounced. Kaylee sprang to the side and the creature brushed past her, carrying the scent of stale fur and plaster. As she landed, Kaylee crouched and spun—just as the saber-tooth attacked again. Vicious fangs tried to sink into her throat but Kaylee blocked with a scaled arm. The cat's jaws clamped around it, inches from her neck. Its claws skittered on the tile, swiping for her exposed skin. One claw caught her shoulder, and her eyes watered with silent agony.

Just as Kaylee's arm was about to give, there was a dull thump and the saber-tooth's weight was lifted off her. Jade leapt after the cat as it was pushed off, continuing to drive her knife into the animal's side. The saber-tooth swiped but Jade yanked her knife out and stabbed again.

"It's not alive!" Kaylee gasped, getting to her feet. "Edwin told me about this. A Slayer's animating it."

"You mean like that guy?" Jade pointed. A man had stepped from behind an exhibit and was calmly walking toward them. He held two magicked gauntlets ahead of him, carving blazing runic symbols in the air.

"And here I thought I'd have the boring job tonight," the man said.

"I'll handle the saber-tooth," Kaylee muttered, eyeing the cat as it prowled around them. "You deal with Mr. Power Trip over there."

They split as the saber-tooth pounced again.

Kaylee slid around the display of a caveman hunting. She wrenched the spear from the display's hands (*really* hoping this guy didn't come to life, too) and gripped it close.

The saber-tooth leapt over the display and Kaylee drew back and swung. The spear snapped on impact and what felt like a ton of fur and fangs collapsed on her. Magic burned the air, singeing the saber-tooth's skin. The cat's next swipe missed and Kaylee kicked out, using a burst of wind to propel her to safety.

"Any time now, Jade!" she yelled.

"Trying!" Jade flipped over another bolt of magic the Slayer lobbed at her. Every time she drew close the man would fire another blast, sending her scrambling for cover.

Then Kaylee remembered the birds. The Slayer was now standing directly beneath them.

"Look up!"

Jade did. She grinned, wound up, and threw her knife. The blade whipped through the air, snipping the cords. The Slayer had only a second to cry out before the display smothered him.

The saber-tooth slammed into Kaylee's side. She expected sharp teeth tearing into her skin, but nothing happened. She waited a second longer for it to move, but the cat had gone stiff. After another moment, Kaylee managed to shift it off her. The saber-tooth had transformed back into its display position, now with the addition of multiple stab wounds and a chipped tooth.

Jade helped her up. "Good thinking."

"Good throw."

The last prehistory bird display snapped its line and smashed to the floor below. One of the cavemen toppled over.

"We should...probably go," Jade said.

They hurried out before anything else could come to life.

The corridor outside was even emptier than before. The sounds of battle were quieter than they'd been before. Either the fight had moved to another part of the museum, or more people were dead or injured than Kaylee had thought.

Jade pointed at a sign at the next intersection. "There's the way to the entrance hall."

"Wait a sec."

Kaylee had spotted another sign. It pointed to the nearest staircase, simply labeled: *Second Floor—Grand Hall.*

"Kaylee, no, we can't—"

But Kaylee was already charging up, focusing on keeping her footsteps light so they didn't echo. After two flights, the stairway opened into a wide hall. A concave ceiling arched overhead. Rows of display cases lined the outside, but it was the center piece that stole her attention: A display of a herd of Wooly Mammoths; and a T. rex skeleton, massive and imposing in the dim light.

"Where's Alastair?" Jade said, her present confusion overriding her earlier annoyance at Kaylee. "The Celtic Gallery is just ahead. His team should be here by now."

"Maybe they already grabbed the Book," Kaylee said hopefully, not believing it.

Together they snuck into the hall, staying as quiet as possible, Kaylee with her claws bared, Jade with her knife out.

"I do believe," a cruel voice said from the darkness behind the T. rex, "the last time we met it didn't turn out well for you."

Kaylee's heart stopped as Lesuvius stepped into the light. In one hand he clutched a leather-bound book. Behind him were two more Slayers, magic gauntlets glowing, and behind them—

Reese, a crossbow in hand, aimed right at Kaylee.

Lesuvius grinned, his face filled with pure malice.

"But I promise, this time, little dragon-kin, will be so much worse for you."

CHAPTER TWENTY-THREE

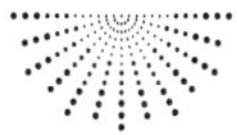

"I wouldn't do that."

Lesuvius held up a hand as Kaylee started toward him. The Slayers on either side raised their glowing palms higher. The weapon in Reese's hand began to shake, though his glare remained firmly fixed on Kaylee.

"Doesn't this just bring back memories?" Lesuvius purred. He cracked open the Book. "You may have stopped me last time, but I won't make the same mistake. Reese."

Reese flinched, as if Lesuvius had hit him.

"Yes, sir?"

"Kaylee is your sister, correct?"

Reese's hand shook more. He put his other one up to help steady it. "She…is, sir."

"You told me none of your family was involved in the Convocation. In fact, I distinctly remember you assured me that wasn't the case. That it would never be the case."

"I didn't know, sir."

Lesuvius' smile widened. He didn't seem surprised at all. "How shocking. If only you *had* known. I wonder, how would your loyalties have changed?"

"Sir—"

"Because not only is your sister in the Convocation, she's their prize player. The rare and powerful storm dragon-kin. Now, Reese, do you know what happens to members who lie to me?"

Reese's eyes flickered to the other Slayers. They shifted their magic toward him. "Sir, I swear I had no idea what she was."

"But you suspected for some time, didn't you? Yet you never said a word to any of us. Do you know how that looks to the rest of us?"

The Slayers' gauntlets began glowing brighter. Lesuvius sighed.

"Normally I'd kill you myself, but I've got a Herald to summon and I'm feeling generous, so I'll give you one chance to crawl back into my good graces. Your sister. Kill her."

"Sir—we have the Book—"

One second Reese was standing, then he was on the floor, nursing a bleeding jaw while Lesuvius hovered over him, his body practically glowing with rage.

"If there's one thing I hate more than liars, it's *excuses*. Kill her, or I'll kill you and then send her to join you." He spat at Reese's feet and swept to face them again. "Oh, and for a little added help..."

Jade pulled Kaylee aside as the two Slayers carved orange symbols in the air. With another push, the symbols sank into the bones of the T. rex skeleton.

"Crap," Jade said.

"That can't be good," Kaylee said.

There was a high-pitched screech. The fasteners in the ceiling snapped free. Flecks of plaster rained from the T. rex's jaws as they snapped shut. Reese was fixed in horror as the T. rex shook itself, bones cracking, then took a step off the platform. Reese's eyes met hers.

"*Run*," he mouthed.

The T. rex roared, a raspy, grating screech. Kaylee swallowed a scream as she dodged its immense jaws as they tried to grab her. The ground rumbled beneath her as she sprinted into the nearest hallway, too scared to look back, her breath tearing in her lungs. The vibrations beneath her grew stronger. Another raspy roar screamed at her back.

Kaylee spun around the next corner, tripped, caught herself, pumped her legs to keep going. The T. rex couldn't stop in time and collided with the opposite wall with a screech of metal and bone. Kaylee paused for breath but already the creature was shaking itself off. Its empty eye sockets fixed on her and Kaylee saw nothing but hollow, ceaseless hate within them.

Her magic wouldn't stop it. Even if it could, the amount she'd need to hurt this thing meant she couldn't run and use magic at the same time.

That left only the winding escape of the hallways. If she could lose it there—

The T. rex's jaws came down just behind her. A hard blow slammed Kaylee's shoulders and then her feet were lifted from the ground. She tensed, just before colliding with a display case. Glass and ancient swords toppled on top of her. An alarm buzzed overhead, washing the area in red light. The T. rex had nearly slipped on the floor again and skidded straight past her. Its massive head whipped around, trying to find where she'd gone. Kaylee stayed motionless beneath the pile of weapons, praying whatever senses this dead thing had been granted couldn't find her.

The T. rex sniffed the air, and Kaylee stifled a scream of horror—but no, it was nudging the blaring alarm. It gave a disgusted snort and stomped down the hallway.

Quiet as she could, Kaylee slid out from the pile of glass and metal. She backtracked into the Ancient Greeks gallery. A replica Trireme sat in the center, surrounded by displays of armor and weapons. She was forced to crouch behind the closest one, letting the pain of her cuts from the glass pass, and her thoughts catch up with what had happened the last few minutes.

Lesuvius. The Book. Jade.

Her brother.

Kaylee forced him and his pleading face from her mind. If she thought too much about him she might start crying, and right now she needed a clear head. Without a doubt, Lesuvius was at this very moment cheerily summoning the ancient Arthurian death dude to come kill them all, and she needed to figure out a way to stop him.

But how? He had the Book, and that bony monstrosity prowling around looking for her put a real dent in any idea that involved directly attacking. She was tired, in pain, and wanted more than anything to bury a scaled fist in Lesuvius' smug face.

"Kaylee?"

Kaylee flattened herself against the display case. In the reflection of the case across from her, she saw Reese enter the room. He held up a crossbow, sweeping it back and forth. "Kaylee?"

Immense sadness weighed her down. She had thought, maybe, when the time came, she'd be able to face him. But seeing him now...she couldn't do this. Not to Reese. Not to her brother.

And in that moment, Kaylee understood once again what Randy had meant; how this life they were all involved in took their family and all the things she once thought stable and untouchable and showed just how fleeting and fragile they really were. How the Slayers could turn Reese into something she knew he wasn't. She *couldn't* fight him.

He would have to kill her.

Kaylee stepped out from behind the display. Reese's eyes locked onto her.

"You're bleeding," he noted.

Kaylee shrugged. "Happens when you're attacked by a T. rex."

"Kaylee, I want you to know I never wanted—"

"Never wanted this? Never knew exactly what Lesuvius and the Slayers were doing?"

Reese opened and closed his mouth, as though the right words might fly into them.

"If you aren't going to shoot me then can you please put that thing down?" Kaylee said.

Reese dropped the crossbow with a loud clatter.

"Lesuvius," he said slowly, "he told me...he promised no one in my family would be hurt. They must have known you were part of it, but they never said anything...*no one* said anything!"

"Would it have changed your mind if you'd known?"

"Of course!"

"So you only stand by their values if you have nothing in the game to lose."

"You don't understand!" Reese's voice was strained, pleading. It cut through Kaylee like a sour wind, drowning out the sounds of battle ebbing and flowing in the rooms around them. "The Slayers...what they're doing is right. They're trying to make the world safer. For everyone."

"By killing those they deem as dangerous?"

"By killing the monsters who threaten us. Who threaten our way of life."

"The monsters? And what am I, Reese?"

"Don't, Kaylee. Don't make me say it. Can't you see how much this hurts?"

"What *am I*, Reese?"

Reese pulled his eyes up to meet hers, but for a moment they weren't Reese's eyes, but Brendan's. They held the same fervor and passion; the same perverted belief that what they were doing was the absolute right thing, end of story.

"You're a freak," Brendan's face said.

"You're my sister," Reese said.

"And a dragon-kin," Kaylee added. "And I promise whatever Lesuvius told you is a lie. He's using you to get what he wants.

Yeah, there are some bad dragon-kin and Convocation members. But we're no worse than any of the other bad things in the world."

Reese let out an exasperated breath. Their argument seemed to be taking a physical toll on him. "Then what…then who…?"

"It isn't as easy as hating the Convocation and blaming all of your problems on us."

Again Brendan's face stared back, and Kaylee had to focus to keep staring at him, even though it hurt.

"It *has* to be that easy," Reese said. "Because if not—if what he's been telling me is wrong…then everything I've done and believed in for the last year is a lie."

Kaylee took a hesitant step forward. "It's wrong. You're wrong. And I'm sorry he lied to you. But I won't apologize for what I am, and I won't make excuses for what you've done. That was your decision, and all the consequences that came with it."

And as she said those words, it felt as if she was speaking beyond the room, speaking to someone other than Reese. As she watched, Brendan's face faded, then vanished for good, leaving only her brother standing before her.

Kaylee put a gentle hand on Reese's ice-cold cheek. He flinched but didn't pull away. Warm tears spilled from his eyes. After a moment, he covered her hand with his.

"Please. Don't hate me."

"I don't."

"You should."

"I don't. We can still fix this."

"How? Lesuvius has the Book. He's probably already summoned the Herald."

Kaylee couldn't help grinning. "It'll be tough, but I'll bet Lesuvius didn't mention that last time he and I met he got his butt whupped."

"Seriously?"

"Worse than the Scarsdale football team during homecoming."

"What do you think we should do?"

"First off," Randy said, "we should stop talking about our feelings and get to actually attacking the guy who's trying to kill us."

Kaylee spun around. "Randy!"

Randy nodded, but didn't stop looking at Reese. Kaylee looked back and forth between them. She was still in shock at finding him here, but it seemed that shock still wasn't quite enough to dispel the grudging feud between them.

"Guys, you can talk about this later."

"I agree," Randy said. "We'll have plenty of time to sort out our differences when we're not in mortal peril. That includes telling your parents about your extracurricular activities, Reese."

Reese grimaced.

Randy closed one clawed hand and the brief hum of electricity Kaylee had just now noticed in the air died. He fixed her with a pointed stare.

"I thought I'd find you here, Kaylee. Right where you can get in the most trouble. A T. rex? Really?"

"I asked, but they were all out of rhinos."

Randy chuckled. "That," he pointed at Reese's magicked gauntlet. "You actually know how to use that thing?"

"Of course."

"Good. Lesuvius is almost done with the spell and Alastair and Zaria have almost broken through to the second floor. I'll take on Lesuvius and I want you two—"

A sudden blast of nausea slammed into Kaylee's gut. The air itself turned acrid. A *wrongness* seeped into her bones, a perversion of magic itself that made her skin crawl.

Randy pushed himself off the nearest display case he'd slumped against. For once, he almost looked scared.

"Crap. He finished faster than I thought. Hurry!"

Kaylee followed Reese back through an adjoining chamber and up another corridor leading to the Grand Hall. Each step toward it weighed her down, as if the strangely emanating light up ahead was pushing her back.

"It's the Herald." Randy put a hand on her back and held her in place. "His very presence affects our kind. You need to fight it. Use your magic to block his out."

"How?"

Randy rapped his knuckles on the top of her head.

"Please tell me all that teaching I did didn't slip right through your skull."

Kaylee crouched, her legs suddenly unsteady. Every pulse of magic ahead battered on her, but she drew from her magic within, dispersing it through her body, creating a dampening shield.

"Better?" Randy said after a moment.

Kaylee stood. "Better."

Reese was motioning to them from the doorway to the Grand Hall. Beyond him, Kaylee could see Jade's motionless form. The two of them had been split the second the T. rex had gone after Kaylee. Now, Kaylee swallowed a sob at seeing her friend lying there. If anything had happened to her...

Kaylee burst into the Grand Hall. Lesuvius stood before a burnt orange portal that had opened in the ground. Kaylee stared at it, her mind trying to grasp what she was seeing. It didn't make sense. Inside looked as though time itself had been shoved into a blender and liquefied into a viscous substance. It was impossible to make out any solid shapes. Just staring at it made her head hurt.

"Ah, the brat returns," Lesuvius said. "Too late, I'm afraid."

He didn't seem surprised when Reese took a place beside Kaylee. "I won't lie and say I had high hopes for you, Reese. Your name will be erased with theirs as soon as—"

"Miss me, buttercup?" Randy said, appearing on Kaylee's other side. He cracked his knuckles, each *snap* sending up a shower of sparks. "Nice portal. Looks like you've been busy."

Lesuvius snarled. A white bolt of magic erupted from his palm, scorching the place Randy had stood just a moment before. The sour taste in the air was replaced by growing static and white-hot electricity. Randy charged and slammed into Lesuvius. The two went tumbling away in a flurry of magic and dragon claws.

Reese pushed Kaylee toward Jade and used his magic gauntlet to conjure a protective shield as the nearby Slayers fired their crossbows. "Get her out of here!"

"What about the Herald?"

Reese grimaced as another volley of shots cracked his shield. The portal remained open, and now Kaylee could make out a figure forming above it.

"We'll stop it somehow. Go!" He leaped toward the Slayers, forcing them to scatter.

Kaylee grabbed Jade's arm. Her insides screamed her friend's name, but she tried to remain calm. A pulse, she needed a—There!

Jade groaned when Kaylee flopped half her body over one shoulder, and Kaylee could have sobbed with relief. The opposite stairwell was directly in front of her. If she could reach it before the Slayers noticed—

An explosion ripped her off her feet. Kaylee went tumbling into the mammoth's display, tucking Jade's body close to her. Through the haze of disorientation, she could make out Slayers pouring from the first floor, firing backward as they ran. Behind them, Alastair's shouts were growing louder.

"Kaylee!"

Okay, now she was seeing things. Specifically, Edwin and Maddox, hurrying over from across the hall, ducking low to avoid any wayward spells.

"Kaylee?" Edwin's voice was murky as the blast noise cleared from her ear drums. "Can you move?"

"Jade," Kaylee said, though her mouth felt like it had cotton balls stuffed in it. "She's hurt."

"I got her." Maddox crouched and easily scooped Jade up into his arms. Some of the Slayers had noticed them now. The group ducked as lancing bolts of light snarled over their heads. Edwin fired back with some of his own, forcing some of the Slayers to cover.

"Get Jade out of here!" Kaylee shoved Maddox toward the stairs and she and Edwin slid behind the nearest mammoth's leg, Edwin hugging her close as another volley of spells tore out chunks of fur and plaster right beside them.

Kaylee whipped up a small frenzy of ice with one hand and lobbed it over her. The ensuing cries of pain told her she'd partially hit her mark.

"Lesuvius finished the spell," Kaylee said. "There's no way to stop the Herald."

A pulse of sick magic even stronger than before washed over her. Edwin held her steady as Kaylee cried out. It was a clawing pain on the inside of her skull. She forced her mind to focus, drawing more of her magic over her, forcing the Herald's out.

When the sensation passed, Kaylee risked a look. The portal was still there, but it was smaller now, shrinking every second. Now, a fully-formed figure stood atop it.

He had no face. Where his features should have been was instead as blank as a wall of rock, yet somehow infinitely more terrifying. He was dressed in Arthurian armor, perched upon a black horse with weeds and swamp moss writhing between the beast's partially skeletal ribcage. In his hand was an ivory horn with a single crack down the center.

The thing turned its face toward her and Kaylee's world stopped.

The Herald had arrived.

CHAPTER TWENTY-FOUR

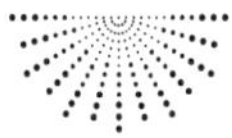

Kaylee couldn't move. Her legs grew so weak that she sank to the ground. Her scaled hands clacked on the tile as they shook.

Then Edwin grabbed the back of her shirt and pulled her into cover.

"Kaylee, focus on me." His voice sliced through her terror, his calming tone grounding her again. "Keep your magic shield up. This guy uses paralysis and fear to win. We can beat him, we just have to keep moving."

As if to prove his point, Edwin suddenly pulled her up again, nearly dislocating Kaylee's shoulder.

"Run!"

Scalding heat grew at their backs as they broke from behind the mammoth's leg, followed by an immense explosion and the creak of an exhibit toppling over. The smell of charred plaster clouded the air.

The Herald lowered his hands, then turned his attention to the other fighters around the room. Kaylee slid in next to Edwin behind the next display.

The Grand Hall was absolute chaos. Maddox had managed to

escape with Jade, but Reese was still holding back the other Slayers. One of their magic gauntlets had flown off and he was scrambling for it. Alastair, Zaria, and Protectors were engaged in a deadly back and forth with a group of Slayers in the gallery beyond. The far wall exploded and Randy landed in a heap on the floor. Lesuvius walked through the hole. His muscles had swelled to an almost grotesque size. There was a barely restrained aura of magic surrounding him.

"Finally going to pay your penance, Conners?" Lesuvius jeered. "You're a few years too late and too weak for that." He gripped Randy by the collar and held him so they were face to face. "When I ask you something, I don't take no for an answer. You *embarrassed* me."

Randy gave a bloody grin. "Oh dear, did I? Thing is, my friend, you embarrassed yourself long before I did."

Randy lowered his voice so that Kaylee missed what he said next, but Lesuvius' eyes bulged with rage. He brought up a swirling ball of magic. "Die."

"You aren't moving your feet," Randy said.

He turned his palms down and shot a bolt of electricity into Lesuvius' legs. Lesuvius jerked, then roared in pain, hurling Randy through the wall of the Ancient Celtic hall.

"What's taking so long?" he barked at the Herald. "I've done my part, Herald! Summon the Hunt!"

"I have not yet regained my strength," the Herald replied, his voice rasping, slithering through Kaylee's senses.

"Then hurry it up! I've wasted enough time already." Lesuvius hurled himself after Randy.

Edwin grabbed Kaylee's arm. "I'll help Randy and Reese. You need to destroy the Herald."

"What?" Kaylee's voice came out as a breathy squeak. "How do you expect me to do that?"

"Remember when we fought the scarabs? Remember what I said then?"

"Of course I don't! That was forever ago!"

"Just look."

Kaylee followed Edwin's finger and peered at the Herald. He hadn't attacked anyone else. In fact, he'd barely moved at all. He sat in the same spot, head bowed, as if he'd simply nodded off in the middle of the fight.

"Look closer at his body," Edwin said.

Kaylee really didn't want to, but she did. She narrowed her eyes.

"He's...see-through."

"Barely," Edwin agreed. "He's not done manifesting in the physical plane. The components of the magic Lesuvius used to summon him are still pulling themselves together."

Kaylee laughed nervously. "Lesuvius does have a tendency to pick the slowest summoning spells."

"And we're going to use that against him. Same principle with the scarabs applies here. There's no counterspell, but if we can hit the Herald—and by we I mean you—with enough power, it'll disperse whatever hold he has here. Hopefully badly enough that Lesuvius can't summon him for a long, long time."

"Edwin..."

"Kaylee." He titled her chin up. His face looked so earnest in his belief that it hurt. "I know you can do this."

Kaylee let out a calming breath. She pulled her focus from how much pain she was in and the battle around her, and instead concentrated on the magic inside. A burning coal of power settled in her stomach, ready to be unleashed. A growl of indoor thunder rumbled overhead.

A single drop of rain pelted Edwin's glasses. "That's my girl."

"You're positive this is the only way?"

"The best way, yes. I would never ask you if I weren't sure."

"You'll owe me big time if I live through this."

Edwin placed gentle hands on either side of her face. "How about I pay a little thanks in advance?"

Thunder roared as Edwin kissed her. No matter how hard she tried, Kaylee couldn't tell if it was his warm lips or her magic that sent a bolt of energy shooting through her body. Her fingers laced through his hair, intertwining even as his own fingers cupped the back of her neck. Sparks trembled up and down her arms. She leaned in, trying to draw closer, wanting to taste more of him.

And then they broke apart. Edwin's glasses were askew. His hair stuck out as if struck by lightning.

"Should have done that a long time ago," he said breathlessly.

Kaylee forced her own heart to stop pounding. "Don't worry, I won't let you forget it."

"Be careful."

He waited until the nearest Slayers were distracted and then leapt into the fight, hurling bolts of magic at their exposed flanks.

Her mind still shooting off a hundred thousand different directions, Kaylee re-focused on the Herald. His head was still bowed—charging, asleep, whatever. Vulnerable. That's all she cared about.

Every cell in her body railed against her as she stepped out of cover and ran at him. She was the prey in this scenario, the rabbit defying the wolf with nothing but a bundle of lightning cupped in one hand.

Kaylee wrapped herself up in her magic and gave another burst of speed. She drew back her arm...

The Herald's head snapped up a moment before Kaylee collided with an invisible barrier. She stumbled back. Her mouth filled with blood as she bit her tongue. Her knee throbbed where she'd slammed it into the wall.

"Interesting..." the Herald's murky voice pulled her away from the sudden pain. "Clearly you don't know how our relationship works, beast."

The Herald's horse stomped its hooves, snorting hissing

steam. The Herald lowered one hand and aimed it at Kaylee. Swirls of magic gathered within it.

"I am your death, and you cannot escape me."

The attack decimated the tiles where she'd stood. Kaylee rolled, pulsing wind magic to shove herself away. Her feet barely brushed the ground as she rode her storm's current of air, keeping one step ahead of the Herald as he reined his horse around to follow her.

Kaylee leaned in and struck again. Her claws raked the barrier, but it didn't do any good. She tried hitting it with ice, her claws, even more lightning, but every time the Herald was there to intercept her attack.

"That is enough!" He roared.

The horse stomped its hooves and a sudden blast of magic threw Kaylee back. Needles of darkness cut into her skin.

"You bore me, dragon," the Herald said. "Surrender, tell all those who fight with you to surrender, and when I call my master he may yet be merciful."

But Kaylee had stopped listening. Her attention was fixed on the still-shrinking portal. The Herald hadn't moved from it. *Couldn't* move from it. Which was why his gross little pony was stomping its feet in place rather than stomping on her.

A weakness.

Shouts of pain made the Herald turn. Alastair and his group had returned to the Grand Hall, drawing more combatants from both sides in to the fight. Zaria and her small group had circled around to close some of the fleeing Slayers in. Kaylee's eyes traveled above them all. Just below her storm hung more replicas of ancient birds tethered to the ceiling.

Leverage. She could attack the Herald from the sky. But how? How could she get high enough? She still couldn't shift her dragon wings. And the only exhibit she'd seen so far that could reach up there was the…

The T. rex exploded through the wall behind Kaylee, its gaping jaws closing around her.

Kaylee couldn't even scream. She pulled her limbs in as tight as she could as the skeleton's teeth closed around her like a trap. Her body was wedged in its bottom jaw, and through its bones she could see the ground now far, far below.

The T. rex's momentum smashed it into the opposite wall. Kaylee saw stars as her head hit the roof of its mouth. Its jaws opened and closed again, nearly skewering her again. Her claws scratched where his throat would have been, but the stupid thing didn't feel pain.

There! An opening!

The back of its jaw un-hinged every time it bit, just wide enough to latch onto if she could…only…just…

Kaylee twisted her body around, shifted her feet, and kicked up with all her might. The top of the skeleton splintered. The jaws cracked open just enough that she was falling, her claws latching onto the neck vertebra, then sliding down the rib cage before dropping to the ground.

Her legs gave. Her head slammed into the tile. But the pain was secondary to the pounding fear coursing through her as she stood. Above her, the T. rex stumbled, its bottom jaw flopping about uselessly.

But it was slowing.

And it was near the Herald.

And it was leverage.

MOVE. Kaylee's mind screamed as she began running. *Faster.*

The wind picked up behind her, carrying her in a way her wrecked bones and muscles couldn't. The air chilled her skin as she leapt for the T. rex's whipping tail, grasping it tightly. Kaylee ladder-crawled end over end, up the spine, her body no longer hers to control but on autopilot. Magic burned fierce and hot as she collected it from the storm above. Lightning crackled and snarled.

Now the Herald was below her. She was high enough now that she knew this fall would hurt. A lot.

Kaylee jumped.

A final burst of air carried her the rest of the way. She drew her lightning-filled claw higher as she plummeted toward the Herald.

The Herald looked up. And smiled.

He caught her by the throat, closing off her gasps of surprise. His other hand clamped down on her hand until her lightning dissipated. Until she heard her fingers snap. Hot tears of pain rolled soundlessly down her cheeks.

"Admirable," the Herald said. "But not enough."

"Then…try…this…" Kaylee wheezed.

Kaylee called on the storm and it obeyed. She felt the lightning descend, felt the prickle at her back and the white-hot bliss as it struck the top of her head and coursed through her body.

The Herald's eyes widened. His mouth opened in a silent scream of rage.

There was a burst of light.

"IMPRESSIVE."

Kaylee didn't know where the man had come from, only that he was *there*. Wherever *there* was. She didn't know. She expected her body to hurt, but it didn't. She expected to remember a struggle—a battle—magic—but that was all strangely distant now.

She was just…here.

The man stood facing away from her in front of a great stone fireplace. The room was heavy with warmth. It resembled Alastair's study, and although Kaylee wished to relax, maybe curl up by the fire, the man kept her on edge. She wasn't quite sure why.

“I haven’t seen this much resistance from a magical being since the days my King’s sister reigned,” the man added.

“Who are you?” Kaylee asked, glad her voice still worked.

The half of his face Kaylee could see gave a bemused smile to the fireplace. “You’ll know soon enough.”

“Where am I? Am I dead?”

“Oh no, my dear, not yet. You are in between. And where you think you are, I can’t say. It is different for everyone, and I have never completed the journey myself.”

The man took a long draught from a mug clutched in one hand.

“I will not try to reason with a being such as yourself, because I know in my heart it will be futile. I have sacrificed much toward the destruction of your kind, yet now my beloved followers see fit to allow you to spread like roaches. Alas.” Another sip. “But I shall fix that soon enough.”

Kaylee found herself reaching for a heavy, iron-bonded candlestick on the desk. She hadn’t intended to attack this man, but the guy was freaking her out. Plus, she wasn’t exactly a fan of getting called a roach.

The man chuckled as she raised it.

“You seek violence as your means. Typical. Though I suppose I do the same, do I not? You might as well put it down, girl. Neither of us can harm one another in this place. But…” He set his mug down and faced her. There was a dull thump as Kaylee dropped her candlestick onto the carpet.

The man could have been Lesuvius. He was not, she could see that now, but the resemblance was uncanny. His black hair was longer and swept back, his face haunting and beautiful and terrifying all at once. His eyes were hot embers, and they pierced her as easily as a Slayer’s spear.

“Yes,” the man said, taking a step toward her. The back of Kaylee’s knees hit the table and they crumpled as she tried to get away. “Yes, remember your will to destroy me and remember it well, for when I rise—and I *will* rise—you will have to strike me down with all your anger and all your hatred, or I will wreak destruction on your kind greater than I have ever managed before."

Those eyes were burning hotter, simmering the air. He reached one hand toward her.

A jolt thudded through Kaylee's chest.

"Ah..." The man's hand faltered in mid-air. "They call you back to the fight. Flee, little dragon-kin. Flee, and grow and thrive, but know that I am coming, and I will be your end."

Kaylee gasped and clutched her chest as another jolt punched through her. Then another. With each hit, the room faded a bit more. Bright white spots danced in her eyes.

Her last vision was the man's fiery eyes, burning her in the dark.

AIR SEARED Kaylee's throat and lungs and she reeled it in desperately. She was suddenly aware of the ceiling. The ceiling of what? The museum. Right? Right. She'd forgotten. But how had she gotten on the floor? And why did she hurt so much?

Randy's face appeared above her. He held up one electrified hand. He looked ready to plunge it into her chest again.

"I'm awake," Kaylee croaked.

Randy sagged with relief, scooping her closer to him. His face was scratched and soot-covered. His arms wrapped around her tighter as he rocked her, tears sticking on his chin. Slowly his rocking turned less desperate and his sobs tapered off.

"You're a real jerk to pretend to die on me like that," he said.

"Whoops. Sorry."

Her muscles were on fire when she moved, rolling over and sitting up on her knees. The Grand Hall didn't seem real. A fine coating of what might have been dust or ash trickled from the ceiling. The Herald, Lesuvius, and most of the Slayers were gone.

"How long was I out?"

"A few minutes. The second Lesuvius saw you'd stopped the Herald, he and the rest of his followers took the Book and ran. I'm sure Alastair, your brother, and that rogue dragon girl are after them right now."

It was then that Kaylee realized the portal—or what was left of it—was nothing more than a puddle of rippling magic, draining away like water at the bottom of a drain.

Randy tugged on her arm and helped her stand.

"We need to get clear. You knocked the Herald back to whatever hellhole he came from for now, but that portal is still unstable."

As if to prove his point, there was a sharp *snap!* A fissure appeared in the tile beneath Kaylee's feet. They looked at one another.

"Run," Randy said.

The portal pulsed outward. Magic tendrils seeped forth and grasped for anything nearby to suck in. The entire Hall shook, the noise like a stampede of elephants. Kaylee and Randy leapt over the tail of the downed T. rex skeleton and bolted for the stairs. The noise grew while they ran, a deluge of sound as the portal snapped and snarled its gasping final breaths.

Kaylee's legs crumpled when they hit the bottom floor.

"Come on!" Randy tried to pull her up, but her muscles had seized. Her magic was all but gone. Striking the Herald must have depleted her more than anything she'd ever done, and now her body was forcing her to stop.

Randy's head snapped up. A large chunk of the ceiling shook free and toppled the giant sloth.

"We need to move, Kaylee!"

"I'm trying!" She gritted her teeth and forced her legs to bend.

But they wouldn't be fast enough. The entire place was crumbling now. Any second, they'd be crushed by—

Reese broke through the curtain of debris and grabbed her other side. The combined effort was the boost Kaylee needed and they started running again.

"The Convocation has a retreat perimeter around the eastern exit," Reese yelled over the noise.

Randy nodded and pulled them that way. The exit door was ahead.

A creak and groan came from above them. The cables holding a model of the solar system snapped free one by one. Jupiter began tipping toward them. Randy's grip grew tighter on Kaylee's arm.

"Hold on!" he yelled.

There was a flap of wings. Kaylee's vision went into warp drive. The falling solar system plummeted ahead of them, then above them, then hit the floor behind with a tremendous crash, and they were stumbling up and out the exit.

The Slayers who had managed to escape the fight inside were beating a hasty retreat across the museum's back lawn, pursued by a collection of Merlins and Protectors. Some attempted to engage the Convocation, but large vines burst from the ground and wrapped them up. The trees of the garden leaned over and plucked or knocked the rest away. Alastair charged after the remainders. Zaria led her small group just behind him.

"This way," Randy said. "Keep to the outside and we'll get clear."

They stepped into the museum's sculpture garden just as three Slayers stumbled through the bushes. Both parties froze. The closest Slayer scrambled to raise his crossbow. Randy swore and shoved Kaylee behind him, but before he could attack, a jet of water burst from behind the nearest sculpture and slammed into the Slayers, knocking them senseless.

Kaylee, Randy, and Reese all gaped at Dani.

"Well come on!" she said. "There's more of them out here."

"Did you *see* that attack?" Randy said as they followed. "She makes all the progress you've made look like a joke."

"Remind me to punch you for that when I'm not half dead," Kaylee said.

Dani and the Convocation scouts led them out of the garden and across the front lawn. The entire time Kaylee felt a prickling growing at her back. The air around the museum was stirring. Then Reese yelled, "Get down!"

Randy grabbed Dani while Reese pushed Kaylee to the ground. An intense blast of heat seared her skin. All she could see was white, and then a beam of light erupted out of the roof of the museum, burning a hole through the cloud layer before vanishing.

Kaylee's muscles trembled. Sparks drifted from the sky and settled in the grass around the museum grounds. Kaylee felt as if she'd exited a long tunnel full of noise to nothing but perpetual silence. Randy was tugging her arm for her to get up, and Kaylee forced her grudging body to obey. She latched onto Reese and together the four of them left the museum and the threat of the Herald behind.

CHAPTER TWENTY-FIVE

Kaylee could hear the screech of voices clear across the safe house living room. Jade, a bandage wrapped across the gash on her forehead, held the phone at arm's length as her parents on the other end let loose. She gave Kaylee a pleading look.

"You want to deal with them?"

Kaylee shook her head as fast as her muscles would allow. "I already paid my price. You'd think Alastair had never given the OK for us to come along with the way my parents acted."

"Parental law overrides Convocation any day," Maddox said.

Edwin snorted. "You're one to talk. Your parents thought what we did was—what did they say? Gnarly?"

Maddox just grunted.

Jade eventually walked into one of the bedrooms to try to continue reasoning with Mr. and Mrs. Azuma. Kaylee could hear her calmly describing the dangers they'd faced ("Really, Mom, their swords weren't *that* sharp.") and playing down the severity of her injuries ("It only bled for, like, twenty minutes.").

She was actually right about the last part. Once Maddox had arrived at the safe house, a Merlin healer had set about stitching

Jade up. Besides the gash and a minor concussion, nothing else was too bad.

"Slayer got a lucky shot," Jade had told Kaylee when she'd returned and squeezed her friend to near suffocation. "Five on one, *plus* they had magic. *Then* they started bringing the Viking mannequins to life. I think it was Erik the Red who finally got me."

Kaylee hadn't been spared from her own form of parental interrogation. She'd awakened in the morning with an I-got-hit-by-a-dump-truck feeling in her bones, muscles, and brain, and a very startled-looking Stephanie holding a cell phone out to her.

"Your parents. They've called ten times and refuse to stop. I'm not even sure how they got this number."

Kaylee had fielded their questions for the better part of an hour. At one point, they'd asked if Reese was with her. Kaylee hadn't known how to answer that. According to Randy, he'd returned to the safe house to make sure she'd been taken care of, then vanished in the ensuing confusion as the rest of the Convocation trickled in and the Slayers fled Rothsburg.

She hadn't heard from him since.

Her parents had persisted in pestering Kaylee with questions until a large hand plucked the phone from her ear.

"She's been with me, Brianna," Randy said. "Yeah. Of course. *Of course* I've taken good care of her."

Kaylee pointed to the numerous scrapes and bumps on her legs, arms, and face. Randy rolled his eyes. "Mostly."

But he had taken care of her, Kaylee had to admit.

Now, as she looked around the living room at the others, she realized they all had gotten off with a lucky break, considering what they'd faced. Maddox didn't look any worse for wear save for a few scrapes of his own. Jade and Kaylee's injuries would heal with a solid week of rest. Dani had been in such high spirits after she'd saved them in the garden that she'd already headed back to Scarsdale with some of the Protectors she'd been assigned with.

And Edwin...

He glanced up and gave her a soft smile. Just that sent Kaylee's pulse racing. She thought of those smiling lips close to her own, kissing hers. And now with the heat of the battle over...

"Oh. My. Gosh." Jade emerged from the other room, tossed the phone on the table and slumped on the couch. "You know, for parents who want their kid to take part in the dangerous Tamer test next year, they're sure making this a waaaay bigger deal than it needs to be."

"Parents will be parents," Maddox said sagely. "Trained fighter or not."

Jade grumbled. She picked at the wrapping around her head.

"Don't," Maddox said, grabbing her hand. "It's only been a day. Let it heal."

"My hero..." Jade fluttered her lashes at him and Maddox crossed two beefy arms in a pout. Edwin grinned. His eyes flickered to Kaylee one more time and she got the impression he wanted to say something to her, but didn't want to say it here.

"Did anyone get the chance to talk to Dani before she left?" Jade said.

"I did," Maddox said. "You would never guess that girl hadn't been in a major fight before. Even the Merlins were impressed."

Kaylee couldn't help feel a small swell of pride for Dani. She was doing better than any of them could ever have hoped.

"What now?" Kaylee said.

"Not sure," Edwin said. "I think we're heading back to Scarsdale this afternoon."

"Back to the mundane," Maddox lamented.

"Back to relative safety," Edwin added.

Maddox swatted him playfully across Jade's shoulders. "All relative, Edwin my man."

"You know the Slayers will be launching a new plan soon enough."

Jade clenched her hands beneath her knees. "Then we'll be ready. Kaylee? Have you…heard anything about…you know?"

All three of them turned to Kaylee, and she could tell Jade instantly regretted asking her here, where Convocation members still moved about and everybody expected her to come up with an answer she didn't have.

Reese was gone, but Kaylee didn't know if he'd returned to the Slayers or not. She didn't see *how* he could after changing sides, but if there was one thing she knew about the Slayers, it was that their logic didn't always match up with anyone else's.

"No. I haven't heard. I thought I'd ask Alastair whether he knew."

"Or Randy," Edwin said.

"Randy's gone too."

"Already?" Jade said.

"I think so. I haven't seen him since he talked to my parents."

Jade still seemed shocked. "But to just show up out of nowhere and leave without saying anything?"

Just like Reese.

It was then that the weight of what had happened at the museum truly hit Kaylee. Reese, with the Slayers. Yet Reese, being the kind of brother he always had been to her. Helping her. Protecting her. Staying by her side. She was as confused about where his loyalties lay as he surely was, and she didn't know what to do about it.

"I'm going on a walk," Kaylee said.

"I don't think that's a good idea," Jade said. "The Slayers could still be hanging around out there."

Kaylee pointed to the kitchen window, the only sliver of the outside world they'd had since coming back to the safe house. "It's the middle of the day. I'll stay in public with other people."

Edwin stood. "Maybe I should—"

"And me," Jade added, wobbling a bit as she tried to stand.

"NO!"

Her friends jumped. Kaylee was as surprised as they were at her outburst. She sucked in a deep breath. "I just need a few minutes alone. Please."

She left before they could argue. She was lucky Stephanie and the rest of the Protectors were still out scouting. They definitely wouldn't have let her go, but Kaylee had the sudden, desperate desire to get outside; to free her body when she couldn't free her mind from everything racing through her head.

Reese. Randy. The Slayers. The Herald. The man she saw in the vision when she was…dead?

Kaylee nearly stumbled taking the stairs down from the apartment. A man in front of his own apartment gave her a concerned look. Kaylee waved before making it the rest of the way to the street below.

The fresh air and steady hum of the mid-day traffic instantly calmed her. Life. Despite all that had happened, life went on, trudging ever forward.

And she would too.

The Slayers had something else planned. They always did. Her brother…her brother had to figure things out for himself, things she couldn't help him with. But she'd get through that too. She was stronger now. She had her friends. And…Edwin.

Kaylee groaned, remembering the slightly shocked expression on his face when she'd shouted at them. He probably thought she hated him.

No…that was silly. He was a smart guy, he could figure out what she'd really meant.

What had she really meant?

Kaylee resisted the urge to bang her head against the nearest brick wall. Some days her thoughts were purposefully trying to drive her insane.

Kaylee cut right at the next street, drifting into the foot traffic frequenting the shops off the main strip. She stopped at an intersection. The museum was to her left. Even from here, Kaylee could see a number of emergency vehicles parked out front. The parking lot had been blocked, but a semi-truck with a tarp partially covering the bed rumbled out. As it turned, Kaylee caught a glimpse of a bony dinosaur arm poking out.

"What do you think happened?" a woman said.

"Robbery, I heard," a man answered.

"Terrorists," another added. "Museum was probably a secret government installation."

"Oh, if only that were true."

Kaylee bumped into Zaria as she whipped around. The other girl smirked. Black circles hung under her eyes. Her hair was more frazzled than usual.

"I see you're still as clumsy about personal space as ever."

"What are you doing here?" Kaylee blurted. "I thought you left with…"

"Randy?" Zaria guessed. "Please. Working alongside Alastair was bad enough. Put me next to Randall Conners and you *would* have a murder on your hands. No offense."

"I completely understand."

The stop light changed, and Kaylee and Zaria stepped to the side as a flood of pedestrians crossed the street. Zaria glared at the museum.

"Where're you going now?" Kaylee said.

It took a moment for Zaria to bring her attention back to Kaylee. She looked amused. "Wherever we want. Perks of being a rogue. Don't have to answer to anyone. You know, my offer still stands."

"Thanks, but no. I'm sure you'll find more than enough dragon-kin to take you up on that, but I've got too many people I care about in Scarsdale."

"Fair enough. It's not…it's not the worst Convocation I've ever come across. You've got something good."

"*You* could always join..."

"No," Zaria said quickly. "But we'll be in touch. I was promised that book and I intend to get it."

Kaylee planted a hand on her hip. "Alastair never said anything about giving it to you. And neither one of us got it."

"Doesn't matter. The Slayers have no right to it, and I'll make 'em pay for taking it."

She lifted a finger. A few of the loitering bystanders threaded their way toward them. Kaylee recognized them as Zaria's older rogues.

"See you soon, dragon girl. Try not to die before then."

"Same."

And with that, Zaria and the rogues melted into the crowd.

"She was exaggerating. I'm not that bad."

Randy smiled up at her, seated at an outside table at the corner Mexican café. The crinkles in his eyes rose when she gaped at him.

Alastair, sitting next to him, pulled out a chair. "Please, sit. I see common sense about staying out of sight has evaded you yet again. Or you, it."

Kaylee sat, still keeping her eyes on Randy.

"Look at her," Randy chuckled. "Probably thinks I'm a ghost." He poked her. "I'm really still here, Kaylee."

"I'm actually in shock that you and Alastair aren't fighting."

Alastair delicately folded his fingers together. "We can act like adults when necessary. And Randy and I have come to understand one another a little better."

"What's that mean?"

"Means after almost dying together, we hate each other just a little bit less," Randy said.

A waitress dropped a bowl of chips in front of them. Randy dipped one and popped it into his mouth. "Try the guac. Place is known for it."

"Why are you still here?" Kaylee said.

"In case you haven't noticed, there was a commotion down at the museum last night. Figured I'd best stick around and make sure everything's A-OK before I go."

"From what I've heard, right after a commotion is usually the time you'd be running."

Alastair snorted. Randy readjusted himself in his seat. "What you heard was only one side of the story. I hope my actions speak louder than words."

"They did this once," Alastair said. "I hope they do again. As I said before, the Convocation could use a man with your skills. And not just us; another could also benefit from having you around more..."

Alastair was bobbing his head her direction. Kaylee rolled her eyes. Suave he might be, but subtle he was not.

"I think I'll stick around a little longer," Randy finally said. "Some of Kaylee's techniques could use some refining."

"Excellent," Alastair said. "You also may have another joining you."

"Is Dani taking lessons?" Kaylee said.

"Not yet, but I'm sure she'll come around."

Randy shoveled a handful of chips into his jacket pocket. "Well then. Bright and early Monday, Kaylee. No excuses."

"Hold on!"

Randy paused as he stepped to the curb and swung one leg over the side of his motorcycle. Kaylee glanced at Alastair and lowered her voice. "Did you see where Reese went after the fight?"

Randy tugged his gloves down over his hands. "I'll let Alastair do all that neat tidying up stuff, okay?"

Customers glared and covered their ears as Randy kicked the engine to life and tore off down the road, weaving his way in and out of traffic.

Alastair cleared his throat.

"Tell me Reese didn't go back to the Slayers," Kaylee pleaded.

"We aren't sure where Reese is," Alastair admitted. "But if we find him—"

"He didn't know what he was doing, Alastair. Lesuvius tricked him. He—he *helped* us."

"Which is why, when we do re-establish contact with him, and we will, it will be to strictly monitor him only. Just to ensure he doesn't return to his old ways. According to what we know of his involvement with the Slayers, he's not so far gone with them that he can't change."

Kaylee sagged into her chair. "Thank you."

"Don't thank me. He may be your brother, Kaylee, but he is not our friend. We'll have to watch him from now on. Especially whenever Lesuvuis makes his next attempt to hurt us."

"He got the Book."

"He got the Book. Zaria isn't happy, as I'm sure you noticed, and neither are we. But you did manage to slow the Herald, and through him, the Hunt. Though for how long, I can't say."

Kaylee couldn't help her eyes drifting back down the street to the emergency vehicles and front of the museum.

"I don't want you to worry about Reese," Alastair said.

"Excuse me?" Not *worry*? That was literally the exact opposite of what she should be doing, save actually getting out there and tearing up the roadways looking for him.

"You have many, many other things that will need your attention. And Reese is, I believe at heart, a good kid. I trust—as should you—that he will make the right choices. In a way, his time with the Slayers can almost be counted as a good thing."

"Okay, now you're really losing me."

"He was on his self-destructive pathway and mindset long before the Slayers got to him. Most of their members are. The Slayers don't convince people to join their cause, they incite what someone's already started to believe, feeding on their perceived injustices in the world. In that sense, Reese was already doomed. But now that he's seen the Slayers' way of trying to solve problems, maybe he won't go down that road again."

Alastair sighed. "I know you've talked quite a bit with Zaria, and I know her feelings about how the Convocation and even some of our kind have treated her and others like her. They're not unfounded. In a lot of ways, the grudge she holds for the slights against her are the same as Lesuvius'. They just have different ways of dealing with it."

"I'm not sure I understand," Kaylee said.

Alastair gave her an amused look. "I suppose I'm blabbering. Do you blame the Convocation, Kaylee, for our failures?"

"Of course not. The Slayers—they were—"

"And what about the things we fail to prevent that the Slayers aren't involved with? What about all those dragon-kin and Merlins we unintentionally miss, like Dani, and Zaria?"

"You're...not perfect."

"But maybe there's a better way. A way in which every injustice and slight is eliminated." Alastair slipped one leg over the other. "At least Lesuvius seems to think so. Maybe at one time he sought to replace the Convocation with something grander, but now I fear he's lost sight of that goal."

The man in Kaylee's vision was still stark in the back of her mind. But she didn't tell Alastair about him, mostly because she wasn't sure how she could explain it. However, the man's resemblance to Lesuvius was something that had been slowly eating away at her.

"Alastair, who is Lesuvius?"

"You know who he is."

"That's not what I mean. Who is he, really? You know a lot more about him than you're telling."

Alastair had gone still. "He is a very dangerous man, and one I pity far more than I fear. That's all you need to know right now."

"Does he have any relatives?"

Alastair looked genuinely confused. "Relatives?"

"You know, brothers? Cousins? Descendants?"

"No. Of course not."

The man's eyes were embers in the dark.

Alastair looked over Kaylee's shoulder. The corner of his mouth twitched. "I will see you back at the safe house. We'll be heading back to Scarsdale today, much to the relief of your parents, I'm sure."

He grabbed one more chip then sauntered off down the sidewalk.

"I know you didn't want company," Edwin said.

He stood out of the flow of the passing crowd, hands in his pockets, an adorable smile on his lips. Kaylee found now she wasn't upset to see him. In fact, she was happy. Ecstatic, even. And maybe a little bit nervous.

Kaylee held out the bowl and Edwin gratefully scooped some guac.

"It's okay. I'm glad you're here," Kaylee said.

Edwin nodded his head. "My dad...did he say...you're not in trouble, are you?"

"Not in the way you think."

"And your brother? And Randy?"

"They're..." Kaylee thought about it. "You know what? They're okay. I'm okay. Is that *really* what you followed me out here for?"

Edwin hesitated. Then he stepped closer to her. He brushed the side of her cheek, the rough callouses he'd gotten from spell-casting gently rubbing over the scrapes she had there.

"Yeah, I was...hoping to ask you something. There's this dance coming up. Some kind of formal. I'm not technically invited, but I was wondering if you'd be interested in going?"

"With you?" Kaylee said innocently.

Edwin cocked an eyebrow. "Um, yeah. With me."

Kaylee pretended to think. "I think...that sounds like fun—"

Edwin kissed her. It was just a brush of his lips, but it sent off fireworks in her head all the same.

"Oh, so *now* you're finally being bold," she said.

Edwin shrugged, but he was flushed and grinning like he'd just run a marathon. "I've faced more monsters in the last couple days than I have in my entire life. I think I can survive asking you out."

Kaylee pulled him closer. A happy feeling expanded in her chest. "Well then, I think I'll have to say…yes."

And when she kissed him again, his lips tasted like guacamole.

KAYLEE DIDN'T HEAR him until he'd made it to his room.

She'd just finished smoothing out the last of any non-existent wrinkles on the dress she was wearing.

"It's just a formal," Jade had said when she'd come over earlier to help her pick it out. "We'll wear something nice, but it isn't like senior prom or anything. When that comes, *then* we can go all out, with limos and everything."

With the way things were going in her life, Kaylee wondered if she'd care at all when senior prom came. When she told Jade this, she'd said to stop being so dramatic.

"Let's just have fun tonight," she insisted. "It's your first date with Edwin. Finally," she added under her breath.

Kaylee rolled her eyes. Ever since she'd told Jade Edwin was taking her, Jade had acted as if their impending relationship had been the most obvious thing in the world. And maybe it had been.

But Jade was happy for her, and after helping Kaylee, she'd left to prep her own dress at her house. She and Maddox were flying solo at the formal. Together. Kaylee had a few choice thoughts about *that* being obvious, but she was a good enough friend to keep them to herself.

But now...Jade was gone. Kaylee's parents were out with Jeremy. There shouldn't have been anybody in the house.

But someone was rummaging around in Reese's room.

Kaylee shifted to claws (she *really* hoped it didn't ruin her nails. They'd taken forever to do). Reese's door was slightly open. The light was on.

"Reese?"

He started when she came in. His room had been picked apart. Most of the things he'd brought home were either spread around the floor, or stuffed into a small duffel on his bed.

Reese just stood there when Kaylee came in. He looked as though he'd been caught halfway through a murder.

"I didn't think anyone else was home."

"They're not. I'm about to go out." Kaylee gestured to the dress. "Spring formal."

A flicker of regret crossed Reese's face. "Sounds like fun. I remember mine."

"So do I. Mostly I remember Mom and Dad having to pick you up from the principal's office at midnight."

Reese smiled faintly. "Nobody could prove we switched the punch with vinegar."

"And the streaking on the football field after?"

Reese just grinned. Kaylee felt herself grinning too, but it didn't come as easily as it once had with him. She looked at his bed, and Reese followed her eyes to the duffel.

"Ah. To be honest, I'm glad Mom and Dad aren't here. I'll call them from college and apologize, but it's best I'm as far away as I can be before they chew me out."

"You're going back?"

"For a short time. As long as I can before...before I have to leave. I'm sure the Convocation will have their eyes on me once they find out where I am, too."

Kaylee only nudged the edge of the carpet, eyes down.

"I'll take that as a yes," Reese said.

"Why?" Kaylee blurted out. She hadn't meant to say it, and she felt like she needed to explain everything she wanted to ask behind that question.

"I can't answer that right now," Reese said. He pushed more things into his bag, then brushed aside some books and dug through the desk.

"I deserve an explanation."

"Well I don't have one. Probably won't for a while. But when I do you'll be the first to know."

"Do you have to go?"

"Honestly, yes. And if I want closure, yes. I pissed off some very powerful people. I may have to lay low for a while. Randy gave me some contacts I could follow up on soon. I might even start working with the Convocation eventually. If they'd take me."

He zipped his bag the rest of the way shut and hefted it over his shoulder.

"I will say this: I never meant to hurt you, physically or otherwise. And I'm...proud of you. Really."

"I know that—"

"You don't. Not really, if you had to ask me why I did what I did. But I *am* proud of you."

He kissed her forehead. "I'll be in touch. Maybe soon we'll be fighting alongside each other again, though that might not be such a good thing."

Kaylee was about to say more when the doorbell rang.

"It's Edwin," Kaylee said quickly as Reese went for something tucked behind his back. "He's taking me to formal."

"The nerdy wizard dude?"

Kaylee lightly punched him. "The smart, strong, handsome wizard dude."

"But nerdy."

"...but nerdy."

If Edwin was surprised to find Reese there when he opened

the door, he quickly hid it, for which Kaylee was eternally grateful. He'd dressed in nice jeans and a designer shirt, his unruly hair moderately tamed. He was carrying a bouquet of flowers.

"I'll take those," Reese said, plucking them from Edwin's hands and handing them to Kaylee. "Bit old fashioned, don't you think?"

"If you knew anything about me, you'd know I'm old school," Edwin said. He did a quick check down the street. "I'd leave now. Most of the Protectors are still on assignment in Rothsburg, and the ones around this section are switching stations for the next ten minutes."

"I appreciate it," Reese said. "I was just going."

He stuck out a hand, which Edwin took. Reese pumped it up and down, maybe a little harder than necessary.

"Make sure my little sister has fun."

"I will," Edwin promised.

"You hurt her, I hurt you," Reese added.

"Reese!" Kaylee admonished.

"I completely believe you," Edwin said.

Reese nodded at them both and threw his stuff into his car. Then he was backing out, giving one final wave before disappearing around the corner.

"He didn't mean that," Kaylee said.

"Oh, I think he did." Edwin grinned. "I could take him, though." His eyes slowly widened as he took her in. "You look incredible, by the way. Not sure if I mentioned that earlier."

Kaylee did a little twirl. "You didn't, but I could hear it a few more times."

"I'll be sure to say it a few more times."

"You're not looking too bad yourself."

Edwin held out his arm. "Shall we?"

Kaylee took it, and together they walked out into the night.

~

The Herald has risen. Now the race to stop him from summoning the Hunt begins…Continue the adventure with *Dragon's Bane!*

Enjoyed this book? It'd mean the world to me if you left a review on **Amazon**

Want more book goodie awesomeness like this? Get a FREE novella and early updates on my latest releases when you **Join My Newsletter**

The adventure continues in ***Dragon's Bane***! The Herald has risen. Unless Kaylee and her friends can stop him he'll summon the Hunt and destroy everything they hold dear…

Grab *Dragon's Bane* on **Amazon**
or
Turn the page for an excerpt!

Thank you so much for taking your time to read *Dragon's Curse*! Writing is one of my biggest passions, and I love connecting with readers and creating stories they love. If you'd like to learn more about my latest books, promos, and exclusive content, sign up for my author mailing list and receive a free novella and bonus subscriber's only content: **Join My Newsletter**

Want to make extra sure you never miss a new release? Follow me on **BookBub!**

I also love hearing from fans on social media:

https://seanfletcherauthor.com

facebook.com/seannfletcher
bookbub.com/profile/sean-fletcher
amazon.com/author/seanfletcher
instagram.com/seanfwanderin
goodreads.com/seanfletcher
twitter.com/seannfletcher

EXCERPT OF DRAGON'S BANE

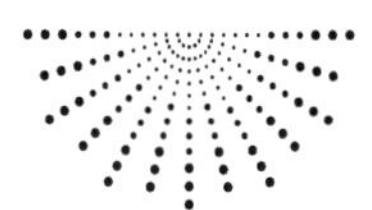

THE INVITATION

Letter Recipient: Jade Azuma, eldest daughter of Graham and Kim Azuma

Status: Tamer-In-Training at Scarsdale, New York, Convocation, under the direction of head dragon-kin Alastair Dumas

Subject: Tamer Test

Miss Azuma,

Congratulations! On behalf of the United States Convocation, being the head committee for all Convocation sections within the United States of America and her surrounding territories, we are pleased to offer you acceptance and invitation to take part in this year's Tamer test. This test will assess your proficiency in the art of being a Tamer for the Convocation you are currently under (Scarsdale, New York, Chapter), and will determine whether your knowledge of Convocation history, science, magic, structure, and Human/Convocation Relations—as well as your physical fitness — are up to standards deemed worthy to bestow the title of

Tamer-In-Full, or Fully-Trained Tamer among the ranks of the United States Convocation.

To be selected for this test is a great honor, and we hope you accept our invitation to participate. Upon review of your past record we acknowledge that you have been involved in a number of instances involving the terrorist organization known as Slayers. These instances include the Scarsdale Incident, as well as the Rothsburg Museum Operation. In both cases you showed a willingness to carry out your Tamer duties in protecting your assigned dragon-kin (Kaylee Richards), as well as the capability to do so. As such, Alastair Dumes (President, Scarsdale, New York, Chapter), has personally recommended you take part in this year's Tamer test.

Note: If you were recommended for the Tamer test and do not feel you are qualified, DO NOT attend. Please alert those who recommended you so that your name can be removed.

Please come prepared for a written and physical portion of the exam. YOU are responsible for your training and the United States Convocation is not responsible for loss of life or limb.

Please bring:

- Your letter of recommendation
- Your own weapon(s)
- Any family/friends (up to three, accommodations not provided for non-participants)

Final Note: With the recent Slayer activity, proceedings for the Tamer test will be held a little differently this year. The United States Convocation reserves the right to cancel or suspend the test in the event of Slayer interference. Participants should be, at any time, prepared to go into battle to defend the rights and values of the United States Convocation and her subsidiaries.

We do not anticipate any problems with Slayers.

We hope to see you in January. Your chaperone will provide the exact location details.

Until that time,

Philleus Johns, Head of Committee, United States Convocation

CHAPTER ONE

As a storm dragon-kin, Kaylee Richards had dealt with a lot during her time in the Scarsdale Convocation. She'd summoned raging thunderheads, fought the forces of darkness, and wrestled with mythical creatures that would cause even the most hardened soldiers to rethink their life choices.

But this…This was going to be the death of her.

"Kaylee, seriously? It's just SAT prep," Jade whispered, pushing the workbook back over to her. "If you want to pass it then you need to study."

Kaylee groaned and plopped her face between the pages, letting her chestnut hair spread across the table. "Easy for you to say. You get to study all the interesting stuff."

Jade cocked an eyebrow and held up the workbook she'd been leafing through. It wasn't a standard SAT prep or even a textbook, but rather a thick, leather-bound volume Edwin had provided her. The pages were full of dense, cramped writing, but it included all the dates, dragon-kin elemental powers, important dragon-kin in Convocation history, and places Jade would need to know to ace the written portion of the Tamer test.

Kaylee wished Edwin had been able to scrounge up something like that for her SAT's. As it was, she'd rather be taking an icepick to her eyes than read any more about vocab words she'd never use (*Vicissitude*? Did anybody born in the last thousand years use that word?), and data analysis for scientific studies she didn't particularly care about.

It wasn't that she envied Jade. Not really. Her best-friend-since-forever and Tamer-In-Training for the past two and a half years didn't want to take the Tamer test any more than Kaylee wanted to take the SAT's. But her parents had practically required it, and Jade had been prepping for years. And with the threat of the Slayers growing every day, especially now that they had the Book of Kells and the potential to summon the Herald of the Hunt, fully-trained Tamers and Protectors were in short supply. The Convocation was practically begging Jade to join their ranks.

Jade flipped to the next page. Kaylee tilted her head to watch, trying not to think about how much in that book she and her friends had already faced. In the last two years alone she'd fended off enough monster attacks and thwarted enough of the Slayers plans to impress even Alastair, the head of their Convocation. Kaylee's Uncle Randy would say that ninety percent of those attacks were a result of Kaylee sticking her nose where it didn't belong. Kaylee thought that was rich coming from a guy who'd made it a life's calling to get involved in things he wasn't supposed to.

Kaylee forced herself to start again on the math portion of the practice test. She and Jade had planned to go shopping and study here in Hansburough, the nearest big city to Scarsdale, before the storm had rolled in. After it had, they'd found the nearest library. The study area was filled with other students their age who were supposed to be on winter break, but instead were confined here while those younger than them frolicked in freedom. Only near-silent whispers and the crusty snap of flipping sheets of paper broke the silence.

Kaylee chewed the remaining end of her pencil. Her eyes kept flicking to the window, legs jostling, eager to be out and moving. Her usual after-school dragon-kin training with Randy had been relegated to a few times per week thanks to bitter winter weather and holidays. Randy was also gone a lot, out on missions for the Convocation he wouldn't tell Kaylee the details of.

"Alastair said I can help with more missions," Kaylee had argued to Randy when he'd come to one of her lessons late, sporting a new black eye, a fresh array of scratches, knife wounds, and a limp. "I've been going on more since junior year started. I should be out there with you."

Randy had paused in pushing his motorcycle to the shed, his bundle of deadly weapons and traps he kept strapped to the back jostling with the stop. Kaylee refused to look at them. She agreed with what he was doing—stopping Slayers—but not with his methods.

"Show me your dragon wings," Randy said.

"Randy, you know I'm still working on that—"

"Eyes of a dragon."

"Okay, that one, too, but—"

"Can you fully control a thunderstorm?"

"A small one," Kaylee had muttered.

"But not a big one. Not like the one you summoned in the Rothsburg Museum?"

Kaylee had grumbled a no. Randy had nodded.

"That's what I thought. You're not ready for the big leagues yet, squirt. Come talk to me when you've mastered those and then we'll see about you joining me on missions."

Then he'd wheeled his motorcycle the rest of the way into the shed and shut the door, leaving Kaylee to drag her feet back to the house before she froze to death.

"Kaylee?"

Jade poked her arm.

"Hello, Kaylee?"

"Yeah?"

Jade held up her backpack. "I'm done for now. Want to grab a coffee or something?"

Kaylee immediately slammed her workbook shut, earning dirty looks from those around her. "Absolutely."

They grabbed their coats, bundled up, and pushed their way outside the warm library. Chilly wind immediately nipped at Kaylee's nose. Passersby hurried past, covered in so many layers Kaylee could only see their eyes. For a brief moment, Kaylee was happy Jade was taking the Tamer test. It was being held in New York City and hopefully—*hopefully*—it would be warmer than this.

"You finish everything you needed to today?" Kaylee asked. Jade shrugged, the bulge of her shoulders moving up and down beneath her thick coat.

"Mostly. The written portion should be a piece of cake. It's like a history test, you know? The practical application's what I'm worried about."

Kaylee couldn't understand how. Jade was by far the strongest fighter she knew, short of Randy and Alastair. She was versed in more types of fighting than the superheroes on TV, could wield a variety of weapons, and hold her own in a fight, even outnumbered five to one.

"You'll be fine," Kaylee assured her.

"I just don't know what to expect," Jade said.

"Ask your instructor. He should be able to tell you a little about it, right?"

Jade shook her head. Or maybe she shivered. Kaylee wasn't sure. Her eyes felt like they had frozen in their sockets so it was hard to look over and tell.

"The Tamer test changes location and requirements every year," Jade said. "This test is totally unique."

"Then maybe Alastair would know."

Jade shot her an 'are-you-friggin'-kidding-me?' look.

"Right," Kaylee said.

Alastair Dumas, Edwin's dad and head of the Scarsdale Convocation, was a powerful forest dragon-kin. He was also a stickler for rules and wouldn't be caught dead giving illicit advantage for something as prestigious as the Tamer test, not even to Jade. He'd been getting on to them the last couple years whenever Kaylee and the others threw themselves into danger against the Slayers. It was only when he realized he couldn't *stop* them from getting in trouble that he'd relented and let them get more involved in Convocation business. Better to regulate their level of exposure to potential death than ignore it, Kaylee supposed.

"Okay, so Alastair's out. I can ask Randy."

"Ha!"

"Okay, fine, not Randy. Edwin then. He's the one who gave you the book to study, after all."

Jade waggled her eyebrows, which had somehow remained unfrozen on her face. "Don't you two waste your precious alone time talking about little old me."

Kaylee bumped her, nearly causing Jade to skid on a patch of ice and into the street. She laughed and the two of them hurried inside the coffee shop.

No sooner had they stepped inside then Kaylee's phone buzzed. She hurried to tug off her gloves and rub her numb fingers until the screen registered her touch.

"Is it Edddwiinn?" Jade cooed over her shoulder.

"Oh hush," Kaylee said, feeling a flush rise to her cheeks. At least she was warm now.

She read the text. "Jade, I'm sorry, but—"

"Go," Jade said, waving her towards the door. "You told me you had something planned. And I know you two deserve the time together."

Kaylee glanced around the coffee shop. It was almost empty

save for a few people tapping away on laptops and sipping steaming lattes.

"I don't want to leave you here alone..."

"I'll call Maddox. He doesn't have anything better to do. We can talk about...I don't know, fighting or something. He's been training with me for the physical portion of the test."

"Oh...the physical portion. That sounds interesting."

This time it was Jade's turn to blush. "Just go on your stupid date."

Grinning, Kaylee gave her a quick hug and again plunged outside. Edwin's text said he'd picked a place for them to have dinner just a few streets away. Kaylee felt a little guilty as she crossed the road and pushed against the wind towards the address he'd given her. Leaving Jade alone was never fun, but her friend had been more than understanding about Kaylee and Edwin's growing relationship. And it wasn't like Kaylee ditched her every five seconds to be with him.

Since they'd started dating almost five months ago, she and Edwin had gone on maybe two actual dates if she didn't count joint training sessions (which she definitely didn't). Between Kaylee's sessions with Randy, Edwin's growing responsibilities as a Merlin within the Convocation ranks, and the murderous amount of work school seemed determined to heave on them, it was a wonder they had time to meet even now.

Kaylee spotted Edwin through the latest swirl of snow flurries. He was bundled in a puffy down jacket, his face and head obscured by a wool hat and scarf, but Kaylee could still tell it was him. If the curly hair and fogging up glasses weren't a dead giveaway, then Edwin's wiry frame, still visible despite his layers, would have given it away.

He turned and spotted her, pulling down his scarf to give her a dazzling smile. Kaylee stopped, nearly slipping on a patch of ice. Her heart had started pounding wildly in her chest. Was it from one cheesy smile? Sure, Edwin had filled out even more through the summer and yeah, he was still skinny as a scarecrow, but now he was a *muscular* scarecrow, his new bulk impossible to hide. His magic had grown too. She might have been imagining it, but the air around him seemed to crackle with energy. As a Merlin, he'd come a long way from the awkward, bumbling magic wielder she'd first met.

"Wow," Edwin said as Kaylee finally reached him. "You look amazing."

"It's freezing, Edwin. I'm wearing at least three coats and you can't see ninety percent of my face."

He gave her a wink, made difficult due to the fact his eyelids looked nearly blue behind his glasses. "But I think it just got warmer with you here."

Then again, maybe he was still awkward. Either way, Kaylee couldn't help snorting and giving him a quick kiss, their frozen lips briefly sticking to one another's.

Edwin opened the door for her. "Shall we?"

The restaurant was far fancier than Kaylee had imagined. Edwin's family came from serious money, but even this seemed extravagant. White tablecloths topped with gently burning candles were spread across a comfortably enclosed room. Murals of rural landscapes were painted over archways leading to more secluded dining areas. An actual violinist played soothing music from one of the far corners.

Kaylee's mouth fell open. "Edwin...wow..." She barely noticed when Edwin gently took her coat and handed it to a waiting server. "Isn't this a little much?"

"This is only, like, the third date we've had," Edwin said. "I figured I'd better make it count to hold us over until the next."

"Fair point."

The server led them to a private windowed alcove that held just a few tables. The space was pleasantly warm and inviting, lit by a single roaring fireplace at their back. They sat and the server brought them water and menus. Kaylee stifled a gasp at the prices.

"Edwin—"

"Just get whatever you want."

She cocked an eyebrow. "You're setting my expectations for any other date pretty high. Sure you can keep this up?"

The freckles on Edwin's face flushed. He put on a cheesy grin. "I sure hope so."

"So you wouldn't mind if I got the Chef's Special?"

Edwin looked where she was pointing. His eyes briefly bulged. "Uh…"

Kaylee burst out laughing. "Kidding! I'm totally kidding."

They settled into more comfortable banter after that. Kaylee hadn't realized how nervous she'd been until that moment. Or even how nervous Edwin was. He acted as though taking her on one date was the greatest thing to ever happen to him; like he had to impress her no matter what, like they hadn't already seen the good and bad in each other.

Kaylee wondered if he knew that's exactly how she felt about him.

After they'd ordered, Edwin relaxed in his chair. His hand clasped hers across the table as they both stared out the window at the worsening storm. Kaylee savored the silence, just sitting with each other, comfortable, content.

"Were you with Jade?" Edwin finally said.

"Yep. SAT's for me, Tamer test for her. That book you gave her has been a lifesaver, by the way."

"Glad to hear it. From what I've heard of the Tamer test, she'll need all the help she can get—"

A log shifted on the fire, the flare of light casting the right side of Edwin's face in sharp relief. Beneath the collar of his sweater Kaylee caught the beginnings of a nasty cut. A knife wound most likely. Kaylee knew what they looked like. She'd been on the receiving end of a fair number of them.

"What's that, Edwin?"

"Kaylee..."

He tried to lean back as Kaylee ran her fingers over it. He let them linger there, before grasping them and gently pulling them away. "It's nothing, you know that. Just a souvenir from my last mission."

"Were you with Alastair?"

"Of course. None of us can go on solo missions until we pass our own tests. The Merlins test won't be for a couple more years for me. Probably longer for you."

"Why longer for me?"

"Dragon-kin's powers tend to be more...volatile," Edwin said. He grimaced. "Sorry, poor choice of words."

"But accurate," Kaylee said.

And they were. As a storm dragon-kin, a half dragon half human who could control thunderstorms, Kaylee's magic had been...temperamental. She'd only recently learned to control a small storm without it blowing up in her face—sometimes literally. Shifting her arms, feet, and stomach to dragon scales was getting easier with each passing lesson, but still not a breeze. The wings, as Randy so kindly reminded her, were a work in progress.

"What'd you guys find out?" Kaylee said.

Edwin put down his water. A server came by and refilled his glass and he waited until he'd left before saying in a low voice, "Good news and bad news. Bad news is the Slayers are mobilizing for something else."

"Big shock."

"Right. We're not sure what yet, but I guarantee it has to do with the Herald and the Hunt they were talking about."

Kaylee shivered. Ever since the battle at the Rothsburg museum, she hadn't been able to get the image of the Herald—as well as the ember-eyed man she'd seen when she'd briefly died—out of her mind. The Herald, it was said, could summon the

Hunt, the bane of all dragon-kin, led by the original Slayer himself, St. George. The Herald had been hard enough to knock back into whatever hell he'd crawled from, but if the Slayers managed to find another way to summon the Hunt then their situation would become ten times worse.

Kaylee felt Edwin's cool hand on her own. "The Slayers don't have the Herald, Kaylee," he assured her. "I mean, they have him, but he's weak. When you hit him with your lightning it knocked a huge part of his essence back into the other realm. He won't be summoning anything any time soon."

"But they'll keep trying."

"Yeah, they will. But so will we. You'd be amazed how much the threat of the Hunt returning has brought all the Convocations, all dragon-kin, together."

Kaylee cocked an eyebrow. "*All* dragon-kin?"

Edwin shifted uncomfortably in his seat. "Well, maybe not all. Zaria and her rogues still won't talk with my dad. At least not without throwing in a dozen snide remarks and impossible conditions we'd have to follow. But if we can get your Uncle Randy to work full-time with the Convocation..."

"Work is a strong word for him. I'd say he'd tolerate the Convocation for the soul purpose of torturing me on an almost-daily basis."

Edwin grinned.

"So where are the Slayers now—"

"Let's not talk about them," Edwin said suddenly. "That's all we seem to do is worry and plan around the next time we'll run into them."

Kaylee folded her napkin back and forth in her lap. "Okay, what do you want to talk about instead?"

"Uh..." Edwin glanced around the room, as if a stimulating topic of conversation would emerge from the bouquets of flowers on the table or tile mosaics set in the walls. "Uh..."

"Having trouble?"

"How's Reese?" Edwin blurted out, then looked furious with himself. "Sorry, I didn't...I mean, I was just wondering how he was...

"Reese is okay."

As far as she knew, anyway. He'd been a Slayer until Lesuvius, leader of the Slayers, had ordered him to kill Kaylee, and Reese figured that maybe, just maybe, murdering his family wasn't something he wanted to live with for the rest of his life.

"Have you been in touch lately?" Edwin said, a note of concern in his voice. Kaylee was grateful for how genuinely interested he looked in her answer. When others asked where her brother was they seemed to do it out of obligation rather than the actual desire to know.

"Not much. When he does call he obviously can't tell me where he is. He thinks he's lost the Slayers tailing him, but you never know. Randy put him in touch with some contacts of his so I'm hoping he stays safe."

Edwin grunted, and Kaylee knew why. *Safe* was not a word often used around anyone involved with the Convocation. "I'm sorry that happened to you."

"I am too. But it did, and I got over it."

Edwin glanced at her. "Did you?"

"As much as I'm going to right now."

"If you ever want to talk about anything..."

Kaylee propped her chin in her hands and fluttered her eyelashes. "You mean like we're doing right now, Casanova? Your smooth chitchat is charming me to no end."

Edwin laughed. Then his eyes flickered to the window. He stood.

"Edwin?"

"Did you see that?"

Kaylee stood beside him. The storm outside was blowing harder, making it difficult to see anything on the street through the sheets of sleet and snow.

"What did you—?"

Something monstrously large slammed into the window. The frame buckled inward, scattering glass across their table. Just as quickly as it hit, the thing peeled itself away and lumbered away. A second later a roar tore from down the street.

Someone screamed behind them. Trays and plates crashed. The waitress had dropped their food and was pointing at the window. "D-did you—d-did you—?"

Edwin glanced at Kaylee. "I hate to say it, but we should—"

"Date later. Let's check it out."

"W-what was that?" The waitress continued sputtering.

"I think it was a bird, right Kaylee?" Edwin said.

"Oh. Yeah, definitely. A…sparrow or something."

The pair rushed to grab their coats, the entire time Kaylee fighting her rising resentment at missing yet another date with Edwin. She shouldn't feel bad. This was important. Whatever that thing was hadn't been natural, and they were the only ones nearby equipped to handle it. She should have been happy to do something. She should have been eager.

So why did she still feel angry?

Kaylee nearly slipped on a patch of ice as they rushed out the front door, Edwin managing to catch her with one arm. He glanced quickly around and, once he was sure nobody else could see, conjured a ball of orange magic in his hand. He used his other hand to shape the magic into a sort of glow stick, which he held out in front of them as they moved cautiously down the road.

It was now that Kaylee wished she was a dragon-kin with a slightly warmer type of elemental magic. Maybe a fire dragon-kin, or lava dragon-kin. But her power over storms didn't lend themselves to anything particularly cozy, or particularly helpful, when they were currently in one. But maybe she could…

"Hold on!" Kaylee yelled. She held her hands up, calling on the magic within. Her hands were soon covered in a thick layer of black scales. The familiar buzz of power raced up her arms, arcing between her fingers, now turned into thick claws strong enough to slice through metal and clothing alike.

Kaylee took a deep breath and pulsed her elemental magic out into the storm, willing it to calm down, telling the wind to silence, prodding the flurry of snow and ice to cease. The storm howled on. But then…

"I think it's working," Edwin said. She could see and hear him more clearly now. A moment later it was almost as if they hadn't been standing in the center of gale force winds. "This is great, Kaylee. Should be easy to—"

A dark shape darted from one rooftop to the next, cutting the distance between them in an instant. Kaylee whirled, already shouting for Edwin to watch out. The lumbering shape lunged.

Kaylee was aware of leathery wings unfolding from the thing's back as it plummeted towards them. She crossed her scaled arms in front, bracing for the blow as it came. Claws raked her chest, luckily protected by the rest of her scales. The force knocked her away like a wad of paper in a wind tunnel. She hit the brick wall across the street and slid to the ground. She was vaguely aware of Edwin yelling, followed by the flash of orange magic as he engaged whatever had attacked her. Another flap of leathery wings and the shape vanished into the sky again.

Kaylee struggled to her feet. Her mouth tasted coppery. Her leg had twisted beneath her when she hit and her knee throbbed where she'd landed on it.

Edwin ran up to her, eyes wide. "Can you move?"

Kaylee gestured to her upright body. "Barely. What *was* that thing?"

Edwin gulped. It took Kaylee a second to realize he looked scared. Like, really scared.

Not good.

"You're not going to believe me…but I think it was—"

The concrete cracked as an immense creature landed in front

of them. Kaylee found herself blinking over and over again. Each time she expected the image to change but it never wavered from the reptilian snout to human-less eyes to thick, scaled arms and legs.

"A dragon," Kaylee breathed. "It's an actual dragon."

~

Continue the adventure with the rest of *Dragon's Bane* on Amazon!

MORE BOOKS BY SEAN

The I Am Phantom Series:

I Am Phantom

We Who Remain

Subject Number One (An I Am Phantom Novella)

In the Depths of Darkness Series:

In the Depths of Darkness

Shadows of the Swarm

The Heir of Dragons Series:

Dragon's Awakening

Dragon's Curse

Dragon's Bane

Dragon's Fate

Website:

https://seanfletcherauthor.com

ABOUT THE AUTHOR

Sean Fletcher was born in the broiling, arid state some people lovingly refer to as Texas. He is the Amazon bestselling and award-winning author of YA and middle grade sci-fi and fantasy, including the I Am Phantom, Depths of Darkness, and Heir of Dragons series, in addition to other forthcoming books whose characters will not give him a moment's peace until they get their turn in the spotlight. When not making things up and putting them on paper, he can be found hiking, biking, or traveling, sometimes all at the same time.

The setting, characters and story used in this book are completely fictitious and come from the author's imagination. Any similarity to real persons, living or dead, is coincidental and are not intended by the author.

First edition published February 2018

Cover Design: Natasha Brown

Always thanks to The Mother (DeLaine Fletcher), Andrea Hurst, Stephanie Mesa, Elissa Rogers, Terrilyn McManus

Printed in Great Britain
by Amazon